LEAVE IT TO CLEAVER

Did I Read This Already?

Place your initials or unique symbol in
square as a reminder to you that you have
read this title.

	J	IL			Jmw
		9			
	LM				

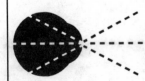

This Large Print Book carries the
Seal of Approval of N.A.V.H.

LEAVE IT TO CLEAVER

VICTORIA HAMILTON

WHEELER PUBLISHING
A part of Gale, a Cengage Company

GALE
A Cengage Company

Farmington Hills, Mich • San Francisco • New York • Waterville, Maine
Meriden, Conn • Mason, Ohio • Chicago

PUb 27

GALE
A Cengage Company

Copyright © 2017 by Donna Lea Simpson.
A Vintage Kitchen Mystery.
Wheeler Publishing, a part of Gale, a Cengage Company.

ALL RIGHTS RESERVED

Wheeler Publishing Large Print Cozy Mystery.
The text of this Large Print edition is unabridged.
Other aspects of the book may vary from the original edition.
Set in 16 pt. Plantin.

LIBRARY OF CONGRESS CIP DATA ON FILE.
CATALOGUING IN PUBLICATION FOR THIS BOOK
IS AVAILABLE FROM THE LIBRARY OF CONGRESS

ISBN-13: 978-1-4328-6648-8 (softcover alk. paper)

Published in 2019 by arrangement with Beyond the Page Publishing, LLC

Printed in the United States of America
1 2 3 4 5 6 7 23 22 21 20 19

LEAVE IT TO CLEAVER

PROLOGUE

February

One year ago, according to her Facebook account, Jaymie Leighton had been suffering through a lonely Valentine's Day thinking about her dead relationship with Joel Anderson, who had dumped her a few weeks before Christmas. This year was wholly different; *this* year she was looking forward to a Valentine's Day date with Jakob Müller.

And to add even more sweetness to the date, it would also be with Jocie, his adorable daughter. The little girl had called Jaymie several times the evening before asking if she liked chocolate *(of course)* and did she like cake *(yes, obviously)* and then if she liked chocolate cake. Jaymie had to laugh, and knew the child was experimenting with the kids' cookbook Jaymie's mother had bought her for Christmas — her favorite present, Jocie confessed.

Then Jakob called to double-check that Jaymie didn't mind sharing their first Valentine date with Jocie. Of *course* not, she told him. Time alone with Jakob was precious, but she loved time with his daughter, too. She was a part of him, after all. Jocie was, as she called it, a "*little* little person"; born with achondroplasia dwarfism, she was, at eight, only about the height of a three- or four-year-old, and doctors weren't sure how much taller she would grow. She would have the typical attributes of her condition, the shortened limbs in particular, but her outlook for a normal life span with only a few medical problems, which were relatively well understood, was good.

But Jakob, Jocie's only parent since her mother had returned to Poland several years ago and subsequently died, made sure she knew she could do anything she set her mind to. As a result she was more mature and confident than many children her age, though as giggling and silly as any little girl should be at times, fond of tickle fights, cartoons, taking pictures with her new camera, tumbling in her tumbling group, and singing. Jakob was a good and loving man. Jaymie felt fortunate to have found him in the most odd circumstances, running as she was from someone who wished to cause her great harm, and banging on his cabin door on a late fall evening.

In February, in Michigan, it was almost dark at five. Hoppy, her three-legged Yorkie-Poo, shivered with excitement as she carried him out the back door of her Queensville home, down the icy flagstone path and through the back gate to her decrepit white van, parked in her spot on the parking lane that ran between two lines of houses facing parallel roads. She set him on the passenger seat, climbed up, and started the motor, letting it run a moment in the frigid air. The heater was unreliable and needed warming up.

Her dog knew that if they were heading out this time of day, they were going to see one of his favorite people in the world, Jocie. Hoppy propped himself up, his one front paw up on the door handle so he could look out, and she drove in twilight away from Queensville to Jakob's log home on his Christmas tree farm, past snow-covered fields and icy bare trees, black limbs like lace against the purplish sky. He, like Jaymie, was a multi-business owner/operator; he helped as much as he could on his family's farm and took care of his enterprise, the Müller Christmas Tree Farm. But he also ran a junk store — The

9

Junk Stops Here — on a back road in a former factory in partnership with a friend Gus Majewski.

Her van rattled and bumped as she turned onto Jakob's road, a back-country gravel lane. There were some ruts from a mild winter and flooding so she slowed, taking the bumps more carefully for Hoppy's sake. Maybe it was time to invest in a newer vehicle. "We're almost there, Hoppy!" she said, glancing over at her little dog. He yapped back and panted.

Ahead, warmly aglow with golden light that flooded out of the front window, was Jakob's log home and happiness. "Here we are, Hoppy!" He yipped, overjoyed to visit Jocie, who he loved with all his doggie heart. She pulled up and jumped out of the van, greeted with a warm, enveloping hug from Jakob. Dressed in plaid flannel and jeans, he looked like a rugged lumberjack, his dark hair beginning to thread with silver and a beard coming in.

When she carried Hoppy in and set him down Jaymie also received a wriggling hug from Jocie, who had her blonde hair pulled back from her round dimpled face with a heart-embellished headband. Jocie's after-Christmas gift — animals should never be given on Christmas day, Jaymie had advised

Jakob — was a kitten she had named Little Bit, and Hoppy had taken to the little tiger-striped devil. Kitten, dog and child frolicked together from one end of the cabin to the other, much to Jocie's delight, and then worked out their giddiness by racing about in circles, Hoppy gamely trying to keep up despite his lack of one limb.

Dinner, Jakob's famous meat loaf, was delicious. Jocie was excited, singing and shooting glances at her father, and so jumpy she could not stay still. Finally she got to present her gift to Jaymie, a heart-shaped chocolate cake sprinkled with heart candies. It was lopsided and messy but delicious, a wreck of its former self after they demolished it. Jocie yawned elaborately after dessert and said she was tired.

"Do you want to go to bed?" Jakob asked.

She nodded and yawned again, slumping in the farm chair drawn up to the rustic table in the dining area that adjoined the living area of the log cabin.

Jaymie eyed her suspiciously, reaching out to coil one blonde curl around her forefinger. She examined the girl's cherubic face, the smooth pink-tinged skin, the high pale forehead, the cupid's bow lips. "Now, Jocie, I thought we were going to watch *A Charlie Brown Valentine* together?"

11

She slipped off her chair and put her hands on Jaymie's legs. "I watched it already with my friend, Gemma. Is that okay?" She stared up at Jaymie, biting her lip and searching her eyes for approval.

"Honey, whatever you do is okay with me, you know that," Jaymie said, hugging her hard and kissing her soft, plump cheek.

The little girl nodded, picked up her kitten and trotted away, calling "Good night" over her shoulder. Odd that she should be so eager to go to bed. Normally it was a struggle to get her to settle when all she wanted to do was spend more time with Jaymie.

"I'll put her to bed and come back down, okay?" Jakob said, and headed for the stairs to follow his daughter.

"Of course." Jaymie wondered why he was so serious that he was almost frowning. She watched Hoppy settle on the rug by the fireplace, basking his limbs in the warmth of a real wood fire. Jakob had seemed off all dinner, so *very* quiet. Fidgety and concerned, she rearranged cutlery, piled plates together, moved restlessly in her seat. Maybe he had something else on his mind and had wanted to call off their date, but felt like he couldn't put her off on their first Valentine's Day as a couple.

She'd have to tell him that if he ever had a family issue he needed to take care of he could tell her. He could break any date, talk to her about *anything;* he could be quiet, noisy, sad . . . *anything.* Just so long as they could talk about it. Her breath caught in her throat. She jumped up, cleared the dessert dishes and ran water in the sink, gazing out into the darkness of the lane and road beyond the kitchen window.

Time to admit it to herself: she loved him. Deeply. Completely. They had only known each other a few months but she was so sure of her feelings toward him she didn't know how she'd stand it if he didn't love her too. But he had to be careful, since he had a daughter. They had already had the awkward conversation when he told her he would always put Jocie first. She had reassured him that she honored that intention and agreed. But maybe Jakob had decided they were going too fast and needed to slow down. She could live with that as long as he didn't tell her he was breaking up with her.

"Please don't let him want to break up with me," she whispered.

She washed the dishes and set them in the drainer, then scrubbed the heart-shaped cake pan and dried it, setting it on the table for Jakob to put away. That was the problem with Valentine's Day; it made everything love-related seem so serious and heavy. Television told you that you had to have the *perfect* Valentine date, or the *perfect* Valentine proposal. Like Christmas, there was too much pressure put on perfection. Jaymie believed that the search for perfection meant you were never happy, because perfection was impossible.

She heard Jakob's step in the hall and turned with a smile. He wasn't smiling, though he usually was. Her heart thudded and the smile died on her lips.

"Can we take a walk?" he asked.

"Outside?" she squawked. "It's only twenty-five degrees!"

He grabbed a blanket. "We need to talk."

Outside of the cabin? It must be serious. She couldn't say a word past the lump in her throat. The door slammed shut behind them and he gently wrapped the blanket around her shoulders, then put his arm around her and led her away from the cabin, crunching across the frozen gravel drive. As they walked they were silent; she was trying to figure out how to take it if he said he needed to back off from their relationship.

Could she handle it without crying? She didn't think so. It was scary how much he and Jocie had come to mean to her in such

14

a short time. She had always drifted into relationships, usually caught off guard by men who asked her out when she wasn't expecting it. But this . . . this was different in *every* single way. Her heart was filled with love for Jakob and for Jocie. It would crush her if he didn't return her love.

"Want to see what I've done in the tree house?" he said, taking her hand.

"Okay." Her voice was small, and she was numb from cold and fear.

He climbed up first. Her freezing bare hands were awkward on the ladder rungs, but he gave her a hand up the final steps. "It's so cold," she said, her breath coming out in white clouds in the dim light from the Müller Christmas Tree Farm sign.

"I'll keep you warm." He wrapped the blanket around her more closely as she leaned against him, feeling his strong arms encircle her. She'd gladly stay this way all evening.

"I don't see any changes," she said, twisting and trying to examine the tree house in the dark. "Do you have a lantern or something?"

"No, but I have a light switch." He let go of her and moved toward the window opening.

"Okay, let's have some light."

"Come to the window. I want you to see something."

"What is it?"

"Come here," he said, his voice gruff. He sounded tense.

She approached and looked up at his shadowy face, wondering what was wrong.

"Look out in that direction," he said, pointing out the window over the sea of dark evergreens, the crop of Christmas trees for next year and the years after.

She did as she was told and heard a click; the illumination was immediate, but it wasn't in the tree house, it was in the evergreen field. Hundreds of lights blazed, making a loopy uneven heart strung from tree to tree and surrounding the sign they used at Christmas to advertise their hours. It, too, was illuminated and held the words *Jaymie: Will U Marry Us? Love, Jakob & Jocie*

Her heart thudded and her breath caught in her throat. She looked up into his face; it was still shadowy. She felt it and traced his grin. He bent his head to kiss her, their warm breath mingling in the frigid tree house.

"Jaymie, I know it's fast," he murmured against her lips, his warm hands cupping her cheeks. "I know we've only known each

16

other a few months." He leaned his forehead against hers. "But I love you so *much,* and I know it's right. Will you marry me? Us? Me and my little girl?"

Her eyes were wet. He touched her cheek, feeling the tears. She couldn't speak, couldn't say a word, and felt him stiffen, tensing. She nodded enthusiastically and then found a way past the lump in her throat to croak, "Yes, *please. I love* you, Jakob Müller!"

From the ground below, she heard a wild cry of "Woo *hoo!*" from Jocie, and Hoppy barking excitedly. In one beautiful minute she had a whole family to love.

ONE

August 1984

Rebecca "Becca" Leighton, fifteen going on sixteen, rode her bicycle along the dirt country road about halfway between Queensville and Wolverhampton, Michigan. It was good to have somewhere to go, because as much as she loved her new baby sister, Jaymie, and her mom, their neediness was suffocating her. A teenager could only take so much diaper changing and burping.

The wind felt good, and her bare legs — she wore cutoff jeans and a tank top — were strong and tanned from two months of wearing shorts. It was a hot summer day, no school for another three weeks or so. She skidded the bike, cornering up the dirt drive of her friend Delores's country home, ditched it on the weedy, patchy grass lawn and raced up the wooden steps as Delores bolted out the screen door, slamming it behind her.

19

"Suck it, Clifford," Delores hollered over her shoulder.

Her cousin's voice echoed from inside, "*You* suck it, Del! You can just —" And he let loose with a string of foul language.

"What's up?" Becca asked as Delores plopped down on the top step of the house-wide porch.

"Just Cliff being Cliff," Delores grumbled, using the heels of her hands on her eyes to get rid of the tears. She pushed her thick hair over her shoulder, the odd reddish-blondish-brownish color a result of using spray-in lightener all summer on her naturally brown hair. It was supposed to use the sun's heat to turn it a glorious blonde, but so far it was a weird mixture of colors, none of them the smooth, silky blonde mane promised by the girl on the box. "All he freakin' does is sit and stare at the TV, smoking pot. He wanted me to make him a sandwich. I told him to make it himself and he went off on me. I *hate* him!"

Becca sat down by Delores on the top step and checked over her shoulder, eyeing the screen door. No car in the weedy gravel lane, so Delores's aunt and uncle weren't home — her Aunt Olga never stayed home if her Uncle Jimbo was going somewhere — and that meant her friend's cousin, Clif-

20

ford, was the only other person present. Becca didn't like Clifford. He looked at her legs and eyed her breasts. Yuck! He had to be thirty if he was a day, and he was a creep-ola.

"Let's get out of here, then," Becca said, standing and hopping down two steps so she was eye level with Delores. "Can we take the horses?" That was pretty much the only reason she had befriended Delores at the beginning of the summer; the Pagets had a barn and two rideable horses, and Becca was now a riding addict.

"Yeah. Let's ride." Delores led the way around the house and back to the barn, the crickets silencing as they walked past, down a beaten and scorched dirt path through the dusty yellowing grass. Behind them the crickets again began to chirp.

The hobby barn, a tin-roofed board structure, was cooler inside than out but not by much, and the horses seemed reluctant to move. They got them saddled — Delores's favorite, a bay gelding named Strider, and Becca's mount, Sally, a gray dapple mare with a black mane — and rode down the lane, across the gravel road and through a gate to a trail that led to the cool copse of trees through which there was a winding path.

"So did Dee ask you where you were going today?" Delores asked Becca.

"I don't tell her everything," Becca indignantly stated. They were speaking of Becca's lifelong best friend, DeeDee Hubbard.

"What about Valetta?" Delores pressed.

This was one of the things Becca didn't appreciate about Delores, the constant badgering about her friends, their reactions, what they thought, what they said about Delores. She couldn't be honest because neither of her two friends liked Delores. It had been a rocky summer so far, trying to satisfy both sides without feeling like a complete fraud. She wished she could take back some of the things she had told her friends about Delores: that Becca had only made friends with her so she could ride; that the Paget home was not clean and not comfortable; that Clifford Paget seriously creeped her out and bragged about all his crimes, like robbing toolsheds for money for pot. As she had gotten to like Delores it felt more and more disloyal.

But it was done and she couldn't unsay stuff. "So, you looking forward to school?" Becca said instead of answering with another lie.

"I guess," Delores said with a shrug. They walked the horses side by side along the path, entering the shady woods. "I'd look forward to it more if I knew I could take driver's ed."

"Why can't you?" Becca shifted the reins to one hand and adjusted her sneaker-clad foot in the stirrup. "My dad said it might be the last year they're offering it because of budget cutbacks or something — I wasn't really listening — so I'm taking it for sure."

"Aunt Olga says we can't afford it. I don't see what the big deal is. I could get a job if I could get my freaking license. I could drive to Wolverhampton in the winter and work at the coffee shop. I'd pay her back, but she won't even hand over my birth certificate so I can get my learner's!"

"Why not?"

Delores shrugged. "Who knows. They're both getting weird. I wish I had parents, like you do."

Becca knew from past conversations this was a dangerous path for their exchange to take. Delores's parents had died in a car crash when she was just a year old, so her aunt and uncle had taken her in, as well as their nephew, Clifford, who had lost his parents some other way. It was all a bit hazy to Becca. They couldn't have kids them-selves but they did have a family, Delores's aunt had said once, when she was acting normal. Other times she and her husband sniped at each other or at Delores, making it uncomfortable all around. Becca preferred visiting when they were out.

Delores glorified the Leightons' home life. She had only been over once but it had clearly made a lasting impression, because she was always asking to come into Queensville and sleep over. Becca wasn't letting anyone come home with her right now. She loved her baby sister, but it was no fun having an infant around twenty-four seven, especially not with Mom sick and depressed all the time and Dad working overtime. With any luck her Grandma Leighton would come back from Canada, where she was staying with her sister, and live with them. Then things would get better.

"At least you don't have to change diapers," Becca said, keeping it light, determined to have fun. "Come on, last one to the stream is a rotten egg." She set Sally to a trot and took off past Delores.

TWO

When the cleaver came at her, Jaymie Leighton didn't know what to do except scream and dive to the left, falling off the stepladder, tumbling and rolling sideways as the blade hit the floor and stuck into the old linoleum.

"What the heck was that?" Becca yelled from the living room.

Jaymie lay on the floor, Hoppy, her little tripod Yorkie-Poo, licking her face as her heart thudded, making her feel sick to her stomach. She took a deep breath, sat up, dusted herself off and said, "Oh, nothing much. I just got attacked by a box of meat cleavers placed dangerously on the top of a set of cupboards!"

"You okay?" her older sister asked, poking her head around the doorway.

"I *said* I just got attacked by a meat cleaver! What part of that sounds okay?"

25

"Actually you said a *box* of meat cleavers." Becca adjusted her glasses, pushed back her silver-threaded dark curls and stared pointedly at the cleaver, still stuck in the stained linoleum floor. "I only see one."

"Ha-ha," Jaymie said and cautiously got to her feet. Hitting the floor that way had hurt her hip; she rubbed it, wincing. She kicked the box. "I was reaching up to get this box from the top of the cupboard, wondering what it was, when it tipped and the cleaver fell out." She shivered, a belated thrill of fear shooting up her spine. "Thank goodness the box landed upright instead of spilling the rest of the cleavers. That could have been nasty."

Becca frowned. "Be careful, ya nutbar! This is a foraging expedition, not a death trap."

Jaymie took another deep breath and lifted the box up onto the counter. "I'm lucky only one fell out!" It was indeed a whole box of cleavers, all different shapes and sizes. "How much meat cutting did this family do?"

Becca joined her at the counter and sorted through the box with her. They laid some out on the scarred butcher-block counter; there were long-handled and short-handled blades, and a couple that didn't have wood handles at all but rather a hook, to hang on a rail. A couple had serrated edges opposite the blades, and one had a wolf atop the blade, stamped from the metal in one piece. There were two other animal ones, a horse and a duck shape atop the blade. "These are plain weird. I don't remember any cleavers from this house way back when. I knew this family pretty well when I was a kid," Becca said. "I even stayed out here a time or two. It's sad they're all gone now."

"How did that happen?" Jaymie asked. "I know that Lesley Mackenzie was hired to liquidate the assets of the estate, but why?"

The Mackenzie auction house was a family-run business that handled most of the estate sales and auctions in and around Queensville and Wolverhampton. Lesley, a much older, very dapper gentleman, was the patriarch, and a good friend of the Leightons' backyard neighbor, Trip Findley, another gentleman of a certain age. Jaymie wasn't asking why the Mackenzie auction house, but rather why the house and estate were being liquidated.

"Nobody can trace their family. It's sad, but no one has come forward, even after a year of advertising and searching. As far as I ever knew there were just the four of them." Becca pensively stared at the cleavers. She explained that the proceeds of the auction would go to the state unless they could find a relative, *any* relative. Michigan law said even someone distant — a cousin, say — could inherit, but so far they had found no one and it had been over a year since the last known Paget, elderly Olga, had died in a hospital without gaining consciousness after a fall at home.

The estate would soon pass to the attorney general if no living relative could be found. Every paper in the house had been gone through, but not a single one indicated any family before 1968, when they had moved into the house. So far most of the furniture that was worth anything had been moved to the auction house. Jaymie and Becca were boxing up the rest of the contents and doing a quick clean so the house could be put up for sale. In exchange for their help, they would get first pick of whatever they wanted.

"The family seemed bound for tragedy," Becca said, helping Jaymie put the cleavers back in the box and setting it by the door. She took one back out and examined its wide blade and polished wood handle. "Some of these are antiques. Maybe the historic house would display them?"

"That's what I was thinking," Jaymie said.

Acquisitions for the kitchen of the Queens-ville Historic Manor, where she volunteered, were in her control and she was gradually gathering a collection of kitchen utensils that would celebrate the most important room of the house, to her thinking. She already had vintage pestles and many other tools, but no cleaver. "I'll go through the box later and pick out the best." She'd have to have them mounted in a locked frame, where they would be safely out of the way of curious guests.

Her sister's words about the family in-trigued Jaymie, so she went back to them. "What did you mean when you said the Pagets were bound for tragedy?"

Becca shrugged and adjusted her glasses, glancing around the kitchen. She tugged her spring blouse, now smudged with dust, down over her generous bosom. "There was never a lot of happiness here. The summer before I turned sixteen I made friends with Delores Paget. Her parents were killed in a car crash when she was a year or so old, so her aunt and uncle took her in. What was his name?" She frowned down at her loaf-ers, polishing the toe of one on her pant leg. "Ah, yes! Uncle Jimbo. Aunt Olga and Uncle Jimbo Delores called them. There was a cousin too; he was older, and I didn't like him. Clifford, if I remember right." She shuddered. "Yeah, Creepy Clifford. Del and I were friends for a while, but Valetta couldn't stand her and neither could Dee," she said about her two best friends from the time, still her friends and Jaymie's too. "I felt sorry for Delores. She was so eager to hang out. I came out here a few times a week that summer. They had horses and I loved to ride."

"I must have been a baby," Jaymie said. She was fifteen years younger than Becca.

"That's why I spent so much time out here," Becca said with a sly grin and sideways look. She rinsed her hands in the kitchen sink under the cold-water tap and dried them on a paper towel from a roll they had brought with them. "Mom had just had you and she wasn't well. Coming out here was a way to escape when I wasn't looking after you."

"So what happened to Delores? I've never met her. Did she move away?"

Becca frowned and balled up the paper into a wad, tossing it into an open green garbage bag. Hoppy yapped once, so Jaymie retrieved it and threw it into the living room. The Yorkie-Poo barked merrily and wobbled after it.

"So . . . what happened?" Jaymie repeated.

Hoppy brought back the ball of paper, but when Jaymie threw it again he had lost interest and went to sniff around the other room.

Becca stroked the worn butcher-block counter, nicked and cut from years of chopping. "She took off the fall after we both turned sixteen. I'd gotten busy with school and was hanging out more with Dee and Valetta again, so I hadn't seen her." She paused. "Well, that's not *quite* true, I guess. She came to my sweet sixteen birthday party in September, and I saw her at school sometimes. She left town in October or November, but no one knew where she went. Just away, I guess. Like I said, she wasn't happy at home." She paused and sighed. "I've since wondered if her cousin . . . if Clifford was the problem."

"Did her aunt and uncle call the police when she took off?"

Hands on her hips, Becca glared up at her "little" sister, who was taller by a couple of inches. "It's nothing weird, don't get that in your head. She took off. Brock knows," she said, naming Valetta Nibley's brother. "He saw her the day she left, if I remember right. She told him she didn't want to live with her aunt and uncle anymore because they were so strict, so she was taking off."

31

"*Brock* saw her before she left?" Jaymie narrowed her eyes, then bent over the box of cleavers, choosing four and setting them aside. They'd be for the historic home, the wolf one and three others. "What *exactly* did she say to him?"

Becca made an exasperated noise. "Good heavens, Jaymie, that was *forever* ago. I don't even remember!"

Jaymie straightened. "But you *do* remember Brock saying he saw her in Queensville and that she was leaving town."

"I can't remember *where* he saw her, he just said he saw her." Becca stared at her younger sister and squinted behind her glasses. "Jaymie Leighton-soon-to-be-Müller, not everything is a mystery! She wasn't happy, and she left. She wasn't the first, and she won't be the last. There was another girl who took off from Wolverhampton about the same time, drove west and kept going. Kids leave. It happens. We had another friend who took off a year or so later."

"But shouldn't Delores inherit then? She'd be your age."

"The state has been looking for her for over a year," Becca admitted. "They searched, advertised . . . even employed a private detective. Nothing. If they can't find her and she doesn't come forward, they have to wrap the estate up sooner or later. They'll keep trying for a while, but what more can they do? Let's get back to work so you can stop imagining things."

They parted ways for another hour, sorting, gathering, stacking, sweeping and vacuuming. It was an old farmhouse and nothing had been done to it for years, so they couldn't make it sparkling clean, but it would be sold "as is" anyway. They then took a break, carrying mugs of thermos tea out to the rickety porch that overlooked a dusty back road, followed by Hoppy, who sat on the top step, content just to be with them. It was only late April, but it was dry enough and warm enough that it felt like late May.

"This must have been a nice place back then," Jaymie said, swinging her legs on the porch swing, hoping it wouldn't shake loose from the rafters and tumble her down. She held her tea in both hands so it wouldn't slosh from the gentle swaying. "I like the view of the fields and the trees."

A car roared down the road, kicking up a cloud of dust that settled, gradually, to reveal the newly planted soybean field across the road, and in the distance, following a creek bed, a narrow band of trees that tossed on the spring breeze. Becca, sitting on the top step of the porch, cradled her mug in her hands and took a sip. "It was okay, but it was always kind of ramshackle. And it was *never* clean. I didn't spend much time inside the house because Clifford was always hanging around, smoking dope and watching TV. Del and I used to ride the two horses across the road and down that narrow lane to the woods." She pointed toward a wide gate and path beyond it. "There's a big hilly open area on the other side, and she taught me to canter."

"I didn't even know you could ride," Jaymie said, staring at her sister. Becca was a tightly wound prissy perfectionist who didn't like sports and who often dressed like a seventy-year-old woman, though she wasn't quite fifty.

"I had my adventurous side," she replied, then drained her tea mug. She stood, dusted her bottom and said, "Let's get this done. We have to finish this job because we have wedding planning to take care of."

Hoppy jumped up, ready to follow. Jaymie felt a tickle of excitement; wedding planning! She would not have thought that possible a year ago, but now it was positively entrancing. She and Becca had consulted with their fiancés and all came to the conclusion that a double wedding would be best, because to gather the aging family together once was hard enough. Twice would be cruel. Jakob got along great with Becca and Jocie had taken to Kevin, Becca's older fiancé, as if he were another grandpa.

"That reminds me," Jaymie said as they stepped back into the dim coolness of the house. She pushed Hoppy in with one foot, since he had stopped to sniff the doorway threshold. "I was thinking of that beat-up dresser in the garage out back, the one nobody wants. I took a picture and sent it to Heidi, and she said it would be perfect. She wants to distress it. I said it's plenty distressed as it is!" They were planning, of course, a vintage-themed wedding, and Heidi Lockland had absolutely *insisted,* as her gift to the sisters, on planning the details. "C'mon, Hoppy. I'll get you some water and a snack."

"What does she want to use it for?" Becca asked, following Jaymie and setting her mug in the kitchen sink. She grabbed another roll of paper towels from the tote of cleaning supplies they had come armed with.

"The cakes. Tami needs something wide enough and sturdy," Jaymie said, speaking of their wedding cake designer, Tami Majewski, Jakob's partner Gus's older

35

sister, who worked as the cake decorator for the Wolverhampton Bakery. She filled the animals' water bowl and set it down on the floor next to a saucer of kibble. "*And* it has a mirror attached, so it might look cool, you know . . . reflect the back of the cakes." They were going to have two cakes, completely different to reflect the differences in the two sisters. "I think it will need to be sanded a bit, and cleaned up, but other than that we want it to look old, so it won't need much work."

"I'm sure it will be okay. Heidi seems to know exactly what she wants," Becca said, pushing her fluffy bangs off her forehead. "I hope it's what *we* want."

"I'll call Mackenzie's and have them pick it up and deliver it for us. Heidi said to drop it off at Bernie's because they'd be fixing it up together."

"Which means that Bernie is going to do the work," Becca said with a snort. She was not Heidi Lockland's biggest fan and thought the girl was childish.

"Maybe. Bernie has more experience refinishing and fixing up her auction finds anyway, so that's probably best. But you know as well as I do that Heidi is doing a whole lot of free work that a wedding planner would charge thousands of dollars for."

Jaymie felt compelled to defend Heidi. Raised rich and spoiled, blonde and lovely Heidi, in her twenties, was doing her level best to grow up. But if that happened in fits and starts, who could blame her when she had been indulged her whole life? She was sweet-natured, didn't have a mean bone in her body, and was trying.

It would have been churlish to say no to Heidi's pleas to do the planning, Jaymie and Becca agreed before they realized how far the girl, who was now engaged to Jaymie's ex-boyfriend Joel, would be taking it. Neither bride-to-be had even considered a theme as such, but vintage made perfect sense since both collected and dealt in vintage and antiques in one way or another. Heidi had done sketches, sent emails, started Pinterest pages, designed invitations and generally run amok in the most tasteful and vintage-gorgeous way. She had also enlisted Officer Bernice "Bernie" Jenkins, their mutual friend on the township police force, to provide vintage barware, *and* design some vintage-inspired cocktails reflecting the joining of the Leighton, Müller, and Brevard families.

It was overwhelming at times, all of the preparation needed for even a modest affair. And Jaymie didn't have a wedding dress yet! The wedding was a couple of months away, in June. She needed to get a dress but she had no clue what kind, though she didn't dare say so to Becca, who had a tendency to take over her younger sister's life if she let her.

The wedding planning was bewildering to Jaymie, though as an inveterate list maker she was generally well organized. As they went back to work rather than dwell on all that had yet to be done for the wedding, Jaymie found it simpler to let her mind wander and think about the family who had lived in this old house. How sad that they were all gone! But what happened if Delores was out there somewhere with no idea she should be inheriting the farm? And what about the cousin, the repellent (to Rebecca) Clifford? Where was he? Jaymie stored those questions away to ask her sister later.

They worked for another couple of hours but finally were ready to call it quits. Hoppy had long ago given up shadowing Jaymie and was curled up on her sweater in the corner of the kitchen, where she had spent hours cleaning out the cupboards and washing windows.

"We're going to have to come back out tomorrow to finish," Becca said, pushing back her dark bangs again to reveal a sweaty brow as she joined Jaymie in the kitchen. Her hair was curling into damp ringlets. "I want to have a look down in the cellar to see how much work we have left to do."

"We have to do the basement too?" Jaymie asked, her voice squeaking in dismay.

"Of course. *And* the attic. When we agreed to do the house, we agreed to do the *whole* house."

"You go ahead, then," Jaymie said, eyeing the cellar door that led off the kitchen.

"Whatsa matter, fraidycat," Becca said, "you scared of the dark?"

"Of course not, I'm not fond of basements. But the electricity is on, so we'll have light, right?"

She followed Becca down a rickety set of almost vertical steps into the dim basement. Hoppy, alerted that something was going on and unwilling to be left out of it, tried to follow her, but she shooed him away and closed the door, afraid he'd fall down the steps. Poor little guy; with just three legs he was not steady enough for the steep descent. The chilly basement smelled musty and damp, like earthworks. There were lights, but they were just hanging bulbs at ten-foot intervals. "Bunch of cheapskates," she mumbled. "I swear these bulbs are fifteen watts at most."

A series of rooms stretched out before them, the smell of decay heavy in the damp air. Jaymie groaned as she saw all the piled junk: old lawn furniture, splitting boxes with mildewed *National Geographic* magazines spilling out, more boxes labeled "Old China" and "Junk," and lining the walls, sagging wood shelves. Those shelves were laden with dozens of Mason jars filled with murky, mysterious foodstuffs. Jaymie slipped past some of the boxes and picked up one of the jars, tilting it sideways and squinting. "It looks for all the world like a pickled lab specimen. What the heck is that?"

Becca took it from her and turned it over and over. "Preserved peaches, I think. Grandma Leighton used to make them. We'd have peaches all winter because of her."

"A peach! That's why it looks like a wee beastie's bum," Jaymie joked, taking the bottle from her sister and setting it back on the shelf, then dusting her fingers off. "Did you ever come down here when you were a kid?"

"No way. Like I said, Delores and I would usually take off and go riding, or walk or bike into Queensville, or catch a lift to Wolverhampton."

"What was she like?"

Becca turned and stared at her through the gloom. "Why are you so fixated on Delores?"

"Just curious. I know most of your friends but I've never even heard of her. And riding horses? That's a side of you I've never seen. It's interesting, I guess. I don't know that much about what you were like as a kid, before I came along."

Becca's glasses glinted palely in the dim light. "I suppose that's right. I never thought of it that way. I know your whole life, but you don't know mine."

"Exactly."

"I liked her, but she was . . . troubled. Let's say I wasn't that surprised when she took off. I knew things weren't all sunshine and lollipops here with her family."

"What about the cousin, Clifford?"

Becca shuddered. "He was an odd duck. Gave me the creeps. Let's keep moving and get all the way back to the front, if you know what I mean."

Jaymie did and clambered back toward her sister over the boxes of magazines. Since the cellar stairs were off the kitchen, and the kitchen was at the back of the house, they were moving through the rooms toward the front of the house. "I wish I'd brought a flashlight," she muttered.

"Like this?" Becca asked as a blade of light cut the gloom.

"Sheesh. You had that the whole time?"

They moved together, following the light, and got to the last room, a low-ceilinged, dank, cobwebby, earth-floored room where the furnace squatted, glowering in the corner, and the rusty water heater sat on a brick pad. The smell was indescribable, a mingling of dead animal — probably a raccoon or possum had crept in through the crawl space and died — and damp dirt, with a soupçon of vegetation rot. Weeds had grown in through gaps in the cracked windows and rotting window frames.

"It is *spooky*! There's nothing here; let's go back." Jaymie shivered, though it was warm and airless in the room.

"Wait, there is one thing: a trunk."

Jaymie laughed, but it came out shaky. "Right, it *had* to be a big old trunk. With my luck it probably has a body in it. You haven't killed anyone lately, have you?"

Becca sighed and trained the flashlight on it. "Well, now we *have* to open it," she said. "Just to show you that it's nothing but old clothes. I don't want my *wittle* sister to have nightmares."

Jaymie groaned at her mocking tone. "All right, okay, let's do it. You know me better than that. I'm not afraid, just creeped out."

It was a very old, rather large trunk, with patches of blue-painted metal still showing through rust. The clasp was rusted, too, but there was no lock on it, so with some effort Jaymie got the hasp open. The lid was stuck. It took both of them tugging to get it to begin to lift. It smelled wretched, like ancient body odor, once they cracked it, but the lid finally came up with a creak.

"Darn it!" Becca screeched.

Jaymie jumped. "What? What's wrong?"

"I broke a nail."

"Oh, for heaven's sake, Becca! You scared the life out of me."

Becca shone the light into the trunk, where some vivid red knitted cloth was visible. "See, I told you; just a wig and some old clothes, probably a tickle trunk."

"What's a tickle trunk?" Jaymie asked.

"Good heavens, you *are* younger than me. A tickle trunk is a costume trunk. It's from an old Canadian show; we got a CBC station from across the border. It was . . . what the heck was it? *Mr. Dress Up!* Yeah, that was the show. I remember Grandma's tickle trunk with all the old clothes from the forties, but maybe you don't. You were too young."

"I think I may have seen *some* episodes."

Jaymie stared, perplexed, into the trunk. "Why would anyone store it full of a wig and clothes in the damp depths of the basement?" There was some other stuff, like a wooden handle of something tangled in with the wig. "So weird," she mumbled. "Maybe it's a Halloween costume?"

Jaymie stared down at the sweater under the blondish wig, a stained hand-knit piece of a weirdly vibrant red synthetic. She reached out to touch the wooden handle, but when she did it felt stuck, and the hair shifted. A low moan erupted from her throat and she bolted to her feet, followed by Becca. They stared at each other and clutched their hands as the flashlight, which Becca had dropped, stopped whirling on the dirt floor.

"Is that . . . is it . . . ?" Becca cried.

"I think s-so, I think . . . no, I *know* . . . that's a cleaver in a sk-skull. It's a b-bo—"

"Jaymie, shut up!" Becca said, her tone strangled. She squeezed Jaymie's hands and stared into her eyes.

"What's wrong?"

"I recognize that sweater," Becca said, her tone agonized. "Delores wore it. Valetta's mom knitted it for her when she was g-going out with Brock! And the hair . . . it's the s-same color, the *exact* shade of light

brownish-reddish-blonde with dark roots."
Her tone was feverish, the words rapid-fire.
"She used . . . she used Sun-In to color it
that summer and it was growing out!
Ooooh," she moaned, swaying. "Jaymie, I
think that's Delores in the t-trunk!"

THREE

Their plans for the rest of the day, admittedly just dinner and nothing much else, went out the window. Jaymie called the police department. There was no need for 911; there was no assailant hiding in the basement to endanger them. Chief Ledbetter, in his last few months of service to the department, came out, with Bernie Jenkins, as well as Detective Angela Vestry, a frosty but competent woman. The chief was a proponent of women in policing and it was widely expected that when he retired in a few months he would be replaced by Assistant Police Chief Deborah Connolly.

The chief and detective interviewed Jaymie and Becca separately. Becca's interview was considerably longer, given that she knew the girl they suspected was the victim of a heinous crime. Jaymie sat on the porch shivering even in the warmth of an unusually mild late April; Hoppy leaned on her lap, snuffling and snoring in a doggie nap, as she stroked him and ruffled his ears. It upset Jaymie that they had been in the house all day, never knowing that below them was the body of a teenager who never had a chance to grow up. All the years that Becca had assumed she was living it up in California or somewhere else warm and far away, her body had been moldering in that trunk.

Jaymie's mind teemed with questions. Had Brock actually spoken to Delores and had she told him she was running away? He had a tendency to exaggerate and embellish, so she didn't trust much that he said. Had Delores returned home first, where something heinous was done to her? Or had she started out hitchhiking, only to be dragged home? Did Delores's aunt and uncle *know* she was in that trunk all those years? Or *was* she in that trunk all those years? She had disappeared in October or November, Becca said. She was apparently wearing the sweater Valetta's mom had knit for her, which fit with the autumn. Was Creepy Clifford to blame?

So many, *many* questions and no answers.

Chief Ledbetter lumbered out the front door and heaved his bulk into a creaky Adirondack chair on the porch. "Come talk to me, Jaymie."

She obeyed, taking the other Adirondack, a little loosey-goosey — it could use some screws and glue — but holding up, and picking Hoppy up to sit on her lap.

He eyed her, then squinted off in the distance, across the road and over the plowed rows of dirt in the rolling fields. "We're 'bout ready to pack it in, once the team moves the body. Not much to see here after all these years."

"We've cleaned and sorted every corner of this place except for the basement and the attic. Too bad we didn't find it — the body . . . poor Delores — earlier."

"Wouldn't have made much difference. We figured out with your sister that the last time anyone saw Delores Paget was fall of 1984, early November, she says now, far as she remembers. We'll narrow it down. That is going back some time for people's memories, but we have resources."

"So you're proceeding based on the idea that it is Delores."

"Becca seems pretty sure about the sweater and the hair. It's going to be touch-and-go since there appears to be no surviving family."

"What about that cousin of Delores's, Clifford? Becca mentioned him but I don't

48

know what happened to him."

"It appears that he was killed in a boating accident in the nineties. The uncle, Jimbo Paget, died in two thousand of a heart attack, then Olga Paget last year. We'll start with blood typing to narrow it down, and do DNA too, of course."

"What about dental records?"

"That's our best hope," he admitted. "She must have had dental work done, but it's going to take some time to go back that far and construct a timeline."

Jaymie pondered the problem as the chief reached out to rub Hoppy's ears. He took the pup from her and rested him on his paunch, letting the little dog curl up there and snooze.

"Becca's friends, Dee Stubbs and Valetta Nibley, both knew Delores. And Brock . . . I guess my sister told you that Brock and Delores dated? And what Brock said, that he'd talked to Delores the last day she was ever seen, and she said she was taking off?"

He nodded. "I've got Jenkins on it right now," he said, referring to Bernice Jenkins, who had been promoted and served as a kind of assistant and driver for the chief. "Your sister didn't know Delores's parents' names, or even if Paget was her legal last name."

"The lawyer handling the estate should know though, right? They would have researched the family to try to find an heir."

"Good point. We're kinda scrambling to find our feet here. I've investigated cold cases before, but this one is in the deep freeze because she was never officially listed as missing, just as a runaway." He got out a notebook and laboriously made a note, huffing and puffing through it. He stuck the notebook in his pocket. "Jenkins wants me to get some kinda digital device to make notes. I said a notebook doesn't run out of battery power."

Jaymie smiled. When she had first met the chief a year ago she had been unnerved and unsure how to take him. Now she knew him better, through a few investigations; he was smarter than he let on, and nicer, too. Becca, looking wan and unsettled, joined them on the porch.

"Detective Vestry said we could go now," she told her sister.

"Chief?" Jaymie said, turning to Ledbetter.

"Sure," he replied, handing a sleepy Hoppy to her. "I'll be in touch."

September 1984
The weather was so weird, Becca thought,

50

disgruntled. One day it was blazing hot and you had to wear short sleeves to school or suffer, and the next you were shivering. She was shivering today; she had left the house in a skirt and short-sleeved blouse, even when her mom told her to wear a sweater. It didn't help that she and her mom had a huge argument that morning about Becca coming straight home from school. She had finally made up her summer-long quarrel with Dee and had promised to go to her place to study, but instead she'd have to go straight home to babysit Jaymie.

Oops, there was Delores coming down the hall. Becca flung open her metal locker door and hid behind it, waiting for the other girl to pass, but instead she felt a tap on her shoulder. "Oh, hey, Del, I didn't see you there," she said, ducking her head around the metal door.

"Yeah, you did. Then you hid." Del's acne-riddled face was red with emotion. Her blondish-reddish hair, dark roots growing out from the summer attempt at dyeing it blonde, was newly but badly layered, so Del had tried to curl it away from her face. It was half successful. "You coming out to my place this weekend?"

"I can't," Becca said. She saw Dee coming down the hall arm in arm with her boyfriend, Johnny Stubbs, and felt a moment of panic. She had to tell DeeDee that she couldn't come over after school, but she didn't want Dee to think she was ditching her for Delores. "I gotta go." She slammed her locker shut, hurriedly snapped the combination lock in place and trotted away toward Dee and Johnny. When she looked over her shoulder, Delores was still standing, watching them.

It was a moment of indecision, but the look on Delores's face decided it. She told Dee to wait a minute, and went back to her summer friend. "Hey, I forgot to ask . . . we're having a pizza party for my birthday this Saturday night. Can you come over and hang out?"

Delores's face lit up, but then she shook her head. "I don't know how. I don't have a ride."

"Maybe my dad can pick you up. He offered to pick up a couple of kids, and I don't think he'd mind swinging by your place."

"Really?" Del's cheeks were rosy. "That would be so cool! Your dad is the greatest."

"I know," Becca said with a smile. "See you in class." She dashed off to join Dee and Johnny, who were in her first-period English.

The birthday party was okay, Becca thought, but they were kind of cramped into the front parlor of their old house, and they couldn't be too loud because her mom wasn't feeling well and Jaymie was still colicky. There were seven of them: Becca, Valetta and her brother Brock, Dee and Johnny, and a couple of others, all crowded onto two finicky antique sofas that faced each other across a low coffee table full of cans of pop and boxes of pizza from the only pizza place in Wolverhampton. There were three separate conversations going, none of which she was part of.

Her mom and dad had given her a boom box, and Dee's gift to her was a Eurythmics tape, but she couldn't play it above a whisper. "Sweet Dreams Are Made of This" was playing for the fourth time. She wished it was Michael Jackson's "Thriller" instead. They should have gone bowling in Wolverhampton. At least they'd be able to laugh out loud without Dad coming in and shushing them with that worried look on his face. This was getting ultra lame.

Delores sure was enjoying herself, Becca thought, eyeing her summer friend, who was glowing with happiness, sitting and talking to Brock Nibley, Valetta's older brother. Becca didn't like Brock much, but he was one of her best friends' brothers, so she had to put up with him. If he wasn't invited to every party he got in a snit, and that left Valetta in an awkward position.

Brock, dark-haired and lanky, not cute but not really ugly, either, was jammed right up against Delores, his hand on her leg slightly under the edge of her denim skirt. Delores was red-faced, the gleam in her eye almost manic. Becca was uneasy, but when she had tried to get Delores away from Brock both had shooed her away. The two disappeared outside for a while and Delores came back hand in hand with him, radiant, joy illuminating her plain face.

The party was over pretty early. It would probably go down as one of the most boring parties in Queensville history. Dee and Johnny had already strolled away hand in hand to walk back to her place. They were happy to go, Becca could tell, but they probably wouldn't get home for hours. The rest of them were all milling around outside, saying their goodbyes, and Becca's dad was lining up who he had to drive home.

Becca grabbed Delores, but the girl pulled away. "Brock's gonna drive me home," she whispered, cupping her hand around Becca's ear.

There was booze on her breath; that meant Brock had a bottle hidden somewhere, the creep. Becca searched Delores's face by the dim light that spilled out through the open door from the front hall. "Maybe that's not a good idea," she whispered back.

Brock was standing a ways away tossing keys up in the air and whistling.

"Why not?" Delores had that look, her brows drawn down with two vertical lines between them; she was waiting for a reason to be mad.

"You don't *like* him like him, do you?"

Delores stared at her. "What's it to you? I thought he was, like, your second best friend's brother. You jealous?"

"Don't be an idiot," Becca muttered, beginning to get angry herself. She watched as her dad politely guided two other girls into his sedan, then looked back toward Delores uncertainly. This was *not* how the evening was supposed to go. This was the most *un*-fun birthday party ever in the history of birthday parties. Wasn't your sixteenth supposed to be special? "I don't even *like* him. It's just . . . he's older than you, you know."

"Only a year and a half," Delores said with

a defiant sniff. "Gawd, Becca, don't be such a prude."

Brock strode over, grabbed Delores's arm and tugged her to his car. She climbed in and he got in the driver's side, gunned the aging sedan, and they sped off in the increasing chill of a late September night, blasting Air Supply's "The One That You Love."

FOUR

Late April — The Present
The sisters couldn't finish emptying and cleaning the Paget house because, despite the chief's gloomy expectation that they wouldn't find anything, they were still searching the house and examining the floor and walls for thirty-year-old blood spatter. Becca returned to London, Ontario, to work on her own business, a china matching service, and Jaymie returned to her multiplicity of jobs, as well as her volunteer work at the Queensville Historic Manor for the Victoria Day weekend event they held, popular with both Americans and Canadians, Tea with the Queen.

It was one of two major fund-raising events each year and accounted for a good amount of their operating budget. Mrs. Trelawney Bellwood was their local Queen Victoria impersonator and presided over the tea table on the lawn of Stowe House with imperial decorum. This year, for the first time ever, she was sharing the duties over the two-day event with her onetime-friend-turned-enemy-turned-friend-again Mrs. Imogene Frump.

Daniel Collins, briefly Jaymie's boyfriend and multimillionaire owner of Stowe House, was going to be in town since he was planning to sell the manor now that his interest in Queensville — Jaymie herself — was over. Late last fall Daniel had swiftly broken up with Jaymie and married his ex-girlfriend Trish, and they were now expecting a child. Jaymie had been relieved by the breakup, not hurt. It had cleared the way for her strong interest in Jakob Müller, and look how that had turned out!

But despite being busy she was not able to get the death of Delores Paget off her mind. How awful that because of Brock telling everyone she was running away no one reported her missing. Not even her aunt and uncle! How was it possible that Delores was dead in their basement the whole time? They must have either been responsible or at least have known.

It gave her shivers whenever she thought of it. Late at night it took two chapters of a romance novel and a phone call from Jakob to get it off her mind.

■ ■ ■ ■

A couple of days after finding the body, it was her Saturday to work in the Queensville Emporium, the hundred-plus-year-old general store that had been in the Klausner family for much of that time. The two very elderly Klausners who currently owned it were training their granddaughter, Gracey, to run it, and eventually she would take over, but today she was driving them on errands and family visiting. Jaymie ran one of her own businesses, Vintage Picnic Rentals, out of the store, so she walked over with two tote bags full of supplies.

It was a lovely late April morning, with robins in full throaty song and red-winged blackbirds chirring loudly, advertising their eligibility as good mates. The air was fresh, but as the sun climbed it warmed up and the various smells of morning floated to Jaymie: good coffee, bacon, freshly mowed grass, and blooming hyacinths, their dense purple blooms bunched in many gardens she passed.

Main Street was still quiet. She climbed the steps in a warm beam of spring sunshine and waited on the wooden porch for Valetta, who was arriving with the keys. Valetta, originally Becca's childhood friend, was now more Jaymie's best pal; she ran the pharmacy counter out of the Emporium from a walled and carefully locked section at the back, dispensing medication to Queensville residents through a sliding glass partition.

Valetta, garbed in her usual colorful sweater and with her enormous purse over her shoulder, was unexpectedly silent and didn't chitchat as she usually did. She went straight to the back, unlocked her domain, and set up for her day. Troubled by her friend's unaccustomed lack of warmth, Jaymie did her job, tidied up her picnic basket rental counter, rang up sales and anxiously waited until their usual midmorning break for tea. They met each other on the porch and sat on the top step with their tea and some cookies Jaymie had made that morning.

The day was brilliant, the sun beaming through the spring green foliage so the leaves almost glowed. But until she knew what was wrong with Valetta, Jaymie couldn't enjoy the day. "So, what's up?" she asked, cradling her hands around her mug of tea and staring over at her friend. "Why are you so quiet this morning?"

Valetta shrugged and stared off across the

street to the antique shop Becca and Kevin were opening in a couple of weeks, in time for tourist season. "Brock came over last night."

"Ah."

"He feels like because you don't like him, you threw him under the bus to the police with the missing Delores Paget thing."

Jaymie watched her friend, who still stared straight ahead. "Seriously?"

Valetta shrugged and grimaced. "That's what he said. I don't want to get in the middle of this. It's none of my business."

"I didn't throw him under the bus, Val. I reported what he told Becca when Delores disappeared. Becca said it too. Why is Brock so upset about *that*?"

"He's not upset," Valetta said, casting a glance swiftly at Jaymie then looking away again. Jaymie knew that her friend often felt caught halfway between her brother, who was not a pleasant man, and the world. "Not *exactly*. He feels like as a real estate agent his reputation is the most important thing about him. And the police spent a *long* time interviewing him. He's sensitive."

Sensitive like a buffalo, Jaymie thought, but did not say. Brock was not one of her favorite people, it was true. He was a bigot and thought a lot of himself. He was conde-

61

scending to her, shouting her down any time she said something about the poor in their country, or people of different races or sexual orientation. He called her naïve and a "bleeding heart." She avoided him when possible but she was reluctant to criticize him too severely to Valetta; he was her brother, after all, and even though Val usually acknowledged her brother's faults, if push came to shove he was family.

Odd that he was upset though. "Didn't he *want* to help the officers out?"

"Of course he did!" Valetta cast her a sharp look, brows drawn down, glasses glinting in the sun. "What are you saying, Jaymie?"

"Nothing, Val, really. But it's important to establish where and when Delores was last seen and what she said. The police will be interviewing everyone, even you and Dee, probably."

"It was a long time ago," she said. There was silence between them for a while, but Valetta finally sighed and sipped her tea. "Okay, I may as well say it," she said, again wrapping her hands around her mug. "I have a feeling Brock fibbed a bit about what Delores said."

Aha, so *that* was it! Brock had lied either about seeing Delores at all or what she said about leaving town. Maybe he even started saying that after the fact when she disappeared. Over the years those subtleties could get lost. That was unfortunate, but it wasn't *her* fault he'd fibbed. "He'll have to tell Chief Ledbetter the truth, then."

"I think he's afraid it's going to make him look guilty."

Jaymie eyed her older friend. There was something more going on. "Val, they dated, right? Brock and Delores?"

"They went out a few times."

"How many is a few?"

But Valetta just shook her head.

"That's why your mother knitted Delores a sweater."

Valetta nodded, but would not be drawn out further. "It's Brock's story, not mine. I'd rather not talk about it."

Jaymie frowned down at her tea. Surely Brock wouldn't *completely* lie about Delores telling him she was taking off. She must have said something to him and he passed it along. Otherwise the aunt and uncle would have reported her missing, unless one of them or the cousin killed Delores. She kept coming back to that; it was the most likely answer, given that she was in a trunk in their basement.

At that very moment Valetta's brother

pulled up in his '99 Cadillac and parked across three spaces that were supposed to be for customers. He got out, frostily nodded to Jaymie, and said, "Val, can I talk to you for a minute?"

She got up and dusted off the seat of her pants with her free hand, clutching her empty mug in her other. "Sure."

They disappeared inside.

Jaymie sipped the rest of her tea, her stomach feeling queasy. Something was wrong, she knew it. But what?

FIVE

She didn't have a chance to speak with Valetta again that day. About five in the afternoon Jaymie's replacement arrived to look after the Emporium and Valetta closed her pharmacy counter. Her friend seemed preoccupied as they said their goodbyes on the sidewalk outside the store. Jaymie watched her walk away, hefted her bag on her shoulder and headed in the opposite direction, trudging home. As always, her home lifted in her spirits. It was a lovely old Queen Anne yellow brick, close to the narrow street. She had planted pansies in the black wrought-iron planters on either side of the door but they were fading. Soon it would be time to trade out the pansies for summer annuals, some trailing petunias and ivy, maybe some lobelia.

She unlocked the front door and entered the welcome quiet of the front hall to the sound of the phone ringing. She threw her bag down and trotted to the kitchen. As she grabbed the cordless phone, Denver twined around her feet and Hoppy yapped, begging to be let out. She said hello as she let the animals out the back door.

It was Heidi. "Don't you ever look at your text messages, Jaymie?" she asked, her usually placid tone fretful. She didn't even use her customary pet name, *Jaymsie.* "Or check your messages or email? I've been trying to get you *all day*!"

She had a million questions, she said, about the wedding. She asked them rapid-fire, and Jaymie answered as best she could. Heidi then had some random complaints about dealing with Becca, as well as a grievance about how cavalier Jakob was being about the wedding. He didn't even seem to care whether his groomsmen wore rose boutonnieres or carnations! And that made all the difference in the world!

Jaymie let the dog back in, fed the cat, fed the dog and rustled around in her fridge, receiver to her ear, waiting until her friend was silent. "Heidi, neither do I care," she finally said. "I'd be just as happy if Jakob was in a plaid shirt with no jacket and no boutonniere at all. He can wear a housecoat as far as I care." There was silence at the other end. Had she offended her friend?

"Heidi?"

"I'm here. I'm wondering if plaid would work."

Jaymie laughed, answered more of her friend's questions to the best of her ability, then, with Heidi calmer, they chatted.

"I heard about you finding that body," Heidi said. "So *awful*! Yuck. I'd be so scared. You do have a talent for finding bodies."

"Don't blame me, this one is on Becca. She's the one who made us look in the basement."

"So, do you think it is that girl, the one they're talking about?"

Jaymie was cautious. "What are people saying?" She wedged the receiver against her shoulder while she fished around in the fridge for salad fixings.

"I heard that it's some girl called Delores Paget who disappeared back in the eighties, and that Becca identified her from her sweater."

"Yeah, I think it's pretty definite. That *was* her home, after all." The fridge needed a good cleaning out, but it would have to wait. There was lettuce, cucumbers, radishes, green onions and some leftover roast chicken, enough for a good dinner salad.

"I was in Wolverhampton to see Tami and everyone was in a dither about it," Heidi said. "I said something to Tami and you know how *she* gets . . . she's a nervous wreck half the time anyway, and it's worse right now because she's trying to quit smoking. She was so upset about the body and all. I guess she knew the girl."

"A lot of people in their age group must have. They all went to the same high school." That meant that not only Becca and Brock, but Valetta, Dee, her husband Johnny, Gus, Tami, and who knew how many others would remember her. She wondered if the police would interview them all. Eventually, perhaps, but this investigation could take a while, given how long ago the murder happened.

"So who killed her?" Heidi asked.

"I don't have a clue."

"Well, it must have been her parents, right?"

"Her aunt and uncle, you mean?" Jaymie chopped cucumber, then tore lettuce into a big bowl.

"Whatever . . . *them.* Whoever she lived with. Since she was in the basement all along it had to be, right?"

It was the logical answer, but that, thank goodness, was up to the police to figure out. She asked Heidi something random about the wedding to change the subject and her friend went happily off on a tangent about colors and flowers and wedding favors. By the time they hung up she had likely forgotten all about the murder.

But it would not leave Jaymie's mind so easily. She wondered if Becca had any idea how bad things were in Delores's home. They must have been awful for her to end up dead. No one got a cleaver in the head by accident, though *she* almost did. Jaymie shuddered. Maybe it happened in the middle of an argument. Teenagers could be prickly, but to pick up a cleaver and give a well-aimed blow to the skull . . . ?

Jaymie enjoyed her salad as the sky outside turned a deep shade of mauve, then indigo. She curled up on her bed to read for a while, kept company by Denver and Hoppy. It was funny, she'd been living alone for several years except for occasional visits from Becca, who co-owned the house, and less frequent visits from their parents, Alan and Joy Leighton, who had moved to Boca Raton years ago. But being alone was different now. She was anxious for her life and Jakob's to be merged.

In fact, she felt lonely, but as she thought that the phone rang and a long conversation with Jakob settled her down. She'd have loved to have taken him up on his invitation

69

to come out to the log cabin for a couple of hours, but couldn't. She cradled her head on her arm and petted Denver with her free hand while holding the receiver to her ear. "I have to get up super early tomorrow and drive up to see Grandma in Canada, and then Monday I have to get up super early again and go out to the cottage to clean up," she said, talking about the Leighton property on Heartbreak Island, Rose Tree Cottage. "Our landscaper is going to be working on the patio behind it to get it done before peak rental season, and I promised I'd send him pictures to start his plan with."

"I miss you."

"Mmmm." She shivered delightedly. "We'll be together all the time, pretty soon," she whispered, even though there was no one else in the house. "June seventeenth."

They had decided not to live together until they were married, partly because they wanted to make the day momentous, symbolic of their joining together as a family, but mostly for Jocie's sake. Her life was going to change enormously, and even though she loved Jaymie and looked forward to the wedding, she deserved time alone with her father before the change happened.

"I'm having trouble waiting," he murmured. "Your little friend has been harassing me nonstop, one more reason to look forward to the day."

"My little friend?"

"Heidi Whatshername. She's called me a dozen times in the last two days, for a million reasons. My best man's name, colors I prefer, my parents' phone number . . . so *many* things! She's bugging Gus, at the shop, and has put reserved tags on a bunch of stuff at the store that she wants to use for the wedding. Are you *sure* it's easier if she takes care of it?" he asked.

Jaymie giggled happily, then gave in to a belly laugh. Denver, offended that the bed was shaking, jumped down and ran out of the room, but Hoppy leaped around; he loved laughter. "Jakob, you have no *clue*! She was on the phone to me as soon as I got home this afternoon. But honestly, she would have pestered me until I let her do it, so it was a foregone conclusion. And this way you don't have to hear me and Becca fighting about all of this. Heidi is our referee. I have no talent for this kind of thing anyway. Heidi does, and she *so* wanted to do it!"

It was true. Her pleading blue eyes had melted Jaymie's heart, so she had convinced Becca that this way the sisters wouldn't argue. But also, she trusted Heidi's exqui-

71

site taste.

"Honey, you could do anything you set your mind to."

She murmured back sweet words and the conversation turned deeply personal. After that, sleeping was easy.

Sunday she drove to Canada with Hoppy and had a long day with her grandmother talking nothing but wedding plans, recipes and the good old days. She and her little dog both came home exhausted late at night and dropped into bed with a miffed Denver, who chose to ignore her.

She awoke refreshed the next morning and took Hoppy for a long walk because she was not going to take him over to the island this time. Then, tote bag filled with cleaning supplies, she headed out, walking toward the river. From there she would take the ferry over to Heartbreak Island, the semi-heart-shaped island in the middle of the St. Clair River that was shared property between the United States and Canada. Rose Tree Cottage, the Leighton family rental property, was a sweet blue-and-white haven with so many good family memories attached that Jaymie had suggested it as a great honeymoon destination. Jakob insisted that he wanted Jaymie all to himself at first, so they were going to go camping on Lake

Huron in Canada for a few days. Then they'd come back to stay at the cabin as a family with Jocie for a week before the rental season began in earnest.

It was another sparkling spring day, with throaty birdsong and the rustle of a breeze tossing the treetops. The Queensville–Heartbreak Island–Johnsonville ferry — officially named the *St. Clair Queen* — was fully capable of taking cars and small trucks across the river to the island and Canada. It had a drive-on portion for vehicles, and a passenger entry for people. Today, though, there were no cars, just a few passengers. She boarded the passenger end, sat on a bench near the prow, and enjoyed the ferry ride over, watching the seagulls circling overhead, then bobbing in contented peace on the boat's gentle wake.

She worked in the cottage all day with only a brief break for lunch and to check in with her neighbors behind, the Redmonds, to tell them about her landscape designer's plan for the back. Sammy Dobrinskie, the son of a man Jaymie had found murdered on the cottage property last summer, was almost done with his first year of landscape design classes. Naturally gifted, he and Jaymie had stayed in contact all winter via email and had continued planning a stone patio, bricked-in fire pit, and gardens to add value to their rental cottage. He would be working on it weekends in May and full-time in June, to be finished before Jaymie and Jakob's honeymoon and prime rental season, July and August. She took photos of the area to send to Sammy, video-chatted with him for a few minutes, walking around with her tablet to show him what she had in mind, sent him the photos, then closed down to let him get back to his homework.

She locked the cottage, and, as the sun began sliding downward in the sky, she started back to the marina, inhaling deeply the fishy scent of the river. The Michigan State Troopers were having diving exercises off the dock. They did that fairly frequently because they were often called upon to perform river rescues, so they had an inflatable dinghy and a dive team working together. The ferry was still on the Canadian side. It would be another ten to fifteen minutes before it arrived, but it was a mellow spring day and she was entertained. She sat down on a park bench and made a few notes for the Tea with the Queen event and reflected on how different her life was from the last May tea event, when she had started dating Daniel Collins, the multimillionaire software company owner who was now going to sell the mansion.

He was a restless spirit, she discovered, and bought houses like some people buy cars, as a collection. He had now lost interest, which was why the house would be going up for sale right after the Tea with the Queen event. She was happy he had found someone else, and happy she had Jakob.

Her daydreams were interrupted by shouts. One of the divers had surfaced out of the greenish depths and was pointing out to a deeper section of the river toward the shipping lane. She got up to see what was going on and hoped the commotion didn't mean one of the troopers was in trouble. The St. Clair River was highly variable for diving, some days being excellent and others murky. There were also some treacherous spots where a diver could get tangled in junk. She hoped that hadn't happened.

She strode to the end of the ferry dock, shading her eyes with one hand from the glimmer of the lowering sun off the water's surface. The trooper boat was anchored about twenty feet off the marina and there was a lot of activity, with much excited chatter and gestures. Ruby Redmond, thin and athletic, wearing a red velour jogging suit, joined Jaymie. Just the summer before Jaymie had saved her from drowning in almost this same spot.

"What's it all about?" she asked, her weathered narrow face alight with curiosity.

"I don't know," Jaymie said. "But they're waving the ferry away. Darn! I hoped to get home soon."

The ferry was turned away and within minutes Robin, the island's only plumber, arrived driving his heaviest truck with the strongest winch. He was the only one on the island who had heavy equipment suitable for using in the river. Soon, word filtered through the growing crowd. The MSP diver had found a submerged wreck. The heavy hook on Robin's winch was taken out by a diver, hooked on to the bumper of the wreck, and the plumber was soon dragging the car out of the water, the high whine of the winch cutting through the chilling air.

Garnet, Ruby's husband and co-owner of the Ice House restaurant, joined them as the setting sun cast a gold light slanting over the glistening water of the St. Clair. "There are so many rumors going around the restaurant I had to come and see for myself," he said, putting his arm over his wife's shoulders. He was a tall man, slim, weathered, and handsome in an aristocratic way. "You'd think no one ever saw a car being dragged out of the river."

More people joined them. Finally the vehicle was hauled out of the river and up the paved boat launch slope.

"Looks like an old Ford Falcon, nineteen seventies, maybe," Garnet said, squinting through the slanting stream of sunlight.

"You can tell that?" Jaymie asked, amazed.

He chuckled, his lean face wreathing in wrinkles. "I was a car-obsessed young man once upon a time. I can tell you the make, model and year by the headlight configuration of any American-made car from the fifties to the eighties."

It was layered in slime and muck, and water sluiced out of one broken window as it was dragged up the sloping boat launch area near the dock. One of the dive-suited state police officers approached the car, his swim fins flapping on the cement. He yelled and motioned for the others. The breeze carried one word to the crowd: *body.*

The islanders surged toward the boat launch and Jaymie was carried with them. Robin had his hose out and was rinsing the car down. The windows were busted, and as she was carried closer Jaymie could see the figure in the driver's seat. Was the driver still belted in?

Horrified, she tried to pull back, but others crowded around her, pushing her forward, and as Robin was shoved, too, his clean water sluiced up into the window and hit the body, spraying mud everywhere. But Jaymie, before she turned away in horror, did see one thing: the figure in the driver's seat was wearing a red sweater of some sort, and it looked a whole lot like the one Delores Paget was wearing in that trunk in the Paget basement.

Six

October 1984

Becca rocked the buggy back and forth on the wood floor of the Emporium, waiting while Valetta served another customer. Val had a part-time job there, and Becca, now that she, too, had turned sixteen, was hoping she'd be able to help sometimes. There weren't many other jobs in Queensville except as a maid at the old Queensville Inn, a six-room guesthouse.

"So I wondered if you know what's going on," Becca said as the customer left, continuing a conversation they had been having before Mrs. Stubbs interrupted with an abrupt demand for service. She was the oldest of all of their friends' moms, more like Becca's grandmother's age, and demanded respect. No one crossed her, especially not her kids, Lyle, the oldest, and Johnny, the youngest (and also Dee's boyfriend), among them. "Is Brock dating Delores or what?"

"Why do you care?" Valetta said, pulling a box of candy bars out of the display case to straighten them.

"Del seems . . . weird lately."

"She's always been weird," Val said, shoving the box back into the case and grabbing a broom. She circled the register desk and began to sweep the creaky wood floors of the aisle.

"I mean *different* weird, you know?" Becca wasn't about to share what she had told Delores at her birthday party, that maybe going out with Brock was not a good idea. "She won't even talk to me. And last week I asked her in biology if she wanted to team up for the genetics and heredity project and she said she already had a partner."

"That's weird? Maybe she didn't want to be saddled with your questionable science abilities," Valetta quipped, pushing up her glasses and tugging down the red sweater she wore.

"That's a new sweater," Becca said, distracted. The baby started to fuss, so she went back to rocking the buggy as Val went back to sweeping. She didn't want to go home too quickly. Her mom was napping, so Becca hoped baby Jaymie stayed content and not needing a bottle or a change for at least another half hour. "Where did you get it?" She picked up the baby and bounced her. "Shhhh . . . Jaymie, it's okay." But the infant squalled and wriggled on her shoulder.

"Mom knit it!" Valetta whirled, her broom like a dance partner. The sweater was bright red, dolman sleeved, and well knit.

Becca reached out and touched the wool; it had an odd synthetic feel to it. "What kind of material is that?"

"My mom went over to Canada with Mrs. Stubbs last month and bought the knit shop in Johnsonville out of Phentex. It's a Canadian yarn, I guess, and it's supposed to last forever. I like the color. She'll knit one for you if you like. She sure has enough of that wool!"

"No, it's okay," Becca said. The last thing she wanted was to dress like twinsies with her friends. Jaymie gave a burp and stopped crying, so Becca laid her back down in the buggy. She straightened and eyed her friend. She was about to tread on dangerous ground. "Is Brock serious about Delores? 'Cause I don't think he should be messing around with her unless he *really* likes her. She's . . . fragile."

Valetta snorted and started sweeping vigorously. "You mean fragile as in peculiar?"

81

"No, I mean fragile as in she's had a crappy life so far, her parents died when she was a baby and she's being raised by an aunt and uncle who don't seem to give a darn about her, *and* she has a creepy cousin around all the time." The baby started fussing again, so Becca picked her up and bounced her yet again, trying to keep the anxiety out of her voice for Jaymie's sake. "*That's* what I mean by fragile."

Chastened, Valetta stopped sweeping, leaned on the broom and said, "I'll talk to Brock and see what's going on. But, Becca, it's none of our business, right?"

"I guess. I'd better get Jaymie home. She's still fussy. By the time I get there Mom ought to be up from her nap."

"I hope your mom is feeling better soon."

"Me too," Becca said fervently, putting the baby back in the buggy and covering her up. "Grandma Leighton is coming to stay for a while. She and Mom don't always get along, but at least she'll be here to help with Jaymie."

"I wish my mom had a baby," Valetta said.

"No. You don't. You can babysit Jaymie next time she has colic. That'll cure you."

April — The Present
It was late by the time Jaymie got home.

Tired and heart-sickened by what she'd seen, she was surprised that her dog wasn't right at the door when she opened it. "Hoppy? Where are you, sweetie?" She searched the main floor, front parlor, hallway, living room, den, all the way back to the kitchen. He never went upstairs without her because he couldn't manage the stairs alone going up, though he could going down. "Hoppy!" she shouted, more worried.

Denver looked up from his basket by the stove with one eye open, watching her. He yawned hugely, then pointedly got out of his basket, stretched and ambled to his dish, stopping and staring up at her.

"Not 'til you tell me where Hoppy is," she said to his pointed, if nonverbal, request for dinner.

He yawned.

"Hoppy?"

She heard a whimper and her heart clutched. She searched again and found him quivering between the Hoosier cabinet and cupboard in the kitchen. "What's wrong, baby?"

His little butt started wiggling but he still wouldn't come out. She moved closer and her sock-covered foot was swiftly soaked. A yellowish puddle on the kitchen floor showed why he was hiding.

"Aw, sweetie, I don't care about that!" she said, plunking down on the floor away from the puddle as Hoppy wriggled out of his hiding spot and climbed into her lap. She hugged him close as he whimpered. "I would have called Valetta to let you out, but she was working and I didn't have my cell phone with me. It's okay, sweetie, it's just piddle."

And why she was explaining to a dog she'd never know, but the tone of her voice settled him down and he snuggled and wuffled his contentment. A short while later her socks were drying, the floor was clean, the animals were happy, a sandwich was made, tea was steaming, and Jaymie sat down in the front parlor with her laptop and phone to check her messages and phone calls. Heidi, Heidi and Heidi, at first. Two phone messages and an email. Phone call from Jakob. Email from Becca. Phone message from Nan Good-enough, her editor at the *Wolverhampton Howler* asking when her next column would be on her desk.

"Good question," Jaymie muttered.

She emailed Heidi, answering the questions from the phone calls and email: turquoise blue; antique rose; roses; pearls; and vintage broaches. The questions had been rapid-fire: Becca's color, Jaymie's color, the preferred flower the two brides had in common, and the jewelry items preferred by Becca and Jaymie. Becca was easy; Jaymie answered by email that no, she didn't have her wedding dress yet and no, she didn't want Becca's help in finding one.

Ever.

Becca was a wonderful, loving sister, but when she found dresses for Jaymie they tended to be things *she* would wear, not taking into account that her sister was fifteen years younger and had a completely different style. So no, Jaymie did not want to go wedding dress shopping with Becca again.

After she hit Send she thought maybe she should have called her sister instead of emailing. That snatch of red she had seen on the body in the submerged car, so like the red of Delores Paget's red sweater, haunted her. And yet, it was mere coincidence. There were many red garments in the world and who knew when that car had gone into the St. Clair River?

There was surely no connection. Why in the world should there be?

Nan she'd call in the morning, she decided. It was far too late for a return phone call, and an email would not allow the back-

and-forth she needed to decide on the next "Vintage Eats" column and discuss what she'd do about it while she was on her honeymoon. The food column had started last year as a way to help her gain experience and some measure of recognition while she wrote a vintage recipe cookbook she hoped to publish someday.

The more she pressed forward with the cookbook, though, the more she realized how unready she was. She had been so naïve when she first wrote the cookbook — it was a grand way to get over the broken heart she was left with after Joel deserted her for Heidi — but she now knew it would take a couple of more years, at least, before the cookbook was truly ready, and before *she* was ready.

Jakob was the only call left. She finished her supper and tea, turned off all the lights, and climbed upstairs, carrying Hoppy as Denver followed. A chat with Jakob was to be relished and savored, not rushed.

Over breakfast the next morning Jaymie checked her complicated calendar, with its numerous notations about hours at the Emporium, Jewel Dandridge's vintage shop, Cynthia's shabby chic cottage shop, picnic basket rentals, the "Vintage Eats" column her volunteer work for the Tea with the Queen event coming up, *and* her time working in the kitchen at the Queensville Historic Manor. Today she would be out at the historic home for a few hours, and then hopefully she could spend some time writing her food column.

Which reminded her . . . she needed to call Nan. She took a deep breath and picked up the phone. Talking to her retirement-aged whirlwind of a redheaded editor, Nan Goodenough, who with her husband had purchased the *Wolverhampton Howler* some years ago, was always exhausting. The woman had been head of a big-city magazine for years and had lost none of her vigor.

Today was no different. After rapidly going through the direction of her column for the next few months and promising two columns to fill in while she was on her honeymoon, Jaymie was ready to sign off and go have a cup of tea to settle her nerves. She stood and headed to the phone receiver to cradle the phone, but her editor was not done talking.

"So, some excitement out at your island yesterday, right?" Nan said. She insisted on calling Heartbreak Island Jaymie's island, though all the Leighton's had was one cottage.

"I was actually there to clean the cottage and saw them pull the car out of the water," she said. It would be the lead in the next newspaper, she assumed, just as Jaymie and Becca's finding of the body in the trunk had been the last headline two days ago.

"So what do you think the connection was?"

Jaymie, puzzled, didn't answer for a long minute.

"Jaymie? You still there? What's the connection between the two girls?"

"I don't suppose there is one," Jaymie said slowly.

"Oh, come on, two girls from the same school wearing the same hand-knit sweater disappear the same day, and then are both found dead? The only coincidence is how both bodies were found within days of each other, but their *deaths*? *That* is no coincidence. They have to be connected, or my name isn't Goodenough."

"Two girls, disappeared the same *day*? From the same school?" Jaymie, the wind knocked out of her, sat back down at the trestle table in the center of the kitchen. "Nan, I haven't heard anything. You'll have to fill me in."

"I assumed you'd know all about this."

"I don't."

Nan then told her all she knew from the newspaper's research and chat with the police spokeswoman, Bernice Jenkins. The body was most likely that of Rhonda Welch, a senior at Chance Houghton Christian Academy, a boarding school outside of St. Clair, Michigan, a few miles north of Queensville, when she disappeared. She had, however, just days before been a student at Wolverhampton High. The car was registered to her parents, who were out of the country on a church mission, which was why Rhonda was at a boarding school.

It was widely reported at the time, Nan said, after checking the newspaper archives from November of 1984, that Rhonda was thought to have run away, which was supported by the car disappearing. Her parents came back to the U.S. to try to find her but all efforts failed. She had been unhappy with her family and at the boarding school. Her aunt, Petty Welch, a researcher at a Detroit newspaper who lived near Detroit, said Rhonda had been asking some odd questions in the weeks before her disappearance about infant abduction that led Petty to believe she was questioning her birth. There was, though, nothing odd about her familial past, as the aunt could attest, since she had known her niece since birth.

"Is there any evidence that Rhonda and Delores knew each other?"

"I don't think anyone knows yet. You've got friends who went there in about the right age range; Rhonda was a senior, while Delores Paget was a sophomore. I thought you could find out."

Jaymie was silent. And they were both wearing red sweaters. Two red sweaters knit by Mrs. Nibley? "I don't know what to say, Nan. Let me think about it. This is close to home." As she hung up, Jaymie realized she now had many more questions than answers. It was time to call Becca.

After the hellos and more info about the wedding, Jaymie told her sister what she had learned. Becca was silent for a long minute. "Holy moly," she said at long last.

"So did you know Rhonda Welch?"

"I knew *of* her, but we weren't friends or anything. Val, Dee and I were all sophomores and she was a senior, a couple of years older that we were, which is worlds apart in high school. That was so long ago! Wait a minute; I want to check something."

She put down the phone and there was dead air. Jaymie in the meantime made a list of things to do out at the historic home and was checking a website on wedding flowers when Becca came back.

"Yeah, I remember her now, very well." The sound of her leafing through book pages echoed in the receiver. "I've got my freshman yearbook — that would be the year before she took off . . . or disappeared — and looked her up. The picture helps. I do remember her quite well. She was *really* pretty. I envied her dark, smooth hair and perfect figure so much. She was in the photography club, it says in the yearbook, and wanted to go to nursing school."

They were both silent again. Jaymie was sadly thinking that the poor girl never got to be a nurse . . . never got to be anything but a written-off runaway. "Do you remember her disappearing at the same time as Delores?"

"Yes, but it was different. She wasn't going to WH anymore, and she had a car. *Everyone* said she took off because she hated her new school. It was a Christian boarding school, something to do with her parents being missionaries, if I remember right."

"Valetta is worried about Brock," Jaymie said, even as she tried to imagine a connection between Delores Paget's and Rhonda Welch's disappearances. "He's angry because I supposedly betrayed him by telling the police he was going out with Delores."

"But that was because of me!" Becca said. "I'll set Brock straight when I come down. And Valetta, too."

"No, Becca, it's okay. I'll handle it. She's just . . . you know Valetta. She'll be okay. It's always Brock. He makes things awkward."

"He's the *king* of awkward. Always was. I even had to invite him to my sixteenth birthday party so Valetta wouldn't be put in an uncomfortable position. Why he wanted to hang out with a bunch of sixteen-year-olds I don't know, but Brock was . . . *you* know." She paused. "In fact . . . I just remembered! Jeez, that's when it started, him going out with Delores."

"Your sixteenth birthday party?"

"I believe so. Val might remember."

"Dee *certainly* will. She remembers everything."

"Hah! You didn't know Dee then. She was hot and heavy with Johnny at that point and would disappear with him any time they got to go somewhere. She was off smooching with him somewhere, probably, and won't remember a thing."

"But there should be pictures from that party, right? Dad *always* took pictures of birthdays."

"He always took pictures of *your* birthdays." Becca paused, then continued. "That year was weird. It was an awful party. We had to be quiet because Mom was lying down and you were finally sleeping after being colicky for a week or two straight. Fun party for a bunch of sixteen-year-olds; pizza and silence."

"I'm sorry."

"Don't be silly, you were a baby. And I *loved* you, even when I was irritated with you."

As they hung up, Jaymie thought how odd it was that she was getting this entirely different view of her sister and their friends, who were separated from her by fifteen years. That didn't seem so much now that she was in her thirties, but it sure had seemed a lot growing up. At times Becca had seemed like a second mother to her, especially when she was four or so and her parents were going through a rough patch. Becca had made life bearable.

"Come on, Hoppy," she said. "Let's go for a walk. I'm going to be gone all afternoon and you need exercise."

She leashed her Yorkie-Poo and headed out on their usual walk toward the river. Queensville, Michigan, and its sister town, Johnsonville, Ontario, faced each other across the St. Clair River. While Queensville was named for Queen Victoria, Johnsonville was named for the unpopular President Andrew Johnson, who gained office after Lincoln's tragic assassination, but was then the first president to be impeached. He was saved from losing his presidency by one senate vote.

Everything was green and fresh and the scent on the breeze hinted at lilacs blooming somewhere close, brought on early by a warmer than usual April. Hoppy tugged and pulled, and she tried to work on his training, which he valiantly resisted. They got to the long walkway that bounded the river and overlooked Heartbreak Island, which got its name from its heart shape being divided by a waterway, and also from what was probably an apocryphal story about an American and Canadian couple parted by tragedy.

Today a blue sky arched over the river and puffy clouds were reflected in the surface of the water that slipped calmly along between the two friendly countries. The ferry pulled up to the dock. Jaymie was surprised to see Chief Ledbetter heave himself off the boat and onto the dock, then make his way huffing and puffing up to the walkway where she stood.

"Jaymie! Just the gal I wanted to see. Walk

94

with me. Bernie is pulling the car around by the public washroom."

Hoppy was barking at some ducks that were waddling along the grassy area, but she gave his leash a tug and he happily tripped along with them toward Boardwalk Park, the greenspace by the river. "I hear you've identified the body in the river as Rhonda Welch?"

He slewed a glance her way. "Yup. Newspapers have their teeth in it. That Nan woman . . . she's a tough nut. Got someone to give the name, but there's no confirmation yet, just likelihood, since the car is right and the remains were found with a school uniform on under the red sweater."

Red sweater . . . a shiver raced down her back, but she made no comment. "The Chance Houghton Christian Academy, right. Becca knew her by sight, I guess, from her attending Wolverhampton High."

"We'll be talking . . ." Huff, puff. ". . . to everyone who knew them. We've had out the school yearbooks. We'll be talking with DeeDee and Johnny Stubbs, Gustav and Tami Majewski."

"Gustav? You mean Gus?"

"Real name, Gustav. Valetta and Brock Nibley, your sister . . ." Huff, puff. "A few others. Something odd about this whole thing, and I want to get to the bottom of it." He paused to catch his breath and slid a glance over at her. "Maybe you could keep your ear to the wall. What do you think?"

"I don't think I understand, chief."

"Keep abreast, keep up . . . keep your nose to the ground and tell me what you hear."

"As in investigate?"

His large paunch heaving with his gasping breaths, he leaned forward, resting his hands on his knees while Hoppy jumped around his feet. "Gotta catch my breath. Most exercise I've done in a year, climbing up from the ferry dock." He straightened, his watery gaze fixed on her. "Don't say I said it, but yes." He scratched his chin, took in a deep breath and let it out in a whoosh. "Want you to sniff around informally. You know a lot of these people."

"But I was a baby when it happened."

"Sure, but still . . . you know them all and this town. This happened so long ago, but people's memories are likely to be jogged when they talk about it, share reminiscences, you know? That's not going to happen when I question them formally."

She glanced down the grassy hill from where they were, near the public washroom, the site of one of her infamous dead body discoveries, which had become far too commonplace for her. Bernie was there by a police car waiting for the chief. She waved and smiled.

"I'll help any way I can," Jaymie said, picking up Hoppy for the descent down the grassy hill. "I suppose I'm in it whether I like it or not."

SEVEN

Late October 1984

"Brock Nibley, you have *got* to stop that girl from calling here all hours of the day and night. I can't get a single thing done with the phone ringing so much. I had to take it off the hook to get a rest and missed a call from Mrs. Stubbs about the church Thanksgiving service! She's my best customer and a beacon in this community and I don't need her angry at me."

Valetta listened in on her mother berating her older brother. Brock had arrived home from his part-time job with Mr. Waterman, who had his own renovation company in town.

"That woman is always angry," Brock griped, jerking open the fridge door, the bottles jingling. "She was born mean."

"I will *not* have you speak disrespectfully of a good woman, a pillar of our community and someone who puts food on your table!"

Their mother cleaned houses for the wealthier members of their community. Mrs. Stubbs, like the local doctor and the pastor of the church, was her employer.

Valetta sat in her room at her vanity table, one she'd rescued from the curb on garbage day and refurbished with some cool neon paint and decals, and stared into the glass. Blinking back at her was a girl with heavy glasses that were out of style and that her mother couldn't afford to replace, unruly hair that she should probably cut short, and a resentful expression. Why did she have to be saddled with a brother like Brock, who made everything she did more difficult? It wasn't fair. Her other brother wasn't like that, but he was long gone from the house.

She could still hear Brock and her mom bickering.

"It's not *my* fault if Delores can't take a hint, Mom. I didn't ask her to phone. I told her not to but she's *crazy*," Brock whined. He was almost two years older than Valetta, his eighteenth birthday coming soon, and still as much of a pain in the neck as he was when he was ten and she was eight.

"You led her on," their mother said, her voice waning and strengthening as she moved from living room to kitchen and back. The scent of onions frying wafted through the house, and fingers of the smell drifted through Valetta's bedroom door, which was open two inches. "You made her think you liked her."

"Did *not.*"

There was a thump; that meant he had clumped into the living room and thrown himself onto the sofa, shoes still on, big feet up, making the furniture bump against the wall, where there was a scar from him doing that all the time. Big galoot.

"All I did was take her for a ride a couple of times," Brock continued.

And kiss her *and* make out with her, Valetta thought, remembering seeing them at a WH football game, and how uneasy she'd felt when the two disappeared for a while. You couldn't do that to a plain girl who had never gotten any attention. It got her hopes up. It made her feel . . . special. Valetta stared at her face in the mirror. Maybe she wasn't so bad after all, she thought. Yeah, her clothes and glasses were out of style and her hair was home-perm awful, but at least her skin was good. However . . . she wasn't any beauty, that was for sure, not like Rhonda Welch. She pushed her glasses up on her nose.

Brock was her brother, but there were times when she wished that wasn't so. She'd never admit it to anyone — not even Becca, her best friend in the world, who had done the right thing and befriended Delores — but Valetta felt sorry for Delores Paget. She knew what it felt like to be second best. Becca was Valetta's best friend, but *Dee* was Becca's best friend.

"I don't care what happened or how," Valetta's mother said, moving back into the kitchen and clattering some dishes. In their small three-bedroom bungalow you could hear everything going on in every room, no matter where you were. There was not a single bit of privacy. "I never would have knit that sweater for her if I thought you were going to drop her like a hot potato and pick up with that other girl. Fastest I've ever knit two sweaters, I can tell you that."

"Nobody asked you to, you know."

Valetta's eyes widened; she wanted to swat Brock. That was *so* disrespectful of their mother! But as always, her mother just went on, paying no attention to his behavior. He got away with murder and she got away with nothing.

"I don't care," their mother said sharply. "I did it because I'm trying to be nice to your girlfriends. Now, you either go back to dating poor Delores or find a way to *make* her leave us alone. I can't take the constant phone calls anymore; my nerves can't handle it. I'll call her parents if you don't do something."

But Delores didn't have parents, Valetta thought. According to Becca, who had hung out with her all summer, all she had were an aunt and uncle, and a weird cousin. A pang of pity moved Valetta; at least *she* had a mother who loved her and a brother who was a pain in the neck, but who she loved.

The very next day at school she'd talk to Delores herself, tell the girl that Brock wasn't worth the trouble. She knew better than anyone, though she'd never be so disloyal as to say it; Brock was a slug when it came to girls. She'd heard him talking big with his friends, Johnny Stubbs and some others, and he'd said all he wanted from Delores was a good feel. After all, you couldn't see her face in the dark, Brock had said, and they'd all laughed. Every *single* one of them, even Dee's boyfriend, Johnny Stubbs.

She slammed her bedroom door closed and threw herself down on her bed. Boys were jerks. Who needed 'em? Not her.

Late April — The Present
Jaymie, in front of the old gas stove in the kitchen of the historic home, was blissfully

happy and forgetful for two whole hours, testing recipes and rearranging displays. Finally done, she tidied, washed dishes and made everything perfect — and secure, which meant locking the knife drawer — for the week's opening hours, which would start on Thursday afternoon with a school tour.

She hung up her apron, then grabbed her sweater off the hook, gave a last glance around the room, and moved out to the dining room, where Mabel Bloomsbury had dressed the dining table with a spring theme, a crisp pale yellow damask tablecloth and chintz china place settings sourced from Becca, of course. She heard voices echo through the house and headed to the parlor, a large room that could be thrown into another large room by opening the pocket doors between.

There she found a cadre of the town's elder ladies: Imogene Frump; Mrs. Trelawney Bellwood, aka Queen Victoria; and visiting in her mobility wheelchair, Mrs. Martha Stubbs, the *grande dame* of Queensville. She was the oldest lady in the village and was still able to remember the old days, right back to the thirties. Thanks to the new wheelchair lift that had been installed a month ago, the main floor of the house was now completely wheelchair-accessible.

Mrs. Stubbs was a special friend to Jaymie. "Finally someone sensible," she said, holding out her hand and gesturing to Jaymie to join them. "These two dimwits want to tear out the built-in bookshelf in the library in search of some artifact they believe is hidden there. They're looking for my support at the next Queensville Heritage Society meeting to do it. I told them I'd rather simmer in a cannibal's stew pot."

Jaymie stifled a groan and eyed the two other stubborn women — the Snoop Sisters, she called them, like on the old TV show with Helen Hayes and Mildred Natwick. Once friends, then mortal enemies for a few decades, and now fast friends again, the two women had become a troublesome duo. They insisted that somewhere concealed in the walls or floors of the Queensville Historic Manor was the Sultan's Eye, a historic and valuable brooch with a painted eye, in a style from the early eighteen hundreds. Noted in diaries from the last century of the Dumpes, who had once owned the house, it had apparently disappeared, never to be seen again.

"We are *not* dimwits!" Mrs. Bellwood stated, crossing her arms under her shelf-like bosom and harrumphing. "And I resent you calling us that. Am I correct, Imogene?"

"Indubitably," Imogene said, and har-rumphed too. The two women headed for the door. "We'll tackle Haskell Lockland," Imogene said, speaking of the heritage society president, as she paused and turned. "And we'll bring it up for a vote. *Then* we'll see who is right and who is a dimwit!"

With that parting shot the two stalked out the front door. Mrs. Stubbs chuckled, a dry, dusty sound from a woman who didn't laugh much or often. "I believe a fight has been joined."

Wouldn't be the first time a heritage society meeting had erupted into a verbal skirmish. Nor would it be the first time Mrs. Stubbs relished the conflict. "Good to see you out here, Mrs. Stubbs," Jaymie said, bending and hugging the woman.

"Edith drove me. We have a van now that will take my wheelchair in the back . . . Edith's idea. She's been good for Lyle, I will say that, and for me, as much as I don't approve of how they're living." Lyle Stubbs, her eldest son, owned and operated the Queensville Inn and now had the help of his live-in girlfriend, Edith. "I don't see why they don't just marry and get it over with, like you and the Müller boy."

Marry and get it over with. That was the

most unromantic description of her wedding Jaymie had ever heard, but you had to know Mrs. Stubbs to realize it was not personal. It was the way she thought and spoke; taking offense would be silly. "I can't wait to *get it over with,*" she said with a smile.

Mrs. Stubbs glanced up at her and clutched her arthritis-knotted hands together, elbows resting on the arms of her mobility chair. "You know what I mean. I can't abide this current fad of either living together as if it's the same as marriage or making every wedding into a big hoopla event. It's the marriage that matters, not the wedding."

"No offense, Mrs. S., but I've *seen* your wedding photos. Your dress rivaled Princess Elizabeth's and it seems your family made a very *big* deal out of your wedding." The Stubbs were one of the wealthiest families in town, along with the Perrys, which was Mrs. Stubbs's maiden name. Her marriage had been a joining of two local dynasties.

A broad smile suddenly wreathed the old woman's wrinkled face and she chuckled. "You're right, Jaymie, you are *right.*" She smacked Jaymie's hand. "I've gotten old and cranky, but that's no excuse for forgetting my own past. You're the only one I let get away with that nonsense, you know, correcting me. Not even my children dare do that."

"I wouldn't dream of correcting you; you have to know that," Jaymie said, stricken at the thought that she had taken advantage of their friendship.

"Now, don't spoil it by taking it back!" The woman chuckled, a dusty laugh more like a cough.

"I'm glad to see you, though, Mrs. Stubbs. I suppose you've heard about the body in the Paget house basement and the one in the car they dragged out of the river."

Her rheumy eyes brightened. She loved to talk about Jaymie's investigations and got a thrill out of helping with any information or reasoning she could offer. Since her knowledge of the town and people in it was vast and her memory rather good, she was often a true help. "I heard you were involved in that, you and your sister. Read the piece in the paper. But wait!" She held up one gnarled hand and glanced around at the gloomy room, with the curtains drawn against the late-day light. "Let's go somewhere comfortable in this big drafty house. Get us a cup of tea and let's talk. Edith is coming to pick me up in . . ." She pushed her sweater sleeve up and checked her old gold watch. "Half an hour. And she is punctual, I'll say that for her, though she can't carry on a conversation to save her life."

"She doesn't talk?"

"Oh, she *talks.* She chatters incessantly, about television and movie stars and the latest diet she's on. But that's not conversation."

"I was hoping to pick your brain. You may have information I need."

"I'll do my best to come out of my shell and tell you whatever you need," she said with her dry humor.

Five minutes later they were ensconced together in the library, a gem of a room with floor-to-ceiling bookshelves filled with old tomes in faded red, hunter green, and umber, picked out in gold lettering and gold raised lines on the spines. The rug covering the hardwood floor was a sturdy commercial-grade imitation antique Turkish rug, taped down to withstand foot traffic, buggies, walkers and wheelchairs. The two women sat in a ray of sunlight that beamed through a side window that looked out toward the evergreen forest that bounded one side of the property. It was a cozy nook with a settee, two club chairs and a low table, a silver epergne with fake fruit centered on it.

As much as Jaymie loved her own home, it was enchanting to pretend to be the lady of Queensville Historic Manor, hosting afternoon tea. She sat in a club chair by the low table, with a china tea service laid out. Mrs. Stubbs, in her mobility wheelchair, was close enough to the table to be able to set down her teacup if she needed to. Jaymie poured tea and set out some of the cookies she had just made in the historic house kitchen.

As they sipped and munched, Jaymie told Mrs. Stubbs, who had been invaluable in one or two past investigations and read murder mysteries by the hundreds, about her and Becca's gruesome discovery and her own witnessing of the car being dragged out of the river. She told her all the speculation, that they were Delores Paget and Rhonda Welch, that both girls attended Wolverhampton High (though Rhonda had recently moved schools) and had disappeared the same day.

"But here's the odd part, Mrs. Stubbs, and you can't share this with anyone."

Mrs. Stubbs leaned closer, her eyes wide with interest. "Go on."

"Both girls were wearing identical red sweaters, supposedly knitted by Mrs. Nibley out of some weird yarn that didn't disinte-

109

grate after over thirty years in a trunk, and even thirty years submerged in water!" She was making the assumption that Rhonda's sweater was the same as Delores's, though it hadn't absolutely been confirmed. "How did Rhonda end up wearing a sweater exactly like Delores's?"

Mrs. Stubbs frowned, her lips wreathed in deep lines in which her face powder settled. "There's something in my memory, something about red yarn, but I can't remember. It'll come to me."

Jaymie continued talking about the connections among Delores, Becca, Valetta and Dee, as well as with Brock. "And it gets weirder; both girls had talked about taking off, which is why both were thought to be runaways." As she spoke, sadness washed over her at two young lives cut short. Two teenagers who never got to experience life as an adult, all the excitement and nervousness of school, dating, travel, love, sex . . . so *many* choices and chances, joys and sorrows.

Mrs. Stubbs spoke of what she had read in the paper about Petty Welch, Rhonda's aunt, and Jaymie told her, in confidence, what she had learned about the aunt's thoughts on Rhonda's speculating on her birth. "That red yarn is plaguing me," Mrs.

Stubbs said, frowning down at her hands, clutched around the teacup. "But I have to leave it alone or it won't come back. Some of it seems like yesterday to me, though I know it's a lifetime for you. Johnny was dating DeeDee Hubbard, as she was then," Mrs. Stubbs reflected. "I always liked Dee; sensible even as a teenager. But I knew what kind of a girl she was. She was not one to put up with tomfoolery. I was afraid Johnny was going to mess it up with her by going after other girls who would put out."

Jaymie gasped at the frank language, and Mrs. Stubbs gave a dry chuckle, eyeing her with satisfaction. She loved shocking people. "Boys have always been after the same thing. He was wilder than Lyle, who was always a plod-along type of fellow, reliable but not much fun."

"What are you saying?" Was she throwing her own son, Johnny, under the bus? "Did he . . . was he going after one of those girls?"

She shook her head. "Pay attention, Jaymie. I said I was worried about it, not that he did anything. I was worried enough that I listened in . . . heard him talking on the phone, and with his friends in the backyard. I eavesdropped . . . snooped. Boys that age, hormones running amok . . ." Her voice was scratchy and she took a long drink of her tea and set the cup down with a clink against the saucer. "Turned out Johnny was okay. He was a good boy, and I think he knew he'd lose Dee if he messed up."

"They've been married a long time."

"They've had their troubles but always make it through. Not like Lyle and his wife; divorced after a few years. No stamina." She paused, took another sip. "Johnny's *friends* were a different matter. Brock Nibley was a filthy liar. He was the worst of 'em all. I didn't like him then and don't like him now, though he seems to have settled into being a good enough father to his two kids. But back then? He'd tell any girl anything to get into her pants."

Jaymie choked on her tea, holding back dismayed laughter. Mrs. Stubbs was occasionally frank to the point of discomfort, but at least you always knew where you stood with her. Nibbling on a cookie, Jaymie considered her own feelings; she had never liked Brock either, but she didn't think he was quite as bad as Mrs. Stubbs thought him.

This didn't seem to have a whole lot to do with anything. "I guess we don't know for sure that the girls were murdered . . . well, except for Delores. If that *is* Delores. She had a cleaver in her skull. I don't know how to find anything out about the Pagets, it was so long ago. Did you know them?"

Mrs. Stubbs frowned and slowly shook her head. "Don't recall. However, the girl's cousin . . . he must have worked somewhere. I wonder where?"

"The aunt and uncle too, I guess."

"What was his name again? The cousin?"

"Clifford Paget."

"I *knew* I'd heard that name somewhere," Mrs. Stubbs said, patting her lap. "They mentioned in the paper that he died in a boating accident some years ago . . . in the nineties? It was August, I think . . . hot that summer. He jumped out, hit his head, his friend said, and disappeared. Both drunk as skunks. Usually the body washes up a while later, but sometimes they're never found."

Clifford Paget's demise didn't seem to have anything to do with Delores's quite a few years earlier, so Jaymie let it slide, and instead asked, "Were there any other teenagers who hung around with each other back then?"

"I worked at the high school on volunteer projects, so I knew a lot of the children. Let's see . . . Johnny and Brock were friends, much to my dismay. A couple of others, too, but they've moved away since then. Two of your Jakob's older brothers went to Wolverhampton High. I knew them from the vegetable stand the Müllers used to have on their road. Best produce anywhere. The parents kept those boys pretty busy; *too* busy to get up to any trouble."

"But they might know what was going on in school with Delores and Rhonda. I never thought of that!"

"They might. And the Majewski kids."

"Gus and Tami? Gus is Jakob's partner in the junk store business."

"I wouldn't doubt if they met through Jakob's older brothers, who are more of an age with Gus. He and Tami may have known Rhonda Welch and Delores Paget."

"That's something to consider." Jaymie took a sip of tea and eyed the older woman. "The chief wants my help."

"No doubt. You're a clever girl." She patted Jaymie's hand.

Jaymie shrugged and began to tidy up their tea things, taking the tray back to the kitchen and washing up their cups. She returned to the library. It was almost time for Mrs. Stubbs to go. The elderly woman was napping in her chair, head bobbing to one side, sunlight illuminating the blue veins and broken capillaries on her face and gently touching her white curls. She awoke when Edith arrived. Jaymie helped get Mrs.

Stubbs into the van and returned to the porch, but she saw Mrs. Stubbs beckoning her to the van and returned, looking up at Mrs. Stubbs securely belted in to one of the backseats.

"Jaymie! There is something nagging at me, something about those two girls."

"Rhonda and Delores, you mean?"

"Well, of course Rhonda and Delores. What other two girls were we talking about?"

Edith, in the driver's seat, compressed her lips, either in a grimace or smile, Jaymie couldn't tell. "Do you mean something you remember?"

The woman squinted her clouded, red-rimmed eyes. She passed one arthritis-cramped hand over her face. "There's something there. And something about that darned red yarn. I'll call you if I think of it."

"You do that. Now go home and have a nap!"

"Got a book I'm reading . . . need to read on and find out whodunit. If only it were so easy in real life!" The van revved and pulled down the lane, with Mrs. Stubbs waving.

Jaymie locked up and headed home. It was a long walk but it was a beautiful day and she had a lot to think about. All she wanted to do was go see Jakob and Jocie, so maybe that's what she *would* do!

EIGHT

Late October 1984

Mrs. Martha Stubbs moved from foot to foot, wishing she had worn her Cuban heels instead of the less practical pumps. It was her day at the Wolverhampton High School library, a boring cement block box of a room lit by fluorescent pendant row lights over scarred tables and gray metal shelves. The sacrifice of her time was occasionally worth it when she saw a student actually checking out a book to read, rather than for homework.

Unlike other parents, she didn't mind if what they were reading was a *Sweet Valley High* romance novel or even a so-called graphic novel, what she still considered a comic book. At least it was reading; *any* book might lead to something more challenging. However, her most frequent interaction with the children was breaking up giggling gaggles of teen girls, or amorous couples kissing in the back corner, also known as Lovers' Library Lane, or a cruder name she preferred not to think about. They all thought she didn't know, but she did. She also knew what the ruder children called her — Mrs. Stubb-up-her-butt — and secretly thought it was mildly humorous, if not terribly creative. Though she'd never tell her Johnny that, since he had gotten in more than one fight with a boy over the epithet.

She patroled, helping the librarian by tidying tables and corralling stragglers. As she strolled between tables, thinking of what to cook for dinner, she saw an unusual sight. At the very back table, partially concealed by a rolling metal cart of books to be shelved, were two girls, heads together, in intense conversation. That wasn't so unusual; it was the identity of the girls that surprised her. Rhonda Welch was one of the most popular and prettiest girls in school, while Delores Paget was one of the most forlorn and homely.

What did those two have in common? Not a thing, except . . . ah, yes! Brock Nibley, that little toad she thoroughly despised. Perhaps she shouldn't feel that way about a teenager, but she'd been a parent long enough to spot a wrong 'un. Martha Stubbs kept her ear to every conversation she was near, and knew that in the last two months that particular unsavory character had "dated" Delores Paget before moving on to Rhonda Welch, who went out with him twice, as far as she had heard, and never again. Going out with Brock had served the very feminine purpose of making Gus Majewski jealous enough that he solidified his relationship with Rhonda from the casual "going out" to the much more serious "going steady."

So Martha did what any responsible — and curious — adult would do: she found a reason to get close, checking the rolling cart for a book she wanted to recommend to a student.

"Do you think she'll help?" Delores was asking Rhonda.

"Yeah, she's cool, *totally* not like my parents," Rhonda whispered. "She took me to my first concert when I was thirteen. The Rolling Stones!"

"Well, I *hope* so. When can we see her?"

"I don't know," Rhonda said, chewing on a strand of her straight black hair. "I wrote her a letter. Everything is so screwed up right now. My folks are leaving October twenty-ninth, but they're taking me to that Christian school first, next week." She groaned, a sound of misery, her face in her hands. "I'm going to be boarding there."

"That sucks. Why do you have to go there?"

"I *told* you . . . Mom and Dad are going to Kenya for two years. It's a Christian mission thing for the church. They don't trust me to live alone, and they won't let me live with . . ." Rhonda saw the older woman lingering and turned her shoulder, giving Delores a wide-eyed look-out-it's-an-adult look.

Mrs. Stubbs ambled away, wondering *What did Delores need help with?* This was a puzzle that required some thought, but the two girls wouldn't resume their conversation until she was well out of earshot. And indeed when she returned to the check-out counter they bent their heads together again.

What could that mean, "help"? And who was "she"? It wasn't necessarily anything more ominous than a planned weekend party, or sneaking out of the house, but they were an odd pair to become friends, especially given their dual connection to the Nibley boy. There were a host of possibilities that would require the help of a female adult, from acquiring drugs to planning an abortion.

It warranted keeping her eye on them.

Late April — The Present
There were a lot of things Jaymie needed to talk to Jakob about before the wedding. So many things they hadn't sorted out yet, not the least of which was . . . where were they going to live, in Queensville or the log cabin? It was important and they needed to talk it over. So when she returned to her sunny Queensville home, after feeding the cat and dog and letting them both out to do their business in the yard, she called Jakob to see what the rest of his day looked like.

"Your little friend . . . jeez, why can't I remember her name? It's like it's blocked again! She's a nice kid, but she can be annoying! It's . . . Heidi. Yeah. Heidi! She keeps coming by the store."

"Think of her with braids and in a dirndl."

"What?"

"Braids and a dirndl, like Heidi from the books!" She paused. "Never mind." Jaymie smiled to herself; any reader of girls' books would have gotten the *Heidi* reference immediately. That was probably a good book to share with Jocie, and then they could watch the Shirley Temple movie together. It was going to be so much fun to have a daughter.

"Anyway, Heidi has tagged a few items in the store, things she wants to use for the wedding. I don't know what to do with them though. They're taking up floor space."

"How much is there? Anything heavy?"

"No, not really. Some boxes of stuff and a table or two."

"Bernie said we could use her garage to store things. Maybe I can pick them up in the van and take them to her place."

"You sure? I could do it with my truck, but I'm not sure when I'll have time."

"Don't worry about it. I'll do it in the next few days."

"That would work. No hurry, *liebchen;* but with the wedding still a month and a half away, I don't want anything to accidentally get sold."

"No problem. Meanwhile, do you have time for coffee and a chat?" Jaymie asked, writing a few things on her grocery list and making a note to herself to pick up the items from The Junk Stops here.

"For you, always," he said, and she could hear the smile in his voice. He was a burly fellow, with a broad chest, and his voice sounded like it came from deep within.

"I'll meet you . . . where?"

"Come to the house," he said, referring to

his cabin. "Jocie will be dropped off by the bus about four fifteen, and then we have to work on an art project. If I'm not there when you get to the cabin, let yourself in."

An hour later Jaymie did just that. She pulled her beat-up van around the back and got out, locked the vehicle behind her, and headed to the house. Jakob had built the log cabin himself by hand on a chunk of the Müller property tucked in the corner of his Christmas tree farm. Surrounded by his acres of pine trees at various stages of growth, it was also overshadowed by a huge old tree in which nestled the tree house where Jakob had proposed to her.

She let herself into the cabin and put on the kettle for tea on the propane stove. Most of the main floor of the log cabin was one huge room with heavy beams supporting the upper mezzanine story, where the two bedrooms were located. The kitchen was along the front, overlooking the porch, which faced the road and driveway; this part of the cabin had a lower ceiling than the big, airy living area beyond, which was bounded on the other side by a huge field-stone fireplace. Comfortable chairs and sofas dotted the space, an ever-changing rotation of furnishings.

She stood and stared out the kitchen

window. That first evening Jakob had welcomed her in and she immediately felt safer, the warmth and comfort of the home he had made for his daughter seeping into her bones. Though she had dated a reasonable amount in the past fifteen years, no man had ever felt *exactly* right until Jakob. He was the kindest, gentlest man she had ever known. Maybe they had rushed into an engagement, but she had never felt one moment of doubt.

He pulled in the drive — his vehicle was the pickup truck version of her beat-up van, dull white and rusty — and jumped out, running around to the back and hauling something out of the truck bed. He was always bringing home something from his store, so the cabin was never furnished exactly the same two visits in a row. His family also benefited from his junk store finds, as did Gus's. Both men kept a list of things their family needed and wanted, and sometimes came up with surprisingly valuable vintage finds! Jakob had told her about his latest discovery, a storage locker with a treasure trove of items from a defunct stationery store — expensive pens, fun and funky paper, vintage journals, and fountain pen ink in fabulous colors — and several lots from an estate sale, including antique cake tins and jelly molds. He knew Jaymie well enough to set aside the best of *those* for her to look at for her own collection and that of the historical house.

This time he hefted onto his shoulder a white painted three-shelf bookcase with intricate molding atop. She ran to open the door for him. He carried it in over his head, set it down, then greeted her in an entirely satisfactory way. The kettle whistling broke it up and she turned, grinning, saying over her shoulder, "Okay, so what is the shelf for?"

"Jocie wanted more room for her books."

"Atta girl, Jocie! Gotta love a kid who reads. She'll take over the world."

"Yeah, well, *someone* keeps buying her more books," he said, grinning at her.

She made a face at him. It was true; she had grown up reading and loving books, so she wanted any child of hers (her heart thudded at that; Jocie would be her child too, in every single way but by birth) to be a reader. Reading fiction made one more empathetic. "She reads them so fast I have to keep up," she said, smiling back at him.

"Let's wait for her up in the tree house. Just going to change into something clean," he said over his shoulder, disappearing around the corner and up the stairs. "Be right back!"

Jaymie made a picnic of it all, with the teapot and some cups on a tray, and a container of treats that she had left last time she was out. Jakob, dressed in a faded Müller Christmas Tree Farm T-shirt and jeans, raced outside ahead of her and stood proudly, holding a rope under the big old tree. "I made a dumbwaiter so we can haul our picnics up to the tree house!" he said, indicating a wooden platform with low sides, like a tray, suspended by ropes in the four corners. "Set the tea stuff on it."

Jaymie eyed it dubiously. "Are you sure it won't tip?"

"Positive. I have it attached to a pulley so it will move smoothly."

She set the tray on the dumbwaiter. She should have had faith, she thought, as she climbed up and waited, pulling her thick sweater closer around her. The tray made it safely to the top, and she unloaded it as he climbed the ladder to join her. He was a good builder, evident by the fact that he'd constructed the log cabin from a kit with his brothers' and friends' help. He wasn't going to want to leave his log cabin home behind, nor was it even fair to ask him to, not with his tree farm and Jocie's life here. But she didn't want to leave *her* house behind, either. She loved her home!

Tea first; Jakob didn't mind tea (though he preferred coffee), so she fixed him a mug, strong with just sugar, as he liked it, and offered him the plate of treats. There were his favorite peanut butter cookies, as well as some chunks of Queen Elizabeth cake, also one of his favorites. Good thing he liked sweets because she was always baking, and someone had to eat it! She checked her watch; it was four. Was fifteen minutes enough time to broach such a serious topic as where they'd live?

"What's up?" he asked after draining his cup and dusting cake crumbs off his fingers. He laid back on the quilt he kept up in the tree house and watched her. "You look like there's something on your mind."

She smiled down at him. He motioned for her to join him, and she did, turning on her side and fitting herself to his strong body. It gave her a warm feeling in her heart to realize that he knew her well enough already that he could tell when she had something she needed to talk about. Staring out the big window with the afternoon sun slanting in through leafy green, she sighed happily as he pulled her close, warming her up. Whatever it took, they'd work it out.

"There *is* something we haven't talked

about yet," she started.

"Where we're going to live once we're married?"

She propped herself up on her elbow and stared down at his face. He was bearded, something she'd never liked before, but on him it was yummy. "How did you know I was going to say that?" She searched his eyes. "Are you developing skills as a mind reader?"

"I've been thinking about it a lot and wanted to raise the topic, but wasn't sure how," he admitted, his brown eyes fixed on her face. He took her free hand and wove his fingers in with hers. "Do you have any thoughts?"

"This is mostly about Jocie. We need to think of her first."

"I agree she's a consideration — maybe the most important one — but not the only one. I want *you* to be happy, too," he said, squeezing her hand, his voice gruff with feeling. "And *I* want to be happy. We're going to be a unit, Jaymie, three sides to a triangle of love."

"How can we manage it? How do we figure it out?" It seemed an impossible task, and she quailed at the thought.

The sound of a heavy motor on the road and a vehicle coming to a halt, the whine of brakes and kids' laughter echoing in the spring air, made them both stand up and look out the window overlooking the road. Jocie clambered down from the school bus and Jakob shouted a greeting. As the bus headed off, Jocie raced toward the tree, dropped her book bag and sweater at the bottom, got something out of her book bag, and climbed up the ladder, her grunts and huffing and puffing floating up to them. With her disproportionately short legs, climbing was never going to be easy, but she'd persist.

Her head appeared first in the hole that topped the ladder up to the tree house. Today her blonde hair was done up in braids attached to the top of her head. Jakob had become proficient in little girls' hairstyles, he had told Jaymie, since becoming her sole parent.

Finally the rest of her appeared and she squealed and lunged at Jaymie, who hugged her fiercely. Jaymie poured her a cup of weak tea, liberally whitened with milk, and handed her a cookie as Jocie showed them her homework.

After a few minutes Jakob exchanged a glance with Jaymie and said, "Why don't we ask Jocie what she thinks about what we were talking about?"

"Okay."

The little girl looked between them expectantly, her expression becoming serious. She was very in tune with adults, more so than most kids her age, Jaymie thought. There was an appealing gravity in her expression when she spoke about things that mattered to her, like books and animals and school.

"Jocie, we were discussing what we're going to do once Jaymie and I get married," Jakob said, taking his daughter's hand.

She frowned. "We're going to go out and stay at the cottage when you come back from camping," she said, cocking her head to one side. "Aren't we?"

"Yes, but your daddy means, where are we going to live." Jocie looked alarmed and Jaymie's heart sunk.

"We're going to trade, right?" she asked, looking from one adult face to the other.

"Trade?" Jaymie glanced toward Jakob, who shrugged. "What do you mean trade?"

"We're going to live everywhere. I mean, we're going to stay *here* sometimes, and stay at your house in *town* sometimes. One of my best friends, Peyton, lives one road over from you in town. If we stay at your house, then I can visit her and have sleepovers easier, right? I can walk over by myself."

It was so simple, so evident, so uncomplicated in her view, and Jaymie laughed with relief. "Well, if that works out for your daddy, then I think that would be simply . . . splendid!"

"I think we'll be able to work something out," Jakob said.

With a smile that reached right down into her heart, Jaymie knew her life was about to get splendidly, messily complicated. And she was going to love every busy moment of it.

Late October 1984

"He's *so* good-looking!" Becca muttered to Dee, staring at Gus Majewski, who was making out with Rhonda Welch. He had her pushed right up against a pillar near the lockers and his hand was almost (but not quite) on her butt; if the principal came along they'd be toast. Rhonda was in senior year, as was Gus, and they were the new "it" couple. Everyone knew Gus was going to go to college on a football scholarship. He had sandy hair that seemed to ruffle into place perfectly. His broad shoulders were always clad in a football jersey, and his jeans were skintight. "What a hunk!" Becca sighed. It wasn't fair; all the good-looking guys had girlfriends.

"Yeah, well, Rhonda has him firmly locked up." Dee was dressed pretty but practical in

131

a wool skirt and sweater. No faddish Madonna lace gloves for her, just good-quality stuff from the only clothing store in Wolverhampton, Top Teens.

There had been an unscheduled fire drill, and they had all been sent out to shiver in the cold of late October. They were now gathered together in the hallway, waiting to get back into class, and every set of eyes was turned to the make-out spectacle between Gus and Rhonda.

"Easy to see why. She's a knockout," Becca said with an envious sigh. Rhonda Welch was one of those girls who seemed to have it all together even in high school. Perfect skin, perfect body, perfect hair. She looked like Phoebe Cates, with dark shiny hair and dark eyes.

"If you're into perfection," Dee said, her tone wry as she hefted her books on her hip. "Johnny says she's cross-eyed."

Becca bumped her shoulder affectionately. Dee was her rock, the friend she could always count on. Valetta was great but there was her brother, who was a pill, and the constant tension he brought with him. "I saw Rhonda out with Brock a couple of times after he ditched poor Delores. I wonder what happened there?"

"I heard Rhonda cut Brock loose as soon

as Gus gave her a promise ring."

"Who wouldn't?" At least she could say that to Dee, who disliked Brock about as much as Becca did.

"Don't look now, but he's coming down the hall," Dee murmured, her eyes widening. "There's going to be trou-*bull*!"

Brock had stopped dead and glowered at the oblivious couple, waiting until he would be noticed, but the vice principal strode down the hall, blew a whistle and ordered them all back to class. Brock stormed off but purposely bumped Gus, sending him careening into Rhonda. Gus rounded with a swinging fist and hit Brock on the shoulder, a glancing blow. The vice principal hollered and separated the two combatants, ordering them both to the principal's office. As the cluster of students cleared, Becca saw Delores standing in the middle of the hall, books clutched to her red sweater, staring after Brock, a look of longing on her plain face.

"Love doesn't seem to be much fun," Becca muttered, feeling a pang for her summer friend.

"Hmph. *That's* not love," Dee said with a sniff. "That is one sad girl looking to fit in."

That was easy for Dee to say, Becca thought. All *she* saw was a loner with no ability to fit in, a homely awkward girl. But Becca *knew* Delores: knew her hopes, to move to Hollywood and become a star, her vowed intention to leave home the minute she legally could. She sympathized with her. Everyone always told teenagers to enjoy their teen years. *It's the best years of your life* her mother always said. *You'll look back and wish you could stay a teenager forever.*

But it wasn't that easy. Becca could see why Delores now felt even worse than she had months ago. Going out with Brock had enlivened her, given her a glow. She had been different while Brock was paying attention to her: smiling, bright . . . bubbly, even. And now that he had dropped her, she seemed lost, the bubbliness flattened like ginger ale left out too long.

"I have to talk to her. She doesn't have anyone else."

"That's because she gives everyone else the cold shoulder," Dee said. "She thinks *we're* the problem? I've tried being friends. She just won't have it, except with *you,* I guess."

Dee didn't realize it but she often gave off a vibe, not like she was better than anyone else exactly, but . . . Becca shook her head. She couldn't even explain it to herself. Dee was just . . . Dee. Becca knew she had a good heart, but she was kind of quick to judge and expected everyone to be as confident as she was.

Becca knew that Delores felt left out. For one thing, it seemed to her that everyone *else* had parents, and she didn't. Everyone *else* had a normal home, and she didn't. Becca understood because right now she felt out of place among all her teenaged friends too, like she had all the responsibilities of having a baby and it wasn't even hers. Her mom was sick, her dad was worn out and Jaymie needed her.

"Yeah, well, everyone is being kind of a jerk to her right now, Dee. I have to talk to her." She headed after Delores, but the girl disappeared in the stream of students returning to class.

NINE

Late April — The Present

Jaymie, invited for dinner at the cabin, had gone home, fed Denver and Hoppy, and brought her dog back with her to play with Jocie's kitten. Dinner had been a frozen pizza and salad, a fast and easy meal for a busy weeknight. Jocie was now in bed with her kitten, Little Bit — the name was well on its way to being shortened to LiliBit — and Jaymie sat on the sofa with Jakob, a nature show on the TV. They talked about the future, immediate and long term, interspersed with pauses for kissing. Hoppy, exhausted from time spent with Jocie and her kitten, was curled up on a bunched-up blanket in front of the fireplace, where the warmth from the fire kept him cozy.

Jakob's cell phone buzzed; he checked a text. "Helmut needs to talk to me about the accounts for the tree farm. Do you mind if he drops in for a minute?"

"Of course not. I should get going anyway," she said, starting to get up.

"No, stay! Please," he said, a hand on her shoulder. "You don't know Helmut very well. He's the shyest of my brothers, but he's a reader and a thinker. You two would love each other if you had more time to get to know him. And he is going to be my best man."

"Okay. I like Sonya and the two kids," Jaymie said, of Helmut's live-in girlfriend and her two daughters. "She's been great."

Helmut, who looked a lot like Jakob except that he was shorter, slimmer and quieter, arrived, and the brothers talked about business while she made a pot of coffee. When she brought the tray to the coffee table, Helmut, his expression lit with curiosity, said, "Jaymie, I saw your name in the paper. You and your sister found that body at the Paget place."

"Becca and I were clearing the house out. It was a shock, let me tell you."

He leaned forward, his narrow face twisted in a serious expression. "Is it really Delores Paget?"

"Did you know her?" Jaymie asked, surprised by his familiar tone.

His brown eyes had an ineffable expression of sorrow. He stroked his beard, a sign of agitation with him, Jaymie had noticed, and nodded.

"From school?" Of course! Mrs. Stubbs had thought the Müller boys might know Delores and Rhonda from school.

He nodded again. "I was a freshman the year she disappeared."

"But you're a few years younger than my sister. How were you in high school at the same time?"

"Helmut was always the brains of the family," Jakob said, punching his brother in the shoulder. "He skipped a couple of grades."

He shrugged, his cheeks pinkening. "I was technically a freshman, but I took some more advanced classes. I liked Delores. We had the same English class. We all had to make a speech. I've never forgotten Delores's; hers was titled 'When I Go,' and it was about leaving behind everything and heading west, like a pioneer."

Jaymie shivered; that may have solidified everyone's sense that she had run away. "And she never got that chance." Sadness for a life cut so short threaded through her heart. It wasn't right. And whoever did it hadn't even been punished for the crime. "How well did you know her?"

"Not all *that* well, I guess. I tried to hang out with her, and at the very beginning of the school year she let me. I think she was lonely. But then she started going out with Brock Nibley and she didn't have time for me anymore."

"Becca did tell me that she went out with Brock. Do you know why they broke up?"

He nodded and took a sip of his coffee. "Brock took her out a few times but dropped her so he could chase Rhonda Welch."

Jaymie's eyes widened. "Wait . . . Brock Nibley *also* took Rhonda Welch out?" That explained the second red sweater, she supposed. How . . . eerie.

"Didn't you know? Your sister must, if she and Delores were friends."

Jaymie considered that. It was all well over thirty years ago. How much of your memory needed a jog after that length of time? "I'll ask her. And I think the sheriff needs to know this," Jaymie said. "Can I tell him what you've said?"

"Of course. Give him my number."

It was uncanny that the more she found out, the more it tied Brock to both Delores and Rhonda. "Did you ever go to Delores's house? Did you know her family?" It was hard to get a complete picture, even with Becca having known them. Becca avoided the aunt, uncle and cousin as much as she

139

could, she had told Jaymie.

"I *kinda* knew them . . . I mean, I met them. I was good at geometry, and Delores asked me that fall to help her. She was good in English, but she had no concept of geometry. No matter how much I tried, I couldn't help."

"So you were at her house?"

"Just once." His gaze became internal and he frowned. "There was a weird vibe going on. That was . . . what time of year? Wait . . ." He thought. "It was after Brock dropped her; she started kind of hanging out with me at school again. It must have been *almost* Halloween, because she was putting together a costume. We joked a bit. I told her I was going out as a scarecrow; I was pretty skinny and my hair stuck out all over the place. She said she was going out as Mr. T if she could find some gold chains at the thrift store. She was self-conscious because she was kind of a big girl."

"So what was weird about the vibe in their house?"

He frowned down at his hands, cracking his knuckles. "Her uncle was a miserable little man. He was balding, thin gray hair, hunched over. He had this whiny voice, like, no matter what he said, even 'What's for dinner?' it sounded like he was whining.

Mrs. Paget was taller than him. She made weird jokes."

"Weird jokes?"

"Like . . . sexual jokes. In front of Delores. About . . ." His cheeks got a patchy red, and he stared off toward the fireplace. ". . . about her breasts getting bigger ever since they'd been felt up. She told Delores if she wanted them even bigger she should . . . should let *me* have a feel." Even Helmut's ears were bright red in desperate embarrassment.

A tingle of apprehension crept down Jaymie's spine. That was *not* a healthy atmosphere for anyone, *especially* not for a teenage girl, and even less so for one probably already sensitive about her weight and physical development. Jaymie remembered what it was like to try to shrink herself, and to dress in baggy clothes to avoid notice.

"Anyway, I got out of there pretty quick. She avoided me at school after that; probably embarrassed. So was I. I never went back, and then a week later she was gone. I didn't blame her for leaving, for heading west. I was . . . I was happy she had gotten way from the Pagets, in fact." His forehead creased as the color drained from his face, leaving pink patches high on his cheekbones. "But all that time she wasn't gone at all;

she was right there in that house, under their feet. For over thirty years."

The next day Jaymie was determined to get a handle on two things: her wedding, and what really happened to Delores Paget and Rhonda Welch. Okay, three things . . . also, what she'd write for her next "Vintage Eats" column. Or maybe four things; she needed to talk to her family about her and Jakob's plans to move back and forth, from the log cabin to the house in Queensville, according to their schedule and whim. It was Becca's house too, and the longtime home of the Leighton family. Becca and Kevin would be in Queensville more often, once their antique shop was open, so they could trade off staying in the Queensville home.

The sisters certainly couldn't stay there together. Becca loathed clutter, while Jaymie thrived in the midst of her vintage stuff, glorious reminders of days gone by. It didn't make for the most harmonious home when they were both in residence.

After a cuddle with Denver and a walk with Hoppy in the light rain that was falling, she set out to Wolverhampton, dressed business-appropriate to talk to Nan. She'd been pondering something for a while; she wanted to move her food column in a slightly different direction, away from just recipes and toward a more general look at cooking styles through the years. She'd still feature vintage recipes, but she'd also do some local and regional food history. Would Nan go for that? *That* was the question. She was the ultimate authority.

Wolverhampton was a much larger town than Queensville with a library, post office, grocery store and other shops. *And . . .* a bridal shop. The rain had stopped, but the sidewalk was still wet and the sky iron gray. Jaymie stopped in front of Her Special Day and stared into the window. She had been in a couple of times and tried on dresses, but nothing seemed right. She didn't even know what she wanted to wear, but certainly not the skirt suit her sister was trying to force on her so they'd "look the same." She didn't *want* to look like Becca. First off, she was younger by fifteen years, and second, they were entirely different people, so dissimilar no one would peg them for sisters. And third, this was her first (and *only*) wedding and Becca's third . . . no, fourth! Her elder sister had recently confessed to a very quick marriage that she had never spoken of before.

What to wear?

Suddenly, with no warning, she was attacked! Arms bound hers to her side and someone was whooping in her ear. She struggled for a moment, then relaxed.

"Jaymsie! My pet," Heidi Lockland shouted, letting go.

Jaymie turned with a ready smile. Heidi was a beauty: slim, elegant, long flaxen hair and big blue eyes. As always, her clothes were perfection: skinny jeans and high heels, a short jacket that showed off her perfect shape and glittering silver-and-blue chandelier earrings dangling from her lobes, tangling with her silky hair. She was the prototype of every girl who had ever made Jaymie feel bad about her larger frame in school. And to top it off, Heidi had "stolen" Joel, Jaymie's boyfriend, a year and a half ago.

But as Jaymie had pointed out to many Queensville friends, you couldn't *steal* a human. Joel was clearly not as committed to their relationship as Jaymie had thought. Looking back, she couldn't even remember what she had found so devastatingly attractive about Joel, though their breakup had only happened a year and a half ago.

"How are you, my friend?" Jaymie asked, giving her a hug.

"Better now. Joel and I were fighting like kittens and pups for a while, but we're moving on. He's got his divorce — finally —

144

and I've met his parents. His don't like me and mine don't like him, so . . ." She took a deep breath and shrugged. "We're even, I guess. We'll see what happens."

"Poor kid," Jaymie said, linking her arm though Heidi's. "I feel like all we've talked about the last few times we've seen each other is my wedding. I'm glad to hear *you're* okay."

For a while, in Queensville, in the wake of the theft of Joel, Heidi had been the subject of terrible injustice. She had been the concentrated target of the small-town chill, a technique of freezing a newcomer out. People — mostly the women of Jaymie's acquaintance — had turned away from Heidi whenever she tried to join a conversation or group. Not willing to put up with that, and even more so, not willing to be "poor Jaymie" the rest of her life, she had befriended Heidi and forced her on the rest of the Queensville populace. The result was that Heidi was very popular indeed now, even more so as a willing volunteer on the heritage society and a generous donor. She was a trust-fund baby, independently wealthy from the Lockland real estate fortune, which had begun a century ago in Queensville before moving to New York City and skyscrapers.

But the couple had hit a speed bump last autumn when Heidi discovered the secret Joel had been keeping: he already had a wife and had never gotten a divorce. It sounded like the couple was moving past that, though Heidi seemed less eager to go ahead with a wedding of her own than she had at one point. Maybe Joel's charm was wearing thin.

"You're not looking for a dress *here,* are you?" Heidi said, her nose wrinkled as they stared together at the wedding dresses in the shop window.

"Where else can I go?"

"Don't go anywhere," Heidi said, grabbing Jaymie by the shoulders and shaking her. "Because I've already bought you a dress."

Stunned, the breath sucked out of her body, Jaymie didn't even know how to react. One of the most personal decisions of her life, and Heidi thought she could waltz in and do it for her? She was about to open her mouth to say something harsh, when she looked down at her friend and stopped.

"Don't get mad, *please,* Jaymsie," Heidi pleaded, her blue eyes welling. "I *do* know I shouldn't have." The girl had been working on being more aware of her failings — namely, her inability to tell when people were upset with her. "But I *had* to! When you see it, you'll know why. It was at an auction, it's vintage, and it's *perfection* for your gorgeous curvy body."

Not just any dress, but an old dress. Lord love a duck. Jaymie did not know what to say.

But that was okay because Heidi was not done talking. "Jaymsie, if you don't love it, you don't have to wear it. But please . . . *try* it. Can you come to Bernie's tonight? That's where it is."

"Okay. All right. I'll try it on, but I won't promise I'll wear it." Heidi did have exquisite taste, and Jaymie owed the dress of her friend's choice a shot. What could it hurt? "What time?"

"Seven. We'll try Bernie's wedding cocktails. Gotta run," Heidi said, dashing away to her car at the curb, a blue Mini Cooper convertible. *"Arrivederci, bella!"* she called out with a jaunty wave.

It was turning into a lovely spring day now that the rain had stopped. The iron gray curtain over the town had evaporated, leaving only a few white fluffies against a powder blue sky. Jaymie wished she could enjoy it, but there was so much to do and think about and plan. Since she was nearby, she thought she'd stop in at the bakery to consult about the wedding cakes with Tami.

147

She entered the Wolverhampton Bakery to the welcoming smells and sights of chocolate. Her love of the flavor was why *her* wedding cake was going to be chocolate with Dutch chocolate frosting, while Becca's choice was vanilla with buttercream frosting.

There was usually a teenager behind the counter serving customers, but today Tami, the head baker and wedding cake creator, was alone. She was sandy-haired and slim, one of those women who subsist on coffee and cigarettes, all nerves and jitters. But locally she was well-liked, her generosity of spirit surpassed only by her love of children. Her volunteer work often meant that there were luscious cupcakes, pies and cookies at school functions and bake sales.

But there was some sadness behind her blue eyes. Jaymie had always wondered why someone who loved children so much had never had any. It wasn't the kind of thing one could ask, though; maybe it was not possible, or perhaps there was never a good time.

As always, recently, that thought brought her back to her impending nuptials. That was *another* conversation she needed to have with Jakob. Did they want children? Did *she* want children? While dating Daniel, it had been a firm no, but she wasn't sure now. Having kids with Jakob, who was a hands-on dad who cooked, cleaned and braided hair, would be a far different thing than having them with a distracted tech millionaire.

"Tami, hi!" she said, approaching the pass-through counter that was wedged between large glass cases of pastries and cookies.

When the baker turned and saw Jaymie she smiled and her eyes lit up. "Just the gal I want to see! I have some ideas for your cake and wanted to run them by you." She grabbed a tablet from the cash desk and turned it on, scrolling through some photos. "Here," she said, handing it across the counter. "What about some of these? You said you and Jakob like books and trees and animals."

Jaymie took the tablet and retreated to a chair near the front window, setting her purse down and scrolling through the pictures. There were a dozen or so cakes, but the prevalent theme was a stack of books with wonderful titles, like *Happily Ever After.* And yet . . . she looked up as Tami came through the pass-through and took the chair beside her. "I love these, Tami. I do. And you're so sweet for wanting

149

to please me. I know we talked about how much I love reading. But I was thinking more of a traditional cake. A two-tiered cake with a topper that shows me, Jakob, and Jocie. She's marrying me too, in a way."

Tami's eyes welled and she touched Jaymie's arm. "I *love* that! I'll go with tradition, then. Your sister's is going to be two-tier as well and done with an antique china pattern on fondant. That's probably enough challenge for one wedding. In the meantime, I have the order for you and your sister's wedding shower to take care of!" Tami took the tablet back and jotted some notes on a pad.

Jaymie took in a deep breath. The joint wedding shower was a few days away. Heidi, Bernie, Valetta and Dee had told her and Becca not to think about it, to let them take care of everything. It was going to be at the Queensville Historic Manor on Saturday afternoon, and it would be traditional, ladies only.

Jaymie wasn't sure how she felt about that. Surely the men in their lives should be able to celebrate the upcoming wedding too? It was outdated to think that only women cared about it. She had insisted that Jakob have as much input as she did into her half of the wedding ceremony. But as much as she would have liked Jakob there at the shower, inviting all the men would have complicated things for their friends, who were already doing so much for her and Becca. She had let it pass.

They did have the best friends in the world, her and Becca. She realized with a start that she hadn't even *talked* to Valetta since their tense day of work. Maybe that's why she felt a sense of underlying unease; Valetta was her *best* friend, the one she talked to most days. She'd have to call her as soon as she got home and before she went over to Bernie's. She grabbed her purse from under her chair, getting ready to leave.

The bells over the door jingled and Chief Ledbetter climbed into the shop, breathing heavily from walking. "Jaymie! Fancy meeting you here. I came in for cookies. Glad I caught you, though; I need to talk to you."

"I'm about done here," she replied, standing up. "I'll wait for you outside, if you like?"

Tami flapped her hand, jumping up and ducking under the pass-through. "Go ahead and talk while I put together his order. I know what he wants. Right, Chief?"

He guffawed. "You sure do, Tami. And add in some cloverleaf rolls. The wife is making Irish stew for dinner. And what the heck; give me a Dutch apple pie for dessert." He winked. "*And* the usual: cookies for the kids at the department! I want them to remember me fondly once I'm retired."

"You know they will, especially if Miss Sour Face Connolly takes over," Tami said.

The chief of police's rumored replacement was his assistant chief, Deborah Connolly, who was all business compared to Ledbetter's folksy — but deceptive — charm, which he used to disarm those he questioned. It had not been made official, but the police chief was lobbying for her with the powers that be, as he called Queensville Township's board of trustees, which was responsible for hiring police officers and firefighters, as well as many others. However . . . township officials were also advertising across the state as well as in Ohio and northern Pennsylvania for a replacement, so her ascension was not certain.

Tami began assembling his order and Jaymie sat again as the police chief sank down in the sturdiest of chairs with a sigh. He was a few months away from his second retirement — he joked that the first retirement, from a big-city police force, didn't take — so this case would be one of the last over which he presided. "We're *fairly* sure that the body in the trunk at the Paget house is Delores, but we don't have official confirmation yet. Tricky, with her. No living relatives, and we can't trace who the Pagets were. We *are* sure now that the body in the car is Rhonda Welch," he said. "Her aunt, Petty Welch, has been helpful."

There was a loud bang behind the counter, and Tami murmured an apology.

"So there's no record of the Pagets at all? That's odd."

"It is," the chief said with a grunt. He folded his hands over his paunch and twiddled his thumbs. "They appeared sometime in 1968, Olga, Jimbo, Clifford and baby Delores. Anyway, we now have a *date* of death, if not *time.* We know that both girls disappeared on November first, 1984. We know that —"

Gus Majewski, Jakob's partner in his businesses, entered his sister's workplace just then. He was a big guy, taller than Jakob, with broad thick shoulders, a shaggy head of hair, graying stubble on his chin and piercing blue eyes. He greeted Jaymie affectionately with a hug, then nodded to the police chief. Tami came to the passthrough and said hello to her brother. "Sis, could you babysit tonight? Nicki and I have to go out."

Tami nodded, her face a mask of sadness

and tears in her eyes.

"What's wrong, Tam?" Gus turned to the police chief and then to Jaymie. "What's going on here?"

Tami glanced toward Jaymie and the police chief, then back to her brother. "I . . . I overheard the chief. That body in that car they dragged out of the river, it's Rhonda Welch!"

Gus appeared stunned and leaned heavily on the counter. "It . . . it *can't* be her. She left . . . ran away . . . she was pregnant, and . . ." He covered his face and doubled over. "She *killed* herself?" he cried, his voice muffled by his flannel-clad arms. He groaned in wordless anguish.

Jaymie was taken aback and exchanged a look with Chief Ledbetter. "Gus, what are you talking about?"

Tami slipped under the pass-through countertop and grabbed her younger brother in a hug, quivering with nerves and sorrow. Her voice choked with tears, she said, "He and Rhonda were dating. They were serious."

"But *pregnant*?" Jaymie asked.

"She'd just found out!" he sobbed. "I was gonna quit school. I was going to get a job and we were going to move in together! Have a . . . have a baby!" His words came out between choking sobs.

Jaymie's heart broke for him as she reached out to touch his shoulder, shuddering under the weight of his grief as Tami clung to him. Gus was the most loving father she had ever seen, other than Jakob. He doted on his daughter, who was two years old and in day care. Jakob said that Gus was committed to giving her the chances he'd never had and making her life the best possible. "I'm *so* sorry, Gus." She glanced at the chief, who watched with a furrowed brow. "And I'm sorry you had to find out this way."

He looked up, his cheeks tear-stained. "When I heard about that car being found and all the speculation, I was sure it *couldn't* be Rhonda. All these years I thought she had taken off, that she got scared or didn't want a baby, and decided to leave. She *hated* that school she was at. She wanted out, but her parents . . ." He straightened, shaking his head, but still spoke between gasping gulps of air. ". . . her folks never would have accepted her having a child out of wedlock. They were strict. They sent her to that boarding school to split us up."

Chief Ledbetter glanced down at his notebook, then back up. "Mr. Majewski, when did Rhonda tell you she was pregnant?"

He blinked. "I don't know. Why?"

"Just think, please."

"Uh . . . the day after her folks took her to that boarding school. She called me."

"What's going on, Chief?" Jaymie asked.

"I don't think I'm giving anything away when I tell you that Miss Welch was *not* pregnant, nor had she ever been."

TEN

Tami burst into tears. "Oh, thank goodness!" she sobbed into her hands.

Jaymie was surprised by the outburst. "Why do you say *that,* Tami?"

"It would have been so awful if she . . . that is, she and a little one . . ." She shook her head, unable to continue, and knuckled the tears from her eyes.

"C'mon, sis, let's go back and get you settled down." Gus turned to Jaymie and the chief as he lifted the counter of the pass-through and pushed his sister to go to the back. As she retreated, he leaned back toward Jaymie and the police chief. "Who did this, Chief? Did Rhonda kill herself?"

"We don't know yet, Mr. Majewski."

"Did the same person kill her and poor Delores, maybe?"

"Do you know of any connection between the two girls?" His expression was neutral, giving away nothing.

Gus looked back, but his sister had disappeared. He paused and wrinkled his brow. "Those two girls couldn't have been more different." His expression became pained and his eyes welled. "Rhonda was someone special. I mean, she was beautiful, but she was nice, too. Kids thought she was snotty but she would do anything to help *anyone,* that girl would. That's why I loved her." He cleared his throat. "I do know one thing: Brock Nibley dated both Delores and Rhonda. He was such a jerk toward Rhonda when she started going out steady with me. I'm not sayin' he did it. I don't like the guy much, but he's never struck me as a murderer. I will say this . . . if you find the bastard that did that to Rhonda, I'll string him up myself."

"We're investigating all possibilities," the chief said. "Tell your sister I'll come back in a while for my order. I'm truly sorry for your loss, Mr. Majewski."

He nodded. "Even after thirty years it stings. My first love, I guess. Who knows what would have happened? I let Rhonda go because I thought that's what she wanted, away from *me.* I thought *I* was the reason she took off."

"I'd like to speak with you about when she disappeared."

"Any time," he said, looking toward the back area, where Tami could be heard sobbing still. "Just not right this moment."

"I'll be in touch. Come along, Jaymie," the chief said, heaving himself up and opening the door for her.

Out on the sidewalk, Jaymie said, "She took that so hard!"

Chief Ledbetter nodded. "Everyone has their trigger, you know. With her, it's babies."

"With me it's animal abuse; I see those Humane Society commercials showing abused dogs and cats and bawl like a child." Jaymie sighed and looked up the street, clearing her head. "I'm glad Gus is there to comfort her. Though Rhonda was his girlfriend; you'd think she'd be comforting *him.*"

"What's he like?" Chief Ledbetter asked.

"Gus?" Jaymie cocked her head to one side, thinking about it. "I don't know him very well. He strikes me as the kind of guy who took a long time to figure life out, you know? He went away and worked different places for years, but about seven years ago or so he came back, and since then he started the junk store business with Jakob and met his wife, had the baby. He's happy now. Why do you ask?"

"We always have to consider the boyfriend."

"Actually, Chief . . ." She hesitated and took a deep breath. She couldn't *not* say this. "Chief, what Gus said is true; I know for a fact that Brock did date both girls, Delores and Rhonda." She told him what Helmut Müller had told her.

"Yup. Helmut called and told us about it, what he knew. He's been helpful."

Thank goodness, Jaymie thought. At least it didn't originate with her, and she didn't have to feel guilty toward Valetta. "I have to go talk to Nan about my column."

"I'll walk with you, if you don't walk too fast." He pushed his shirtsleeve up to show a black wristband around his meaty wrist. "One of them walking counters. M'wife says she wants me to lose twenty pounds before retiring." He sighed heavily. "She says she doesn't want to be married to an old fart who can only be ballast in the fishing boat."

As they walked, the chief told her more about what they had discovered about Rhonda and Delores's last day. School records showed the last day the two were marked as in class at their schools was November first, a Thursday. Police records revealed how soon they were each reported missing. Rhonda was reported missing

160

almost immediately. She didn't attend her two afternoon classes, and teachers alerted the office. The evening of the day she went missing it was reported to local police; the school was some miles from Wolverhampton, but it was noted in the official police report that her car was missing too, and a schoolmate at Chance Houghton admitted Rhonda may have been planning to run away. Delores wasn't reported missing by her aunt and uncle until the next day — Friday, November second — after she didn't return home from school the previous day or evening.

"Odd that they didn't call the evening she disappeared," Jaymie said. "I sure would if a fifteen- or sixteen-year-old was missing after school and didn't come home by bedtime. Did they call friends to see if she was staying over?"

"The Queensville Township PD notes said the officer asked them about friends, but the Pagets reportedly said she didn't have a single one."

Jaymie shook her head and looked over at the chief as they walked, tucking a blowing strand of hair behind her ear. "But that's not true. My sister was a friend. Enough so that she spent time out there riding horses that summer. *And* invited her to her sweet sixteen birthday. That's a pretty big deal."

The chief's gaze sharpened. "I knew 'bout some of that, but I didn't realize the friendship continued after the summer. Will you ask your sister to give me a call? I'd like to speak with her again."

"She's not in town right now, but she's coming for the weekend. Is that soon enough, or do you want her to call you from London?"

"This weekend is fine."

"Did you talk to Brock Nibley about seeing Delores that day?" The chief nodded. "What did she say?"

The chief paused to catch his breath and sat down on a wrought-iron bench; Jaymie sat beside him.

"He said that he was at the Queensville Emporium just sitting there, and she came into the village looking around, like she was looking for someone. He talked to her, and she told him she was taking off."

"Hmm. What was he doing in town in the afternoon of a Thursday? Shouldn't he have been at school?"

"Yeah, about that . . . he says he just took a break. He didn't have another class scheduled until after lunch, which gave him a couple hours free, so he hitched into town, then hitched back out and went to his afternoon classes."

Would any kid do that, hitch all the way from the high school to Queensville only to hitch back out again?

"Anyway, Jaymie, I'd better get going," he said, standing back up. "Cold cases take time, sometimes years, and we have lots to do. We're starting from day one, in a way, now that both bodies have been discovered. We're still trying to make more of any connection between the two. One bit of information I don't want spread around . . ." He looked undecided, squinting his perpetually watery eyes.

"You know you can trust me, Chief."

He nodded. "We do believe that Delores — if the body in the trunk is hers, and I think it is — was killed right there in the kitchen of the Paget house. We pulled up some of the linoleum, and there was blood seepage into the board floor underneath. Jenkins did some research and found that the linoleum in that kitchen was likely installed sometime in the late eighties. She's a peach, is Jenkins," he said with an admiring nod. He was referring to Bernie, of course. "She tracked down the style and it wasn't available until 1985."

Jaymie stopped dead and stared at the police chief. "Are you saying the linoleum was installed to hide the blood from Delores being murdered?"

"Not making that assumption. Not yet. And we still have some testing to do on the floorboard sample. We're also trying to dig up blood typing from Mr. and Mrs. Paget. We think we can get it from the hospital, once we have permission. Olga Paget was given transfusions after her fall."

"Oh. So you're checking the blood type for . . . why?"

He shrugged. "One more piece of the puzzle. Trouble is, if Delores had the same last name as Jimbo, that might mean she was *his* niece, not Olga's, and we don't have a blood type for Jimbo Paget."

Blood on the kitchen floor. It was sobering, and sickening, to realize that the murder had perhaps happened right there where the cleaver came at Jaymie in the kitchen. "Chief, what about Clifford Paget? I know he drowned in the river, but . . . is he a suspect?"

"He is, at least in Delores Paget's murder. But if there *is* a connection between the two girls, it's hard to make a case against him in Rhonda's death."

"Though the amount you don't know means there could *be* a connection, you just don't know what it is."

"We have a long ways to go yet," he said, nodding. "Like I said, cold cases can take years. So, your sister is coming for the weekend?"

Jaymie nodded and flushed, putting her face up to feel the spring breeze on her cheeks. "It's our combined wedding shower this weekend, out at the historic house."

"Ah, yes. Looking forward to the wedding, Jaymie. You've got a good fellow, one almost worthy of you."

That was the gushiest thing he had ever said, and she'd known him almost a year. Inviting him and his wife to the wedding had been an impulse, but one she didn't regret. He had been kind to her.

"I'm going out to talk to Ms. Welch again," he said, walking again, determinedly picking up the pace. "She lives outside of Queensville."

"Ms. . . . oh, Rhonda's *aunt*! Do you think she'd talk to me about her niece?"

He glanced over at her, his face red, his breath coming in huffs and puffs. "I'll ask her. You got your cell phone with you?"

"I do."

"I'll get Bernie to text you the answer. Whatcha thinkin'?"

"Nothing really," she said, trotting to keep up with his pace. "Trying to piece it all

together. Trying to help any way I can."
They arrived at the *Wolverhampton Weekly
Howler* office and paused, the chief taking
in a long gasp to catch his breath. "Chief,
unless the two deaths are related, it's a heck
of a coincidence."

He nodded, the color gradually subsiding
from his flushed cheeks and his breathing
returning to normal.

"So it's likely they're related. Two girls
who knew each other, who went out with
the same guy and who had gone to the same
school until days before their deaths, killed
two different ways? It's weird," Jaymie
mused. "If the deaths *were* related, I can't
help but wonder, was only one of them the
real target, and the other got in the way?
And if so, which one was the target?"

"All good questions, Jaymie."

After saying their goodbyes, Jaymie
strolled into the newspaper office, buzzed
through to the back by the receptionist. Nan
was in her cubicle, chewing on a coffee stirrer. She fairly radiated agitation. On her
computer screen was some information on
the disappearance of Rhonda Welch and
Delores Paget.

They greeted each other, Jaymie sat in the
visitor's chair, and she got down to business, going through her ideas for her column

and how she wanted to change it up. Nan gave her her complete attention.

"I know I started out saying I wanted to do vintage recipes so I can work toward the cookbook," Jaymie said. "But I'd like to do some columns on foods of the past, like how packaged mixes became fashionable between the thirties and the fifties, and how televisions and TV dinners changed eating habits in the fifties and sixties."

"I was a kid in the sixties. No one I knew was eating TV dinners," Nan said as she scribbled notes. "We couldn't afford it in my house, even though both my mom and dad worked. Do you think readers will be interested?"

Jaymie looked down at her nails; they were a mess. Another thing to think about before the wedding. "It will depend on how I present it, don't you think?"

Nan frowned at her computer screen, jiggling her mouse to get the resting computer to restart, which it did with a beep. Rhonda and Delores's pictures popped up on the screen again. "Jaymie, I have mixed feelings about this. Why are you considering changing your format?"

"I don't want to become complacent, you know? Shouldn't I be thinking of ideas to move ahead?"

"Change for the sake of change is rarely a good idea." The editor smiled and twiddled her coffee stirrer between her fingers, leaning back in her chair. "You think you need to get serious, or change things up, or something like that?"

Jaymie nodded.

Nan sat up, with a squawk of protest from her swivel office chair. "Did you know I get more people stopping me in the supermarket to talk to me about 'Vintage Eats' than any single column?" she said, pointing her coffee stirrer at Jaymie. "Sure, readers ask me about the news items and sometimes opinion pieces, but the regular columns? You know we have a pet column, and ones on gardening — popular, but seasonal — local history, crafts, some rotating columns. Without exception, your 'Vintage Eats' is the one I get asked about most."

Jaymie was taken aback.

"Look here," she said, grabbing a newspaper from the stack on her desk. It was from mid-March. Among the ads for a special on asparagus at the supermarket, an article about the Queensville Methodist Church's pancake supper, and a notice of a thirtieth-anniversary celebration for Tovey's Hamburger Joint, was Jaymie's column with a vintage recipe for corned beef hash to use

168

up all the leftover corned beef from St. Patrick's Day. "I had four people stop me in the grocery store to comment on that, and quite a few letters to the editor about how it brought back such great memories."

"So don't fix what ain't broke; is that what you're saying?"

Nan smiled, a rare flash of humor. "You could say that. Your blog traffic is up, yes?"

"I hit three thousand followers this week." She tried to update every two to three days, but it got difficult at times to come up with blog ideas. "I've started to think about putting in some kitchen utensil blog columns . . . you know, on old utensils, antiques. With photos."

"Then maybe *that's* where you should write your articles on food fads of the past, too. Stick with vintage recipes rethought for 'Vintage Eats.' "

"Okay, I get you." She grabbed her purse, ready to be dismissed.

"Now, about these two girls," Nan said, pointing toward her computer screen. "I understand that your sister knew them both?"

"Everyone in town knew them. Everyone around the same age, anyway. Valetta Nibley, Dee Stubbs, Brock Nibley, Gus and Tami Majewski . . . all of them. Even Jakob's older brother, Helmut, knew Delores."

Nan's lips twitched in a smile. "Lord, sometimes I forget how insular this place is. I grew up in a big city. Everyone dispersed after the school bell rang, so we didn't hang out with kids from our school, you know?"

"I guess."

"It's funny, isn't it, that you and Becca were clearing out the home of a girl she knew?"

"Not really funny. That was through the Mackenzie auction house, who are auctioning the contents for the estate. We're old friends of the Mackenzies and go to all their auctions. I buy stuff for the historic house all the time through them, and I've done odd jobs for them in the past. Mr. Mackenzie has even started to contact me about vintage kitchen items coming up in sales. I've cleared out old houses before, so when it came to clearing out the Paget place, they thought of us. It was just chance that Becca decided to help."

"So what's going on with that house? Do you know?"

"On the record or off it?" Jaymie asked cautiously.

Nan hooted with laughter. "You're learning. Off the record for now, then."

"The chief trusts me not to give stuff

away," Jaymie explained. "He's asked me, since I have a nose for this kind of thing and in this case know all the players, to sniff around."

"Chief Ledbetter has been pretty noncommittal. All he'll say is it's early days yet."

"Let me talk to the chief. I'll see if there's anything I can share. I think it's safe to say that right now they're investigating the house as a crime scene. But in the meantime . . . maybe you can give *me* some information."

"Quid pro quo?"

"Quid what what?"

"How about, *I scratch your back, you scratch mine.*" She picked up her coffee stirrer again and jabbed it at Jaymie. "I trust you. I'll give you anything we've got, *if* you'll promise that whatever you *can* say, you'll say to us first. The wire services are panting for this stuff — two teenage girls, cold case, missing over thirty years and found within forty-eight hours of each other — and it's a chance for us to get our name out there. It's tough sledding for newspapers these days. We need to get noticed."

"Got it. Hey, I gave you the exclusive on our story of finding poor Delores, right?"

"Okay, I've been digging." She turned to her computer and quickly moused around

171

some documents. "The Pagets arrived in the area in March of 1968, according to school enrollment for Clifford Paget, who was sixteen at the time."

"How did you find that out?" Jaymie asked.

Nan waggled her reddish arched eyebrows. "We have our ways. I've got some hints of employment for Jim — nicknamed Jimbo — Paget, though mainly, at least at first, he worked on the farm for an elderly woman who owned the house they lived in. There are a few mentions in newspaper archives on Mrs. Olga Paget. But I can't find anything before that, no birth records that fit, no military service records, no work, no school . . . *nothing.* It's weird, as if they arrived from another planet. I put my best researcher on this, and we got . . . nothing."

"That's pretty much what the chief said."

"What does that tell you?" Nan watched her expectantly.

"Well, that they were using fake names, at the very least."

"And what else?"

"They were hiding something from their past."

"Bingo!" Nan pointed the stir stick at her.

Jaymie had been trying to figure out what could cause Delores to be murdered in her own home, as appeared to have happened. A crime, maybe; infant abduction? That would bring a lot of emotion to the family. Maybe that's really why the chief was trying to find blood typing on Mr. and Mrs. Paget; he wanted to establish Delores's family history.

But there were other things that were nagging at her, like how Clifford Paget creeped Becca out as a teenager, and Olga Paget's disgusting remarks to Helmut about Delores's physical development. It was not a healthy environment and there were other possibilities she didn't even want to consider until she knew more. "Anything on Clifford Paget? He drowned in the nineties."

"I found a bunch of stories on that. They never found his body." She pulled up some articles on the disappearance. A grainy black-and-white photo of Clifford Paget sitting in a lawn chair, beer in hand, popped up. He was skinny and scruffy-looking, with a hangdog expression.

"I wondered about that." Jaymie shook her head. "There are almost too many possibilities."

"Almost," Nan said with a twinkle in her eye. "But not quite."

"What about Rhonda Welch? I know she was sent to a Christian boarding school days before she disappeared because her parents were going somewhere for a missionary job, or something. Where are they today?"

Nan brought up an archival newspaper clipping. "Her parents were embarking on a two-year mission to Kenya, but came back after learning their daughter — and only child — was missing. Their church offered a ten-thousand-dollar reward for information leading to Rhonda's discovery. It was never claimed, though lots of tips came in at the time."

"What kind of tips?"

Nan read the pieces, her lips moving. She grabbed a flash drive and said, "I'll put some of this stuff on this for you to look over."

"And put the articles about Clifford Paget's death on it . . . whatever you have. I'll read it all."

"From what I've read the tips were the usual missing person sightings of her in other towns as far away as San Francisco — we now know those were false — and some sightings of the car."

"Was there ever a reward for Delores?"

Nan met her eyes and shook her head. "Nothing of note."

"And the two cases of missing girls . . . weren't they ever connected back then?"

"Only when it was supposed there might be a serial killer or rapist on the loose. But I think that idea faded. The police at the time seemed to figure it was a coincidence, two runaways decided on the same day for different reasons to take off."

"That's an awfully big coincidence."

"But not impossible. There was a big murder case in late December that shoved the two girls' disappearance off the front pages and out of people's attention. That happens if no new leads come in."

Jaymie took the flash drive Nan handed her and stuck it in her purse. "I'm trying to wrap my mind around it. Which one was killed first? And why both of them?"

"That's the question." Nan paused and eyed Jaymie, tapping her coffee stirrer. "My first thought was, what about murder-suicide? I mean, that only works if Rhonda killed Delores, and then herself, but . . . maybe?"

Jaymie shook her head. "Not likely, Nan. Delores was killed in her home. I can't even imagine a motive for Rhonda to go there, kill her, then kill herself by driving her car into the river. The Paget family seems a good place to start, though I can't figure out how Rhonda ended up dead, if that's the case. It doesn't seem to hang together."

"You make some good points. Look, I've got one of my reporters on this, but sometimes women are better at getting information out of older folks. I was thinking of handling it myself, but I'm not much better than he is. I have a couple of names here." She scribbled some names and information on a piece of paper. "Mr. Welch died a couple of years ago, but Mrs. Welch is in her eighties and in a retirement home. And there's a retired detective, Lenny MacDonald, who investigated both cases. He might remember something that will help." Nan cracked a smile as she stuck out the piece of paper. "You missed your calling, kiddo; maybe you should have been an investigative reporter instead of a food writer."

"*Or* maybe I should have become a private detective." Jaymie smiled, staring at the names, phone numbers and addresses. "Though you know, it's never too late for that."

ELEVEN

Jaymie walked back to her van, parked on a side street near the bakeshop, and threw her purse in, leaning against the door and looking up at the sky. Her mind was a jumble of thoughts, worries, and curiosities.

Mostly worries, many of them minor.

She worried about the wedding shower; she had always disliked being the center of attention. There was nothing she could do about that but be appreciative that people wanted to come celebrate her and her sister's marriages and try to enjoy the day. This was all about the love people had for Becca and her.

She worried about the wedding: so much cost and trouble! Slipping away to elope had been her number-one choice. She'd never been one of those girls who dreamed of her wedding her whole life, but her family would have been crushed if they hadn't been invited to celebrate a special day with

Jaymie, and so would Jakob's. All she could do about that was plan a wedding in keeping with her and Jakob's modest wishes, be grateful for her friends, and know that after it was all over she would have a family. That was most important. She was marrying a man who truly valued her for herself, and a daughter she already loved.

She worried about the murders, even though they were committed over thirty years ago. Those two teenage girls, with so many plans for a future they never got to experience; they deserved at least to have their killer brought to justice, even if that killer was also long dead. What she could do about this was help Chief Ledbetter solve them. She'd done it before, she could do it again.

She worried that Valetta was truly upset with her about Brock. She perked up . . . now *that* was something she could fix immediately. When she got back to Queensville she'd go talk to her friend. Surely their friendship would withstand the stress. Valetta must know that Jaymie would never purposely do anything to harm her or her family.

Calmer for having mulled it all over, she climbed in the van and checked her cell phone. There was a text from Bernie's official police number, and it confirmed that Ms. Petty Welch would be pleased to talk to her. Anyone who would help solve her niece's death was welcome. Jaymie jotted down the address and headed toward it, a place between Wolverhampton and Queensville, the home of Rhonda's aunt.

November 1, 1984
Petty Welch smoothed back her permed and hairsprayed mop of hair, tucking it behind one ear, and held the phone receiver up as she punched in the numbers. She loved doing her hair every day — teasing it into the exaggerated tangle that was fashionable — and wearing jangly earrings, but the earrings especially probably weren't a good idea when you were on the phone as much as she was. She glanced around the room, a thicket of gray fabric cubicles, each holding a researcher or fact checker for the Detroit newspaper, then up at the big round glass-covered clock. It was five, and she wasn't done at work until six. But she couldn't wait. This was a personal call; if anyone found out she'd be in major crap, but with her brother and sister-in-law out of the country, Rhonda didn't have anyone else to call for help. If her damn boss wasn't such a dick, Petty would have gotten the call that

came in to her earlier.

"Chance Houghton Christian Academy. How may I direct you?"

"Hello. My name is Petty Welch," she murmured, turning away from the other cubicles as much as she could. The hum of voices and jangling of phones was a constant backdrop to her workday, and she was used to it. "My niece, Rhonda Welch, is a new student there. Her parents just left the country. I got a call from Rhonda earlier this afternoon at my work number, but no one passed the message on to me until now. May I speak with her?"

There was a pause on the other end of the phone. "Miss Welch, it is not unusual for students to be homesick the first few days of their residence with us and to try to engage family in their problems. It's best to let us help them work it out. I'll make note of your concern, but —"

Petty firmly said, "Rhonda is seventeen, not ten. If she called me, she had a damn good reason —"

"There is no need to swear at me, miss. Please keep your temper, or I will end this call."

She took a deep breath, then let it out slowly. "My apologies. But nonetheless, Rhonda is seventeen, not ten. She called me for some reason. With my brother out of the country, I would like to be there for my niece if she needs me. Would you be so kind as to find her and bring her to the phone?"

"I'll see what the headmistress says."

She was put on hold.

When the young woman came back on the line, there was a distinct difference in her tone, a deference, almost. "I'm sorry, but Miss Welch isn't available right now, Miss . . . uh, Welch. The headmistress asked that you call back in an hour, if that's okay?"

Petty looked up at the clock again. "Would six thirty be all right? I'll be on the highway until about then. It's a long drive home." Surely whatever her niece was calling about could wait until then.

"Six thirty will be fine," the young woman said, her tone relieved.

Petty hung up and stared at the phone for a long minute. She talked to dozens of people every day and had become proficient at reading voice tones. Why relief? One of her few friends in the department wandered by.

"What's up with you?" she asked, pausing.

Petty, still staring at the phone, said, "I don't know. I feel like something's wrong, you know?"

181

"Whatever it is, happy hour will cure it. Drinks later?"

"No, I'd better not," Petty said. "I have to drive home, and then I have to call my niece at boarding school to check in. I'll feel better once I've talked to her."

"Suit yourself."

Late April — The Present

Daffodils nodded in the spring sunshine, and abundant greenery laden with buds was thickly planted in mulched beds. Petty Welch's house was a perfect country cottage. It could have been taken out of the pages of an English fairy tale, constructed of cobbles and blue painted shingle. Jaymie parked in the lane and got out, standing for a moment to gaze at it, bathed in spring sunshine. It was the kind of home where you'd bet nothing bad had ever happened. A woman came out to the porch and shaded her eyes, waving to Jaymie as she approached the cottage.

"You must be Jaymie Leighton," the woman said. She was petite, with damp, curly gray hair, and she wore wire-framed glasses. "Petty Welch," she said, thrusting out her hand.

Jaymie shook hands. "Nice to meet you."

"I read your column, 'Vintage Eats.' It

takes me back to my grandmother's house in the sixties. She's the only reason I know how to cook today. Come in, come in!"

Jaymie stepped up onto the low cement porch, abutted by cobblestone pillars, and followed the woman through a screen door that slapped closed behind them with a creak and smack. They entered directly into a small living room with a huge picture window that overlooked the gardens outside.

The walls were painted pale blue and the room was decorated the way only a woman who lived alone could decorate. It was the essence of shabby chic, with sofas slipcovered in sturdy white broadcloth, white painted tables, the paint rubbed along the edges to show the raw wood underneath, and lots of pale blue lanterns, vases, and reed baskets. The fireplace mantel was painted white and over it hung an extravagant painting of cabbage roses in a glass vase. The overall effect of the design choices was breathtaking.

"Your home is lovely, like it's out of a design magazine!" Jaymie said as Petty waved her toward an overstuffed chair.

"I'll give you a tour after, if you like. I'd love to show you my collection of pastel Pyrex! You're one of the few people who would appreciate it. It's my passion, I will admit."

Jaymie hesitated, but then forged ahead: "If you've got a collection, would you mind if I profiled it on my blog? I'm always interested in anything vintage and kitchen-related."

"That would be so wonderful," Petty said, blushing. She put her hands to her cheeks. "I was hoping you'd say something like that!"

Ten minutes later they settled with tea, served on a blue bar cart topped by a tray with a transfer of a Little Bo Peep–style lady, and in a pastel multicolored tea set. Jaymie wasn't sure how to get down to the matter at hand, but Petty launched into the topic.

"You're here about Rhonda." Her expression sobered. "My niece. I can't believe they found her, and so close to home! I *knew* she was dead."

"How?"

"If she was alive she would have contacted me even if she was running away. She tried to, the day she disappeared, but I never got the message until much later in the day. I kept waiting for her to phone in the days after but . . . she never did." She leaned forward, her expression earnest. "And she *would* have. We were close."

"I'm so sorry, Ms. Welch."

"Petty, please," she said with a quick smile that lingered on her lips only a second, then disappeared. "Rhonda and I had a special bond. I always felt sorry for her. My brother was a . . ." Her lips tightened. "I won't speak ill of the dead. Roger passed away two years ago."

"But your sister-in-law is still alive, I understand?"

"Yes. I feel bad for her. Iona only *ever* wanted to be a mother. She had several miscarriages, then had Rhonda and had to have a hysterectomy immediately from complications of the birth. Rhonda was her miracle child."

"And yet they left her in a boarding school as they were taking off for two years."

"My brother's doing, not Iona's. She didn't want to go but Roger forced it on her, and her church's command was that a wife must obey her husband. All she ever wanted was to keep house and dote on her daughter. Afterward she blamed him for Rhonda's disappearance and it soured their marriage. Roger wouldn't hear of divorce, so they lived together in misery for the last thirty more years."

Jaymie frowned down into her teacup.

"I'm sorry to be blunt, but why are *you* asking about Rhonda? I've spoken to the police already and identified . . . identified some of Rhonda's things from the car." Her voice had thickened, and tears gleamed behind the glasses. "They were going to ask Iona to do it, but I wouldn't hear of it. She's been through so much in her life. Bad enough I had to break the news to her that Rhonda had been found. She always thought perhaps Rhonda had just left, gone off to make her way in the world."

Jaymie told Petty a bit about Becca knowing Rhonda and Delores, and how it had hit them all hard. "I've poked around for the police chief before. I seem to have a nose for trouble . . . or actually for solving trouble."

"I've seen your name in the paper attached to investigations." Jaymie's explanation seemed to be enough. Petty poured more steaming tea into her cup. "I feel so guilty, so responsible. If only I'd gotten the message that day; it mightn't have changed anything, but the thought nags at me. I hope I can help, but I'm not sure how."

"Tell me whatever comes to your mind about Rhonda."

Petty spoke quietly but with deep emotion about her niece. They had a kindred bond, more like sisters than aunt and niece. Petty took her to concerts, let her drink wine, and they shared long phone conversations, even though Petty lived near Detroit for her job in newspaper research.

"How was her relationship with her parents? You spoke of some estrangement?"

Petty frowned. "Rhonda was in her senior year. She didn't see why she couldn't live in their home alone. She could drive; she was responsible. But Roger wouldn't hear of it. That was one sore spot. Another was that she was dating."

"Gus Majewski."

Petty nodded. "I never met him, but Rhonda seemed smitten."

"Was there anything else to their troubles?"

The woman frowned and set her cup down. "There was one thing that was a bit weird. She wrote to me a few days before she disappeared. She was asking strange questions, like, could I look up accidents in Michigan and Ohio, ones where two parents had died leaving a baby girl?"

"Did she think she was adopted?"

"I thought that's why she was asking at the time. I didn't write back because I was coming to see her at her new school on Saturday to take her out to dinner, make sure everything was okay. I thought I'd leave it to talk to her then, in person. It didn't make any sense. We had *had* conversations. I'd told her since she was little about seeing her just an hour after she was born, and how precious she was."

"Petty, I know you hadn't met him, but do you know anything about your niece's relationship with Gus Majewski?"

"It was pretty new, I can tell you that. But it seemed more serious than others she'd had. She was popular, but she always told me life was too short to have a steady guy."

"Yet it seemed more serious, you say. Why?"

She shrugged. "I don't even remember why I thought that. It's an impression left from something she said, I guess."

"What was she like?"

Petty reached over the arm of the sofa and grabbed a slim album from a basket. "I got this out recently for the police. It has photos of Rhonda." She paused, took a deep breath, and cleared her throat. "She would be fifty," she said, tears welling, and one trailing down her cheek to her chin. "We'd be friends. If she had kids . . ." She cleared her throat. "I loved that girl so much. I was devastated when she disappeared, but for a long time I held out hope we'd find her.

Then the hope faded and I accepted what I'd known all along, that she was dead."

Jaymie took the album and leafed through it, letting the woman rein in her emotions. There were the typical grainy color photos, faded with time, of a baby in a bassinet, then a chubby toddler with dark curls, then a slim child: playing baseball; wearing a confirmation dress in front of a church; having a birthday party. Then there were more of the two of them, Petty recognizable despite the years, dyed blonde hair in eighties curled profusion, and dark smooth-haired Rhonda, a slim and gorgeous girl with a direct and intelligent gaze. Arms over each other's shoulders, they did look more like sisters than aunt and niece.

And that was it; Rhonda Petty never aged past her last photo, almost eighteen, with her aunt at an exhibit at the Detroit Institute of Art.

"She was kind and capable," Petty said. "She was smarter than my brother ever was. Always got the best of him in arguments and that drove him nuts. She was *stubborn.* She was good in science. Wanted to be a nurse."

"What do you think happened?" Jaymie asked, remembering Nan's wild and improbable theory that Rhonda killed Delores and then herself.

"If it was just her that died I'd think she was leaving the school — maybe that's what she wanted to tell me — picked up some bad dude hitchhiking, and he killed her then ran the car into the water."

"Is that the kind of thing she'd do, pick up a hitchhiker?"

"Oh, absolutely! She always thought she could judge a person just by looking at them; I guess that's the naïveté of youth. When you get older you realize that jerks also come in pretty packages." She gave a rueful smile, and Jaymie thought that was perhaps hard-won personal knowledge on her part. "But if it was tied to Delores Paget's murder? I don't know."

"Did she ever mention Delores to you?"

Petty shook her head.

"What about friends? Did she mention Brock Nibley, or anyone else?"

Petty shrugged as she shook her head. "I'm sorry I'm not more help."

"Did Rhonda keep a diary, or write you letters, other than that one? Do you have any of that kind of stuff left?" It was unlikely, but still . . . things you would normally get rid of you might not, if your niece disappeared and it was all you had of hers.

There was a shift in Petty's expression and

her eyes widened behind the glasses. "I should have remembered this when the police came to ask me for photos! I kept a bunch of totes with stuff from when Iona went to the retirement home after Roger died. Iona was a saver, not like me, so there *may* be some things in there of Rhonda's. It was Roger and Iona who collected her things from the school." She moved to the edge of her seat. "I could look through that stuff, see if there's anything."

Jaymie felt a tingle of excitement. "Would you? You never know what may help."

"Should I give it to the police?"

Pausing, Jaymie thought for a moment. "Would you mind if I saw it first? The police should definitely have it, but I would like to get an idea what was in it. Chief Ledbetter knows I'm talking to you, of course. Do you have anything yourself? Like the letter she wrote asking about babies and accidents?"

Regret on her face, Petty shook her head. "I'm a scrapper, not a saver. All this collecting," she said, waving her hand around at the stuff crowding her neat and pretty living room, "is recent. Since I've retired I find myself holding on to more, I don't know why. I don't have anyone to save it for."

Jaymie surreptitiously glanced down at her watch. If she was going to check in with Valetta, do the other half dozen things she needed to get done that day, have something to eat and then go over to Bernie's, she needed to get a move on. "Is the stuff easy to get to?" Jaymie asked. "Could I look through it now?"

"It's up in the attic. I have a few totes up there of mine and many more of Iona's, but only a couple will have Rhonda's things in it, if they do at all. Can you come back another day?"

Jaymie stood. "That's a good idea. I'm on kind of a tight schedule today. As much as I'd like the tour of your kitchen — and your garden, by the way, which looks beautiful — maybe I can come back and do that all at once? I'll bring a camera and get some shots of your Pyrex so I can feature it."

Petty agreed to call her when she had it all together, and Jaymie left.

Home, dog, cat, lunch, catching up with Jakob and a brief call with her dad from Florida about their travel plans for returning to Michigan for the weddings. Just as she was getting ready to slip out the door, the phone rang again.

It was Mrs. Stubbs. "Jaymie? That you?"

"Yes, it is. Is everything okay?"

"I remembered something. One day, a few

days before they disappeared, if memory serves, I saw Rhonda Welch and Delores Paget together in the library. I eavesdropped, and I'm trying to remember what they were talking about."

Jaymie felt a chill of excitement. This was the first real memory anyone had of a connection between Rhonda and Delores, but it didn't do to hurry Mrs. Stubbs.

There was a long pause, the sound of the elderly lady's breathing on the line. "I think I've got it. First, those two together was a real mystery to me. They were so unalike! Ran in different circles, one popular, the other a loner."

"You're right about that."

"But the two girls were thick as thieves that day, heads together, whispering and scheming. Saying something about going together to see someone, a 'her.' "

"Going to see a 'her,' " Jaymie mused. Slowly, she said, "I *think* I may know who the 'her' is, and I may even know the why."

"What is it?"

"Mrs. Stubbs, I'd love to tell you, but I have got to run. May I visit with you tomorrow sometime? Becca is coming into town and I have to go to her new shop with her. I also need to stop in at the Emporium for my vintage picnic baskets. But I'm sure I can fit in a visit, either before or after, if that's okay?"

"You know where I'll be."

Jaymie was off again then, walking this time. She had a dear friend who she needed to smooth things over with. It was late afternoon, and though the Emporium would remain open for another few hours, Valetta would be locking up her pharmacy counter at the back. Jaymie caught her as she was leaving to walk home, lunch bag and purse over her shoulder.

"Valetta, can we talk?" she said, racing up to her friend, who was stepping down to the bottom step of the wooden stairs that led from the store.

"Jaymie! I'm so relieved. I've wanted to call you every night the last few." She blinked behind her glasses and played with her purse strap. "Can you come over for a cup of tea? I need to talk to you. *And* I've got some things to show you."

They headed to Valetta's nearby cottage, talking only of inconsequentials on the way. Neither got down to business until they were ensconced in her living room, in which every surface was cluttered with knick-knacks of vintage origin reflecting Valetta's varied interests: cat figurines, collecting magazines, bowls, lamps, candle holders, pop idol figures, and dolls.

There was silence for a moment. Jaymie was about to speak but Valetta held up one hand. "I have to say . . . I know what you and Becca and *everyone* think of Brock." She hugged her knees and looked down at the carpet. "He can be hard to take." She looked up at Jaymie. "But he's my brother."

"I know that, Val, and I'd never —"

"Jaymie, hold on. Though he's my brother, if I thought for one second that he had done anything like . . . like hurt those girls, I'd turn him in. I'd never stand for it."

"I know that, Val."

"I've thought about it a lot, and I want to help. If we uncover who killed Rhonda and Delores it will clear Brock. I don't want people looking at him funny." She pushed her glasses up her nose. "A real estate agent has to have people trust him. *Women* need to trust him. They have to meet him at vacant houses. This is important to me."

"Okay."

"But I won't let Brock pit me against the rest of you anymore," she said with a shake of her head. "He does stuff like that all the time. He's always felt like an outsider, in a way, and he expects me to feel like an outsider too."

Jaymie decided against saying that Brock

was Brock's own worst enemy.

"But I know as well as anyone that Brock is his own worst enemy," Valetta continued. "He's not going to change now, though. Not at his age."

Jaymie held back a smile and nodded, patting her friend's hand where it rested on her knee. "Val, you're my best friend. I care about you and I want you to know that none of us thinks any differently about you, no matter what Brock is like. He's just . . . Brock. We *know* that."

Val nodded with a sigh. "Anyway, I have some things I want to show you." She disappeared into her spare room and came back out with a battered cardboard box labeled "Old Stuff." She dropped it on the floor between them and flipped open the flaps. "This is stuff from my teen years. I pretty much have everything I ever owned, even my old clothes. I was never sure why I don't get rid of stuff, but now I think it was because when I was growing up, we didn't have much. Dad died when I was four, and Mom struggled. So we did well just to have a roof over our heads." She shrugged and pushed up her glasses, meeting Jaymie's eyes. "So . . . I've saved everything. This is stuff from the eighties." She reached into the box and took out an old diary that was covered in loopy pink hearts and stickers of John Cougar and Joan Jett.

Jaymie smiled. "Isn't his name John Cougar *Mellencamp*?" she asked, pointing to the sticker.

"Well, yeah. But before that, in 1982 or so, he was just John Cougar, and I was totally in love with him. I always said if I had a daughter I'd name her Diane."

Jaymie was mystified for a moment, then remembered his song "Jack and Diane." She took the diary from Valetta. "So is there anything in here about Delores or Rhonda?"

"Some. If you think it will help, you can take it home and read it."

"You don't mind?"

Val smiled. "It's so long ago. I may have had a few hurtful things to say about Becca — I was jealous about all the time she spent with Delores that summer — but it was kid stuff."

"I'll take it. Anything else?"

In the end there was a small pile of notes, school papers and a journal.

"Val, I keep wondering about those sweaters," Jaymie said, straightening. "I know Brock went out with both girls."

Valetta nodded.

"But he apparently only went out with Rhonda once or twice. Why did your Mom knit *both* girls sweaters?"

"She was always trying with Brock's girlfriends. He never managed to keep a girl for long, but she tried so *hard* to make friends with them. In fact, even years later she tried so hard with Brock's wife that the poor girl eventually stopped answering the phone 'cause Mom called at all hours, wanting to gab." Brock was a widower; his wife had died a few years ago.

"So, your mother knitted them both sweaters because she wanted Brock to do well with them?" Sounded crazy.

"You had to know my mom. She was always so overwhelmed by life; I feel bad, looking back. I, at least, tried to help, but Brock was useless. He sat around in the living room complaining. She thought if he had a steady girlfriend he'd change. You know, the love of a good woman, all that stuff. He was always a good worker, when he had a job, but he never did seem to have a clue with women."

And he had repellent views about women right up to the present day, which made Jaymie dislike him, though she tried to hide her dislike for Valetta's sake. There was a niggling worry in the back of her mind that Brock was somehow involved. It was the kind of thing she could see him doing;

maybe not the murder itself, unless it was an accident, but the attempt at a cover-up.

"Anyway, Mom knit the sweaters and then made Brock give them to both Delores, first, and then Rhonda. I was *deadly* embarrassed, but both girls seemed to like them. I had one too from the same pattern and same wool and I loved it. Mom was a fast knitter. In fact . . ." Her gaze became unfocused. "Yes, I *remember*! I actually saw Delores and Rhonda one day in the halls talking . . . must have been just before Halloween, because the Halloween dance banner was being put up. They were both wearing the red sweaters! I overheard Rhonda say, joking, that they were going to form a red sweater club."

And days later they would both be dead. Jaymie shivered, but then jumped to her feet, reached out and hugged Valetta. She gathered the stuff up, ready to go. "I've got a full day of running around tomorrow," she told her friend. "I'll be stopping in at the Emporium to update the vintage picnic basket rental book." She paused, but then said, "I may be fulfilling the bookings I have and then stopping with the business. With the wedding and spending time with Jakob, I don't think I'm going to have much time."

"You do what you have to do," Valetta

said. "It's been a good run, but you have too much on your plate. See you tomorrow, then."

TWELVE

Jaymie returned home, had a quick dinner, and sat at the kitchen table to work on the next "Vintage Eats" column. The difficult parts of any vintage recipe were details like weights and measures, and oven temperatures, which were often only alluded to vaguely, or estimated. But this time it was complicated by the handwriting, which she was trying to decipher to transcribe onto her laptop. She had dug out her grandmother's decrepit recipe book from the 1950s, and decided to try her hand at salmon loaf. She'd tried a different recipe for salmon loaf once before and it hadn't turned out great. But surely it shouldn't be *that* complicated.

However, the difficulties began with the can of salmon; it asked for a one-pound can. Did anyone even make a one-pound can of salmon anymore? The largest she had seen was fourteen-point-five ounces, shy of a pound. She could use three six-ounce cans, maybe. And . . . what kind of salmon? Pink was bland, red or sockeye horrendously expensive. This was not a budget-friendly dish for the family, as the recipe book claimed.

But she could use the pink salmon and spice it up, so the flavors improved. Or she would use canned flaked ham, or turkey. With a sigh, she set it aside to think about. She felt scattered, like her mind was in a million places at once: wedding, murder, writing, working, historical house . . . Jakob. *Ah.* Jakob and Jocie. She sighed and sat back, closing her eyes. It was all going to be okay because soon she would have Jakob and Jocie full-time, her husband and her daughter; everything else would work out.

But not yet. She sat up straight and glanced at the clock on the wall over her Hoosier-style cabinet. Time was speeding, and she had a date to look at her wedding dress . . . or at least the dress Heidi had picked out for her. She felt the need of some emotional support, so she called Heidi to ask if Valetta could come along. That okayed, she called Valetta, who enthusiastically agreed and would in fact pick her up. The distance to Bernie's place was walkable, but it would be faster to drive.

"I don't know what to expect, Val," Jaymie said as they drove over through the spring dusk in Val's sensible sedan with a bobble-head cat stuck on the dash. "Heidi has good taste in clothes, but for me? I'm not so sure. Even though she *did* help me choose a pretty dress for the shower. I love a thrift store, you know that, but a used *wedding gown* . . .? I'm not sure."

"If you don't like it, don't wear it," Valetta said, glancing over at her. "Your wedding, Jaymie, not hers."

"I have a bad feeling about this," Jaymie fretted.

They parked in Bernie's driveway behind Heidi's car and headed to the door. The sun was very low on the horizon and it set the yellowy red brick of Bernie's mid-century ranch-style home aglow. Jaymie hiked her purse over her shoulder and rang the door-bell.

Bernie, also known as Bernice, threw open the door and welcomed them both with hugs, her dark eyes sparkling. With dark skin and dark eyes, her hair short-cropped and natural, gorgeous smile and full lips, she looked like a slightly shorter version of the actress and singer Jill Scott. Bernie was compact and medium height, but strong and athletic, as it behooved an officer of the law to be. She and Heidi went to the gym in Wolverhampton to work out together all the time. They had invited her to go with them, but Jaymie's idea of exercise was a walk by the river with Hoppy.

"Come on down to the rec room. I've started the cocktails . . . your wedding cocktails, Jaymie!" she said with a bounce. "A Müller Mull and a Leighton Pink Lady!" She led the way down some steps of the back split ranch to the rec room. As heavily into the mid-century modern look as Heidi, Bernie had found at auction a highly lacquered all-in-one unit that held her collection of vintage barware, as well as bottles of alcohol. Heidi was putting a record on the stereo and the sounds of Dean Martin, followed swiftly by his Rat Pack pal Sammy Davis Jr. floated out of the speakers.

But all Jaymie could focus on was a white clothing bag hung from a floor-to-ceiling pole light near the stereo. Even as Jaymie was staring at it, Bernie shoved a drink into her hand and said, "Try this!"

Jaymie sipped and her eyes widened. She looked at Bernie, who was handing a drink to Valetta. "This is del*ic*ious! What is it?"

As Bernie recited the recipe, which had apple brandy and some other ingredients, Heidi waltzed over and grabbed Jaymie, dancing her around the room so violently her drink sloshed on the hardwood floor.

"Drink up!" she crowed. "And another!"

Ten minutes and two drinks later, Jaymie sat down on the sofa, feeling woozy. Valetta, biting her lip to keep from laughing, joined her. "I think you'd better slow down, kiddo."

"I know. I'm not used to drinking."

Bernie shoved another drink into her hand.

"Nooo, Bernie, I can't!"

"Relax, lightweight, it's ginger ale. I know how to pace myself and others too."

"Now, for the reveal!" Heidi said, unzipping the clothing bag. She pulled out the dress. "Ta da!"

Jaymie stared at it, doing her best to clear her mind. It was ivory lace, long lace sleeves with satin buttons at the wrists and with a fitted bodice, but no corseting or any of the other uncomfortable structures she disliked about the wedding dresses she had tried on. The front bodice had a chevron design of satin ribbon, and a satin cord laced it all the way from the waist up to a sweetheart neckline.

It wasn't as bad as she had feared, but it was impossible to tell if it would be right for her. "Do you think it will fit?" she asked with some apprehension. She was a solid woman, not slim, like Heidi, or compact and well-muscled like Bernie.

Heidi, one hand on her hip as she held up the dress with the other, glared at Jaymie. "Do you think I'd have bought it if I didn't know it would? Honey, I'm good at this. I've been shopping my whole life for myself and everyone else I know. You *have* to try it on!"

What did she have to lose? She had not been able to find a wedding dress on her own, particularly because she was not willing to spend a couple of thousand dollars for a dress she felt certain would be the recipient of wine and food spills, doggy hair and kids' sticky hands by the end of the night. An elegant and expensive gown was fine for others, but not for her.

It was becoming torturous and upsetting to even think about it, considering that her wedding was a month and a half away. Heidi grabbed her hand and hauled her into the furnace room, where she had a makeshift dressing room set up with a full-length mirror and a dressing table, along with accoutrements: makeup, a veil, and a hair piece.

Jaymie decided to give herself over to the process and let Heidi do what she wanted. Soon she was laced into the dress, her luxurious hair — long, light brown and wavy — coiled up and pinned, with a long wavy pony over one shoulder, and the veil pinned to a pearl clip ornament. Heidi fussed at her some more, putting some lip gloss and mascara on, things Jaymie didn't wear unless it was a formal occasion.

Finally, Heidi stood back and nodded. Were those tears in her eyes? Jaymie wondered how bad it was.

"What's wrong?" she asked, her voice croaky with worry.

"You're so beautiful," Heidi said, her voice thick with weepiness. "My *friend.* I've never had a friend like you." She shook her head, swallowing hard. "I can't imagine what my life would be like in Queensville if it wasn't for you."

Jaymie was touched, but heavens . . . she wasn't perfect. She had been so *very* jealous of Heidi at first. It had taken *months* to get over that. When Joel first moved out of her home and into Heidi's, she had driven past the house many times, her heart aching, hating the woman inside.

Until she got to know her. "Heidi, everyone loves you for *you.* You must know that. I may have got the ball rolling, but the rest is all you."

Heidi nodded. "Maybe. But you started

207

that ole ball rolling. I might not have stuck it out, you know. I might have sold and moved back to the city. Even if I never marry Joel, I have a home here now." She rushed at Jaymie and hugged her extravagantly. "Thank you."

"Aw, sweetie, it's okay." Jaymie hugged and released. "How do I look?"

"You look like an angel. Come over to the mirror." Heidi grabbed her hand and hauled her to the full-length mirror. "Look!"

Jaymie took a deep breath, faced the mirror and opened her eyes. She looked . . . she looked like a fairy-tale princess! She had collarbones and slight cleavage and good skin, and her hair was nice . . . she actually did look beautiful, as Heidi had said. "It's *perfect*! Oh, Heidi . . . it's kind of fairy-tale princess-y, but not in a bad way. Jocie is going to *love* this!"

"I told you, I told you!" Heidi leaped around and crowed.

"Come *out*!" Bernie yelled from outside the door.

"We want to see!" Valetta said. "We *need* to see!"

"Go sit down!" Heidi yelled back. "And we'll come out."

Shy, but determined to moved forward, Jaymie emerged from the furnace room and faced her friends. Val and Bernie were both silent, staring, setting Jaymie's nerves aflutter.

"Well?" she said. "What do you think?"

Bernie bounced up out of her seat, rushed her and hugged. "It's perfect!"

"Val?"

Valetta stared at her, tears gleaming behind the glasses. "I think my best friend is getting married," she said, her voice thick. "It fully hit me. Jaymie, you look lovely."

"Jaymie Leighton," Heidi intoned, standing beside her. "Do you say 'I do' to this dress?"

Jaymie nodded, tears spontaneously welling. "I do," she croaked.

Back in her regular clothes, Jaymie and the others chatted for a while over retro snacks: French onion dip and chips served in a glass chip-and-dip bowl from the sixties, platters of tiny sandwiches, including white bread spread with peanut butter, wrapped around a banana and cut into thick round slices, as well as shrimp cocktail in vintage champagne coupes and tiny grilled-cheese sandwiches. It was all delicious and had Jaymie thinking of doing a "Vintage Eats" column on party foods of the past.

Bernie's rec room was comfortable, with a

brick fireplace that held a modern gas insert, which she turned on since evenings in April are chilly in Michigan. She had furnished the place with Danish modern repro sofas, as well as real vintage coffee tables and side tables. The retro blonde-wood-paneled walls were adorned with kitschy cool "big eye" and black velvet paintings. Over the fireplace hung a thrift store find, a vintage Hawaiian sunset paint-by-number that was not quite done. It gave the whole room a quirky finesse.

She had made a nonalcoholic punch for them to try. "I have to work tomorrow night," Bernie said with a smile as she served the drinks over ice in vintage highball glasses. "Can't have any more alcohol. Gotta keep it sharp if I want to move up!" She was ambitious but had a ways to go to advance to the heights she intended. Her first goal was to become the first female African-American detective on the Queensville Township PD. She was taking online certificate courses to prepare to work on a master's in Law Enforcement Intelligence and Analysis from MSU.

The group chatted, and Jaymie was happy that Valetta was so comfortable with Bernie and Heidi. It was important that all her friends got along. The topic of conversation moved naturally from Jaymie's upcoming wedding shower, her wedding, and finally, to what was in the news and on people's lips: the finding of the two teenagers who had disappeared in the eighties.

"I don't understand how nobody connected the two girls. They did disappear the same day, right?" Heidi looked around the circle.

Valetta, as the only one who was there then, nodded. "I know it seems obvious now. I don't know what the officials were doing back then, but I do remember what they were saying at school."

"Which was . . . ?" Jaymie asked.

"So much!" Valetta loaded a chip with dip and munched, her gaze thoughtful behind her thick glasses. She swallowed and took a sip of her punch. "At first we didn't know about both girls disappearing, remember. Rhonda had been sent to a boarding school because her parents were off to a missionary position in Kenya."

Heidi snorted and caught Jaymie's eye. "Missionary position!"

They all chuckled, but the matter was serious, so they sobered in a second. "From what I understand the police *did* connect the two missing girls and considered a serial killer or rapist," Jaymie said. "But then

Rhonda's car never surfaced and a school-mate said she'd talked about leaving, so they figured she ran off. Delores's people also said she was likely a runaway. I'm surprised they didn't consider that the two girls had taken off together, but not many people knew they were acquainted, or thought they were close enough friends to run away together."

She wasn't willing to share what she knew of Delores and Rhonda being seen together by Mrs. Stubbs. And she certainly wasn't going to bring up that both girls had dated Brock Nibley. Valetta met her gaze and nodded, gratitude in her eyes.

"It's so sad," Heidi said.

Bernie nodded, but didn't add anything. She usually did go silent when any conversations came up concerning police business.

"I hope they can figure out what happened all those years ago. I don't like unanswered questions," Valetta said, her tone grim.

"I think I'd better get going," Jaymie said. "Val, are you ready?"

She got up and tugged her sweater down over her hips. "I am. Work tomorrow!"

Jaymie stood. "Bernie, this has been such a nice break. Thank you!" She turned to Heidi and drew her into a hug. "I don't

212

know how I'm going to thank you for the dress," she murmured. "How much do I owe you?"

"Not a thing," Heidi said, pulling back so she could look up into her friend's eyes. "It's my wedding gift to you. Leave it here and I'll take care of it. I know Valetta's your maid of honor, but I'll be your maid of the dress! I'm going to get it professionally cleaned and there are a few alterations I want done."

It was all a bit unorthodox, perhaps, but Jaymie wasn't going to say no. She and Jakob were paying for most of their share of the proceedings themselves, even though her father wanted to help. He was going to pay for the catering for his daughters' wedding — he had insisted — but the rest was up to the couples.

"Do you know what jewelry you're wearing?"

"My Grandma Leighton has a set of pearls she wants me to wear as my 'something borrowed,' a lovely necklace and earrings. Becca wore it for her first wedding, and now it's my turn."

"Perfect."

They all trooped outside into the chill night air, hugs all around, but then Heidi put one finger in the air. "Wait! I just remembered. I came over before Bernie got home from work to set up the dressing room, and the auction house delivered that dresser here." She dashed away back into the house.

Jaymie turned to Bernie. "What is up with that girl? I can't thank you enough for taking care of the dresser, Bernie. It's a weight off my shoulders."

"You don't have to thank me. I'm happy to do it! And that reminds me, I have to lock my garage because Heidi won't remember!" She strode away, key in hand.

"I've got to give you this," Heidi said, coming back from the house with a plastic grocery bag. "There were some things in the dresser, kind of a bundle of stuff, and I thought you may as well do something with it. I don't want it." She wrinkled her nose.

"What is it?"

She shrugged. "No clue. Papers. Junk. You can toss it in the garbage here if you want."

"I'll throw it out at home. We have to get going. Good night, all!" She bundled the plastic bag under her arm, waved, and she and Valetta got into the car and drove off.

On the way home Valetta said, "I appreciate you not raising the thing about Brock dating both girls."

"No need to thank me, Val. It has nothing

to do with anything anyway." As far as they knew.

"Still, I appreciate it." She was silent for a moment, but then said, as she turned down Jaymie's parking lane behind the house, "I talked to Delores about Brock, you know. I forgot until now, but I was worried about how Brock treated her. He was a louse; typical guy. I thought she'd be angry, but she seemed almost philosophical about it for a fifteen-year-old, you know? *If* I'm remembering it right." She pulled into Jaymie's parking area. "That was a long time ago. But I remember thinking afterward that she must not have been that crazy about him after all."

"Maybe that's true; maybe she didn't care about him much." Or maybe she wasn't going to confess her feelings to the guy's sister.

Valetta frowned and pushed up her glasses. "I don't know. She seemed so intense whenever she looked at him. While she was dating him she dropped by our house one day; that's the only time Mom met her, I think. She wanted to ask Mom what Brock would like for his eighteenth birthday."

"That sounds pretty serious," Jaymie agreed.

"I know. And yet a few weeks later she

blew it off — her feelings for my brother — as if it were nothing."

"I guess teenage emotions blow hot and cold."

"Not that I remember," Valetta said dryly. "Seems to me that teenage girl feelings blow hot, hotter and blazing inferno."

Remembering what Mrs. Stubbs had said about Delores and Rhonda being close in conversation, Jaymie asked, "Do you think Rhonda may have talked to her, changed Delores's opinion of Brock? And why did Rhonda dump Brock . . . if she did?"

"Oh, she dumped him all right. It was the only thing we heard about for a while. He moped around the house whining." Val shrugged. "I don't know. I figured that she got sick of him. No girlfriend ever lasted long with Brock."

"*And* she started going out with Gus Majewski."

"That's true."

"Was that serious?"

"*Serious?* They were kids."

"Val, kids get pregnant all the time. It can be serious."

Valetta cast her a shrewd look. "You know something."

Oh, crap, Jaymie thought. She hadn't intended to say anything about pregnancy, but there was time to back off. Keeping her face blank and her tone even, she said, "I do *not* know anything. I'm speculating that teenage love can be pretty serious." Rhonda's pregnancy scare was not her secret to tell. If the police or Gus Majewski chose to talk about it, then fine, but she wouldn't leak it.

"I don't know if Rhonda and Gus were serious. They were all over each other, I do remember that. Gus was the hot shot in school; Becca had a big old crush on him. Football hero, you know. He had a football scholarship to U of M, it was rumored. I don't know if he ever went."

"And she was the popular girl."

"Rhonda *was* popular. She wasn't a cheerleader, or anything like that. She was pretty and popular."

"Did you like her?"

"I didn't know her."

"Even though Brock went out with her?"

"Once or twice, at the most. *After* he dropped Delores. Didn't mean I ever hung out with her."

None of this seemed to have any bearing on the double murder that put Delores in a trunk with a cleaver in her head and Rhonda in the river in her Ford Falcon. "I gotta go. Thanks for being with me tonight. I was

217

afraid of what Heidi had in store. I'm lucky it turned out the way it did. If I'd hated the dress I would have needed you to back me up."

"I'm standing in for Becca whenever I can. You're like the little sister I never had, you know?"

Jaymie reached across and hugged her, then released, patting her friend on the shoulder. "I have about a hundred things to do tomorrow," she said, thinking of what Nan wanted her to do, to go talk to the former cop, Lenny MacDonald. "I have to come in to the Emporium briefly, and Becca is coming to town. We're going to have a look at how the antique shop is coming. She wants to be open by the Victoria Day Weekend." The late May Canadian holiday, the weekend before the American Memorial Day weekend, was the unofficial start of the tourism season in Queensville, since Canadians flooded across the river on the ferry to attend the annual Tea with the Queen event. "But I'll see you when I stop in at the Emporium."

"See you tomorrow, then," Valetta said.

THIRTEEN

November 1, 1984

Valetta, skipping a class for the first time ever in her life, clutched her books to her chest and lingered outside the science lab, ducking her head every once in a while to look through the metal-mesh-reinforced glass in the door and make sure Delores Paget was indeed in this class. The bell rang, and the rumble of students — pushing out chairs, opening doors, chattering, laughing — roared through the halls like a tornado.

Aha! There was Delores, in the red sweater knitted by Valetta's mom. As the girl trudged out of the class in the flood of other students, Valetta grabbed her sleeve and pulled her aside. "Can I talk to you?"

"What do *you* want?" Delores said, glaring at Valetta, her tone dripping with hostility.

How the heck could she say this? *What* could she say? "Look, Delores, I know we're not friends —"

"No kidding," the other girl said, pulling her sweater sleeve out of Valetta's grasp. "I gotta get to next class."

"Just wait!" The flood of students was already thinning, and Val had to get to *her* next class, too. "I wanted to . . . I had to tell you . . ." She sighed and blurted out, "Look, my brother can be a *jerk.* I know he treated you crappy —"

"You think I care about *him*?" Delores said, eyes wide, incredulity on her pimpled face. "I'm moving on. He's history."

She should have been reassured by the girl's combative words, but it felt like there was still a world of hurt behind them. "If you ever want to *talk* about it —"

"With *you*? Hah!" She hooted in laughter. "That's a real knee slapper. I'm so *sure*! You never had a single second for me before this and you got Becca jerked back into your tight-knit circle of three, so don't pretend you give a flying f—" She glanced around at a teacher who was coming toward them. "A flying fig about me."

"Girls! Class. *Now!*" the woman said.

"You can forget about me because I'm *fine,*" Delores hissed, poking her finger in Valetta's chest. "I've got other things on my mind than your ugly, cheap, *dork* of a brother." She whirled and headed down the hall as the teacher glared at them both.

"Fine, whatever. Glad to know I could help," Valetta muttered after her, turning in the opposite direction and hurrying down the hall to her next class.

Late April — The present
Once inside her homey, warm kitchen, with the golden pool of light from the fixture over the sink illuminating the dark room, Jaymie tossed the plastic bag aside, then went through the familiar routine: animals fed, cat out, dog out, dog in, cat . . . search, call, and finally go out and find Denver lurking in the holly bushes and drag him back in for the night. Jakob had texted her. They would normally talk last thing in the evening, but he was at his mother's place helping his parents with something, so he'd call her the next day.

It was late, but she was restless. She prowled to one of her bookcases and let her eyes slide along the spines; nope, she wasn't in the mood for reading a romance novel. That happened once in a very long while when she had something on her mind. She *should* be working on her column, due in three days, but it was too late to start. Actually, she was more interested in finding out what was on the flash drive Nan had given her. So she retreated to her room and sat on the bed with Hoppy on one side, Denver on the other, her legs wedged firmly under the covers between them. She opened up her laptop and inserted the flash drive, transferring the contents to a new folder, labeled Delores & Rhonda. She then started to peruse the files, sorting them into categories.

There were news clips about the two girls, as well as yearbook photos, school records, interviews with kids they went to school with. There was a lot of raw data, transcribed reporter notes from interviews with Delores and Rhonda's school friends. One name leaped out at her: Sybil Thorndike; a friend of Rhonda's, according to the file. That was the exact same name as the principal of Jocie's school. Could it be the same woman? Was she the school friend of Rhonda's from the Chance Houghton Christian Academy? Jaymie made a note of that. Sybil told a reporter that Rhonda had said she was desperately unhappy and had no intention of finishing the school year at CHCA.

There were pieces on Clifford Paget from when he went missing, including a bit from the friend who was with him when he disappeared, a fellow named Henk Hofwegen. She jotted down the unusual name. Alongside that article was a real estate ad with Brock Nibley's name, and it triggered her memory: the box of stuff from Valetta! She jumped up, much to Denver's grumpiness and Hoppy's excitement. She dashed downstairs, got the box and brought it up, dumping the contents on the yellow and cream floral-patterned quilt.

That was enough for Denver, who jumped down in a huff and stalked off, heading downstairs to the peace of his basket by the stove. Hoppy, meanwhile, sniffed the papers on the bed and sneezed, falling over from the effect. She laughed as he crept closer and put his one front paw on some of the papers and sneezed again. "I know, sweetie; dusty, huh? This stuff is old!"

There were notes, an old address book, a few fan magazines. She leafed through some of those, noting the stars of the day, many of them still on tour! And there was the 1984 diary. Valetta had said she was free to read it, but she hesitated.

This was all so strange, like slipping through a wormhole for a view at life thirty-plus years ago when her sister and friends were all teenagers. For a long time she had felt out of place with Valetta, DeeDee,

Johnny, and even Becca, especially when they all got together to talk about the good old days. Now, of course, she had her own relationships with these people, and so her memories of them were her own. But this was a step back in time. Would she learn anything she didn't *want* to learn about them all? Would it change her view of them?

Hesitantly, she opened the diary. Valetta's was typical handwriting for a teenage girl, with self-conscious loops and curlicues, hearts dotting *i*s. Out of the slim volume slipped a couple of photos, the kind you get — or got — at drugstore photo machines. Nobody used those nowadays, Jaymie realized, because everybody, even teenagers — especially teenagers — carried a camera in their pocket in the form of a cell phone.

The photos were of Valetta, Becca and Dee as teenagers. Jaymie smiled and set them aside. She flipped through the diary, still uncomfortable. But Valetta had said it was okay to read it, if it might help with getting a sense of what was going on that fall. So she dived in.

She started in summer. Valetta recorded the weather, what she did, what TV she watched. She was a big fan of *Dukes of Hazzard* (John Schneider — sooo cute! Hearts hearts hearts), *The Facts of Life* and *That's*

Incredible! She adored *Little House on the Prairie.* She loved John Cougar, The Go-Gos and Kool and the Gang. She absolutely idolized Michael Jackson.

And she missed her friend Becca. There was a strong thread, through the summer, of jealousy, that Becca had made friends with Delores Paget and now took off to go riding every chance she got instead of hanging out with Valetta, or even DeeDee. There was an acknowledgment that Dee was Becca's best friend, but Valetta hinted that she was at least second best until Delores came along. Valetta also wrote how she wished she had a baby sister to cuddle, and that Becca was so lucky to have Jaymie.

Loneliness oozed from the pages; it was heartrending. Jaymie identified, because at that same age she had felt awkward and unwanted, out of place and out of time. Her parents were older, already in their mid-fifties and looking toward retirement. Maybe that's why she and Valetta had ended up such good friends; even though there was an age gap of fifteen years or more, they were similar.

But then September came and school started. Valetta sounded upbeat and hopeful about the new school year. She listed her classes and the clubs she had signed up for:

Poster Club, Creative Writing, Junior Band (she played the clarinet, to Jaymie's surprise), and Chess Club. She mentioned boys she liked, and a football game she went to with Dee and Becca, when Gus (Juice Man) Majewski was especially impressive.

Jaymie smiled as she thought of Gus, now a fifty-year-old father of a young child. That he was a football hero and the object of countless girls' adoration was funny now, when he was a worried father with silver in his hair and a spare tire around his middle. What had happened, she wondered, to turn his dreams of a college football career into dust? Because he never did go on to college, she now remembered, from something Jakob had once said. Had the loss of Rhonda been so devastating? It seemed to hurt him even now, over thirty years later.

She skimmed on in the diary and came to Becca's birthday party, and Valetta's concern over Brock taking off with Delores in the family car. She was angry partly because he was supposed to give her a ride home. She was suspicious of his intentions with Delores. Fury at her older brother threaded through the next two months as he kept going out with Delores, disappearing with the family car instead of teaching her to drive, like he was supposed to be doing.

Then there were angry passages when Brock apparently ditched any relationship he had with Delores to go out with Rhonda. *Why SHE would go out with my crappy brother, I can't figure out,* Valetta raged at one point. A few days later, the snicker was almost audible when she wrote, *I get it now; Rhonda was just using Brock to get Gus jealous so he'd stop playing around with cheerleaders. Ha-ha to Brock, I say!*

Interesting. Brock had reason to be very angry at Rhonda. Did Valetta realize that when she gave Jaymie permission to read the diary? She was intent on clearing Brock from suspicion, but this didn't do it.

Jaymie settled back and read more carefully as she came to the days in questions, late October, before Delores and Rhonda disappeared, never to be seen again. There wasn't a whole lot. November first she wrote that she had tried to make friends with Delores but that the girl was sulky and didn't want anything to do with her. November second was a long tirade: school was crappy; her Sony Walkman, which had cost her a bundle of the money she had saved from working all summer to buy, was broken. She blamed Brock, who had borrowed it the day before and come home late that night with the car, which he had borrowed

227

without permission. He had tried to sneak it back into her room broken, but she had caught him at it.

Also, *someone,* she said, had been in her room the day before and *someone* had used her perfume. Who would do that? Not her mom, and not Brock. It was weird.

Monday, November fifth's entry was written in a scribble, with an undertone of unease. Gossip was buzzing through the school. Delores Paget was missing. She had been at school last Thursday, Valetta knew that, she wrote, because she had talked to her then; Delores was again wearing the red sweater Valetta's mom had knit. It must have been a favorite. Sometime after lunch period Delores left, according to gossip. Valetta scribbled more, worry running through her words; Brock, who was skipping school that day, said he'd seen her in Queensville and that she'd said she was taking off. But she hadn't said that to anyone else, not even Becca, just about her only friend at Wolverhampton High. Where had Delores gone?

This was a lot to think about. Jaymie set the diary aside, deeply troubled. Something didn't add up. The more she learned, the worse Brock looked. Valetta was always apologizing for him: the way he acted, things he said, things he did. But Jaymie had never considered him malicious or dangerous before.

Was it time to rethink that?

Fourteen

November 1, 1984

Brock Nibley glumly slumped on the top step of the Queensville Emporium, huddled in a beat-up leather jacket he'd found at the Goodwill. It was damn cold and getting colder. He was trying to figure out how to spend the rest of the afternoon, having skipped out of school at lunch. That last joke from a couple of the guys about his girlfriend-less state had been enough. Everyone was a jerk anyway. School was for suckers.

Delores Paget hiked into view, backpack over her shoulder, sour look on her face. She stopped, scanned the whole green area near the store, then continued on toward him. Hmm. Why was she in Queensville?

The poor girl was probably looking for *him;* probably came to find him when he wasn't in school. She was *crazy* about him, after all. Until recently she had been calling his house almost every day. She hadn't called for a while, true, but . . . maybe he had been hasty dumping her when Rhonda had agreed to go out with him. A girl in the hand, and all that. He chuckled at his own wit. Nobody appreciated how smart he was, not even his own sister.

He jumped off the step. "Hey, Del! *Hey! Del!* Come here."

She glanced over, saw him, and stopped but didn't approach.

Brock stretched, smiling and beckoning her. "Come here. I wanna talk to you."

She approached slowly, blinking and fidgeting with the strap of her backpack.

"Hey, how are you doing?" he asked, reaching out, caressing her shoulder. "You're wearing the red sweater Mom made for you. That's cool!" he said, touching the knitted red yarn under her heavy, lined blue jean jacket.

"What do you want, Brock?" she asked, her voice cracking.

"Just to talk. Come on, sit down with me."

"I don't *think* so, jerk."

So . . . she *was* still mad at him for dumping her. That proved even more that she liked him a lot. He licked his lips. She was dumpy and nothing to look at, but he could still remember how eagerly she had kissed him in the car when he took her out to a back road to neck. "You're still mad 'cause I said we couldn't go out anymore."

"You mean because you dumped me for Rhonda Welch," she said swiftly, anger hardening her voice.

Probably not best to remind her what he'd said and done. He hadn't been as nice as he should have been when he told her he didn't want to go out with her again. Next time he dumped a girl he'd lie his ass off in case he wanted to pick up where he left off. "It was a mistake, Del," he said, a wheedling tone in his voice. "I'm *really* sorry. She can't hold a candle to you; *you* know that. You're *way* smarter than she is."

"And brains are what you're looking to feel up in the dark?" She whirled and started trudging away, but turned back. "Is there a pay phone somewhere?"

"Why?"

"No reason." She paused, an uncertain expression on her face. "I was supposed to meet someone, if you have to know."

"Someone? Like someone *who*?" Did she have some other guy on the hook?

"None of your beeswax," she said, walking backward, slowly. "Is there one?"

There was a pay phone in the Emporium but he wasn't going to tell *her* that. "If you need to make a call, you can come back to my place where it's free." He thought quickly; this was his mom's day to clean old Mrs. Stubbs's house, so she wouldn't be home. He might even get lucky. His heart started to beat faster as he waited for her to respond.

She looked doubtful.

"Come on," he wheedled. "It's free. And you look cold. Let me make it up to you. I feel bad for how we ended things."

She shivered and huddled in her coat. "No funny stuff?"

She was a little squirmy last time he had tried to put his hand up her top. Maybe he needed to take it slower, use more finesse. He'd take her to Val's room, which smelled a lot nicer than his, and sweet-talk her. "No funny stuff. Scout's honor." Not that he'd ever been a scout.

"Okay. But just to use the phone."

"Who you calling?" he asked again.

"I told you, none of your freakin' business."

Snotty little witch. Grimly, he grabbed her hand. He didn't need to like her, he just needed to get her alone. "Come on. Let's go."

His house was empty, like he'd hoped. "Where's your phone?" Delores asked.

"Right there," he said, indicating the wall phone in the kitchen. As she picked up the receiver, he raced off to check Valetta's room. Okay, neat enough, he thought, scanning it. Too girlish, but whatever. The flowered wallpaper was covered with posters of John Cougar and John Schneider cut from a magazine. Anyway, her bed was made.

He grabbed her Sony Walkman off the bed and tossed it onto the desk, where it clattered loudly, then he picked up her Love's Baby Soft perfume atomizer and squirted some on the pink chenille bedspread. He propped up Valetta's furry cushions against the wall on the single bed and examined the effect, rubbing his hands together. Perfect.

He returned to the kitchen as Delores was hanging up the phone. "Hey, want a Coke?" he said, ambling to the fridge. "We got Orange Crush, too."

"No. I have to make another call," she said, her expression filled with tension. She kicked her knapsack to sit between her feet, as if she didn't want it anywhere near him, and picked up the phone again.

"You said one call!"

"What's it to you? It's not costing *you* anything," she said.

He snatched the handset from her grasp

and slammed it onto the cradle. "You don't have to be rude. I'm being *nice* to you. You ought to be *grateful.*"

Her eyes narrowed and she picked the receiver up again. "Lay off, Brock. Just one more call."

"Then you'll have a Coke?"

"Sure," she said. "Just let me make this call."

She glared at him until he ambled out of the room, but kept his ears perked. Trouble was, she mumbled. Sounded like she was asking a question, then there was silence. Then she asked another question. He edged closer to eavesdrop.

"Okay," she said, then hung up.

He came back into the kitchen as she hoisted her backpack.

"I have to go," she said.

"But you said —"

"Forget it, Brock. I have to get home right away." She headed to the door.

"Why? Your parents there?"

"No."

He thought fast. "How you gonna get there?"

"I don't know. I'll hitch."

"Let me give you a lift," he said, thinking he had one more shot at some fooling around.

She eyed him, squinting. "Okay. But straight to my place."

"Straight to your place," he agreed. "Clifford isn't there, is he?"

"He's not supposed to be. He's doing someone's roof in Wolverhampton. Why?"

Brock shrugged. "I don't like him, that's all."

"That makes two of us," she muttered. "You giving me a ride or what?"

"All right, okay. Don't be so crabby."

"I'm in a hurry," she said, and eyed the clock on the wall, an orange-and-yellow relic of the last decade.

"Then let's hit the road." He grabbed the car keys from the holder near the door, glad that his mom walked — to save gas — when she went to Mrs. Stubbs's place to work.

April — The Present

It always seems, Jaymie thought the next morning over tea, *that the moment you meet someone, or learn about them, you see their name everywhere.* Jaymie read a story on her tablet in the *Wolverhampton Weekly Howler* — which was weekly in print but updated daily on their website — about Henk Hofwegen, who had been hit by a car on the highway and taken to Wolverhampton General for observation.

With a name like that he *had* to be the same guy in the boat when Clifford Paget went into the St. Clair River. Interesting, but not particularly relevant to anything, since Clifford Paget's death was probably unrelated to Delores's. Clifford *may* have been the one who killed her and Rhonda, but that wouldn't have had anything to do with Hofwegen.

She turned the tablet off, set it to recharge, then washed her mug and cereal bowl. It was going to be a busy day, no time to linger. Becca and Kevin were coming over from Canada and would see her at the new store to check out the final décor and fixtures, ready to load in the antiques for their grand opening weekend. The question was, in what order should she do all that needed doing?

She got Hoppy's leash and jingled it, but he would not be moved from a spot under the table. "What are you sniffing, fella?"

She bent over and discovered the plastic bag of stuff from the dressing table that had been delivered to Bernie's place. "No, don't touch that, honey." She picked it up in two fingers and tossed it out on the summer porch, which lined the back of the house, providing a nice barrier from the cold in winter, and a lovely place to get some bug-free cool air on a summer evening. She had no clue what was in the bag, and worried it had already brought vermin into the house. She'd have to look into it later, because she could never just throw something in the garbage until she knew what was in it, but for now it would stay on the summer porch.

She clipped Hoppy's leash onto his collar and exited through the back door — after tugging him away from the bag once more — and set out on their walk, leaving Denver behind in the backyard to recline under the holly bushes. She strode full-speed to the river, her favorite walk, and then headed through town to the Queensville Inn. Mrs. Stubbs was at her best first thing in the morning, so she would do her promised visit while walking Hoppy.

The Queensville Inn, the largest accommodation establishment in the village, was an old Queen Anne yellow brick home extensively renovated and added onto in the eighties to make it a welcoming hostelry. Lyle Stubbs provided a wheelchair-accessible suite on the main floor for his elderly mother. Jaymie breezed in through the glass double doors with Hoppy bouncing beside her, waved to Edith at the registration desk and went down the long hall directly to Mrs. Stubbs's room. She tapped on the door. Cynthia Turbridge opened it.

"Cynthia!" Jaymie said as Hoppy yapped a greeting. "What are you doing here?"

Cynthia, a slim petite brunette in her late fifties, had given up a high-profile career in finance to move to Queensville. Bored with semi-retirement — she taught some yoga classes at the community center on the other side of the village — she had opened the Cottage Shoppe, where she sold up-cycled items, mostly shabby chic. Forks and spoons became wind chimes; old wood crates became chic glass-topped side tables; teacups became pendant light fixtures. She was also an alcoholic who was battling back after a recent brief relapse, throwing herself into her healthy lifestyle with a vengeance. "Have you forgotten I'm a yoga master?" she asked. "I'm volunteering with the hospital outreach. I've developed a program to help seniors regain mobility and strengthen generally, and I've been working with Mrs. Stubbs on chair yoga."

"That is wonderful!"

"Is that you, Jaymie? Come, come! We were about to drink some of this dreadful green tea that Cynthia insists on pouring down my throat."

The other woman made a face, lines creasing around her mouth and across her forehead. "She's stubborn as a mule."

Jaymie let Hoppy off his leash and he waggled, hobbling, over to Mrs. Stubbs, who usually had a treat for him: a corner of cheese, a bite of cookie. She did not disappoint and leaned over in her chair to offer him a tidbit. Jaymie explained about her busy day and her decision to come over early to talk to Mrs. Stubbs.

"I heard about your discovery," Cynthia said, packing up her equipment, which included some light hand weights. She was the lithe and glowing picture of health, a tribute to her own practices. "Finding bodies, *again*!"

"I know. I'm going to get a reputation if I don't watch it," Jaymie said. "Oops, too late!"

"Come, Jaymie, before I forget what I want to tell you," Mrs. Stubbs said, beckoning her. "Sit. Drink this ghastly green swill."

Cynthia waved goodbye and headed out. The moment the door closed behind her, Mrs. Stubbs commanded Jaymie to dump the green stuff and get her a hot cup of the good black stuff, instead. As she obeyed, Hoppy settled on Mrs. Stubbs's feet and curled up with a sigh.

Mrs. Stubbs drank some of her black tea, a good English breakfast blend. "This is better. Now . . . I told you I remembered those girls talking, Delores and Rhonda. Unlikely pair, for friends. Anyway, Rhonda said that she had written a letter to 'her,' whoever her was, and that maybe 'she'd' help Delores. What could that mean?"

"Is that all you heard?"

"Unfortunately, yes."

"I think it does show the connection, and I have a feeling I know who 'she' was, and what problem Rhonda thought she'd help Delores with." Jaymie explained about Petty Welch, Rhonda's aunt, that she was a newspaper researcher and that Rhonda had a strong bond with her. She also spoke of the letter Petty got from Rhonda about baby abduction and fatal accidents.

Mrs. Stubbs nodded and drank her tea. "That makes sense. I suppose many girls fantasize about not being their parents' child, especially when they're estranged, but Delores may have had good reason, given her aunt's and uncle's story. Do you think there may be a motive there?"

"For both girls' murders?" Jaymie thought it over. "Possibly. It's certainly something I'm going to mention to the chief. If Delores was stolen or abducted as a baby, that's a federal crime. If she found out, and the Pagets were afraid of her going to the police, they could have killed her. But why Rhonda?"

"If Rhonda knew what Delores was investigating, that would make her a danger. They needed her to die, perhaps, before she went to her aunt to ask her help in discovering the truth."

"You may have a point," Jaymie said. "But how did they get to Rhonda?"

Mrs. Stubbs thought for a long moment. "Is it possible that Rhonda went to the Paget home to pick Delores up for some reason? Do you think they could have been on their way to see this Petty Welch, wherever she was?"

"That could be it!" Jaymie felt a tickle of excitement. "I always wondered why Rhonda left the boarding school in the middle of the day. And Delores skipped out, too. Maybe she was going to pick Delores up to take her to Petty Welch to ask for help in tracking down the truth. Ms. Welch, being a newspaper researcher and fact checker, had access to more information in the pre-Internet days than most would have, and what she didn't know, she knew how to find out. Kids then didn't have Google to rely on. Petty would have been an ideal ally for two teenage girls trying to find something out."

"I wonder if there's a way to establish some kind of timeline for that day, the day the two disappeared. If you should discover that they met up, or were at the same place at the same time, or even if you could place Rhonda at the Paget residence, you'd have something."

"Mrs. Stubbs, you are a genius."

"Just the George to your Nancy, my dear. I also remembered something about the red yarn."

"Yes?"

"Nothing important . . . just that it's Phentex. I went over to Johnsonville with Valetta's mother and we bought out the store. It was all the rage back then, Phentex yarn. We made slippers, hundreds of slippers."

"And Mrs. Nibley made sweaters."

"The thing about Phentex? The color never fades and it is virtually indestructible."

"Even after being in a trunk for thirty years." Jaymie shuddered, remembering the water sluicing through the broken window of the Falcon. "Or even after thirty years in the St. Clair River."

Jaymie returned home with Hoppy and let him off his leash to piddle in the backyard while she called the chief. She explained what she and Mrs. Stubbs had spoken of, and he was cautiously optimistic that she may have figured something out, certainly about why Rhonda and Delores disappeared on the same day. If any of it was true, it may provide a motive for the Pagets, one or all, to kill the two teens.

"By the way, Chief?"

"Yup?"

"Was there any thought that Clifford Paget may have faked his death?"

"You're thinking that if he killed the two girls he may have faked his death so he could disappear. I'll do some digging and find out if he was considered a suspect, or if he had an alibi, but it was years later that he died."

"I heard that Henk Hofwegen, the fellow who was with him the day he drowned, was hit by a car and is in the hospital?"

"Yup. Drunk again."

"Maybe he'll be willing to talk to you. He's a captive audience."

"Might do. I'll talk to him. I'll also see if there was anything in the nineties being done that might have triggered a sudden need for Clifford to flee."

"Chief, I'm also reading some friends' diaries and things from 1984," she said, purposely vague. "I'll be sure and let you know if I figure anything out. Is that okay?"

"Yup, as long as you turn them in to me. We don't have time right now to go through them, but the longer we go without figuring this thing out the more detailed we're gonna get."

"Also . . . I was given the name of the detective in charge at the time, a Lenny MacDonald. I was thinking of talking to him. Would you object?"

"Not at all. I've talked to him a time or two myself. Interesting fellow. You tell him it's okay by me if he wants to talk to you. Now, you will remember to have your sister call me about her memories of Delores and Rhonda, all righty?"

"Will do, Chief."

Becca was already in town. She texted Jaymie to meet her at the new antique store. Jaymie was about to walk out the back door when the phone rang. Keys in hand, she stared back into the kitchen. To answer or not to answer? With a sigh she knew what she had to do. She ran back in and snatched the phone up before it could go to voice mail.

"Jaymie? This is Petty Welch. I've retrieved Rhonda's stuff out of my attic. Do you have a few minutes today to come by?"

Three million things to do; of course she

didn't have time. However . . . "Sure. Will after lunch be okay?"

"Do you have a luncheon date? If not, you could come by here and I'll make you lunch. I have the prettiest vintage luncheon set I never get to use!" Jaymie was about to say maybe not, when Petty added, "I don't have many friends, or at least not many around here. It would be so nice to serve lunch for once!"

"Sure. Will one o'clock be okay?"

"Perfect."

That changed her day. She retrieved her camera from her room, put down a pee pad for Hoppy in case she was late, made sure both animals' bowls were full, Denver's up on the table so Hoppy couldn't eat all the cat food — Becca was going to freak about that, feeding the cat on the table, but cat food was not good for Hoppy — and grabbed her van keys.

Becca's car was parked by the antique store, but Jaymie knew once she was with her sister she'd never get to the Emporium, so she started at the store. Mrs. Klausner was behind the counter knitting while her granddaughter Gracey, who was working more and more these days, stocked shelves. Jaymie had a feeling she would soon be out of one of her part-time jobs, as the granddaughter and a couple of other grand-children were gradually making her presence less necessary. And that was okay.

Once she was done consulting her vintage picnic basket rental book and spoke with Mrs. Klausner for a minute, telling her about her decision to close out the small business, she caught sight of Valetta, who was beckoning her from her pharmacy counter in the back.

"What's up?" Jaymie asked, coming to the pharmacy window.

Valetta hushed her with one finger to her lips. "Can I talk to you out back?" she muttered.

"Sure." Jaymie went out the front, waving goodbye to Mrs. Klausner, then circled to the left of the Emporium, up the grassy rise, past the old oak tree and to the back parking lot behind the store. Valetta came out the back door, her lab coat still on and her arms crossed over her chest. Something was wrong. "Valetta, what is it? You look awful!"

Valetta, her voice catching on a sob, said, "I don't know what to think of Brock. He's lying to me, Jaymie."

"About what?"

"About where he was the day Delores disappeared."

Jaymie felt her stomach twist. "Val, that

could mean nothing. You *know* that."

"But why would he lie, Jaymie? *Why?* He's trying to tell me that he was in school all day that day, but he wasn't. I was in phys ed, running the track out back of Wolverhampton High. I *saw* him leave. He didn't see me. I was going to call out, but I whammed into another slower girl. He left at noon that day. But he told me this morning that he was in school all day that day." Her words caught on a sob. "Jaymie, why would he lie?"

FIFTEEN

This was not news to Jaymie, and was what had troubled her about Valetta's diary and the police chief's relation of what Brock had told him. Brock had told Chief Ledbetter that he did see Delores in Queensville, yes, but that he hitchhiked back to school that afternoon and never saw her again. But Valetta's diary said differently, stating that Brock was gone all day. Jaymie had little comfort for Valetta, but *did* tell her it could just be a matter of Brock forgetting because it was *such* a long time ago. Her friend went back to work somewhat mollified, but still . . . it wasn't good. Unless he truly did forget, there was no good reason for a lie.

Heading across the street to the antique store, Jaymie tried to shake off Valetta's gloomy and fearful mood. There was no way that Brock, who she had known her whole life, could have done such a thing as kill Delores.

Could he?

Her sister and brother-in-law-to-be's antique store was in a small cottage, one of a string on the main street in Queensville that were gradually being turned into touristy shops specializing in vintage, antique and retro goods. The external walls were covered in what Kevin, who was English, called pebble dash but what Jaymie thought of as stucco. Pebble dash was certainly a more accurate description of the pebble-covered cottage exterior, now painted a medium gray. With black window awnings and the trim painted white, the effect was tailored and modern.

As she approached she saw a Wolverhampton sign company's truck parked along the lane. The couple had tossed around many names for the shop but had settled on the prosaic and descriptive Queensville Fine Antiques, to differentiate themselves from Jewel Dandridge's retro and funky shop Jewel's Junk, and Cynthia Turbridge's Cottage Shoppe. Becca and Kevin's would sell antique furniture as well as fine china and other good-quality antiques.

Becca strode out the front door with a guy in green work pants and a paint-stained T-shirt. She trotted down the front steps and pointed to the roof of the cottage-wide deep front porch, about midway along. That was where the signage would go, front and center, hard to miss. He beckoned to his workmate, a guy who had been smoking a cigarette and plucked it from his mouth, flicking it off into the grass. Becca upbraided both guys. He sheepishly retrieved the butt, stomped it out, and stuffed it in his cigarette pack.

Jaymie hid a grin. No one messed with Becca, her property, or her family. The two sisters greeted each other with a hug and chatted while the two men constructed a mount for the sign, simple black and white but with the shop name, phone number and website on it. After catching each other up to date on wedding news and about the wedding shower, Jaymie also murmured what Valetta had spoken about, her worries about Brock.

"Do you think he'd ever do anything like that?" she whispered. "I feel creepy even asking. I mean, I've known him my whole life."

Becca adjusted her glasses and watched while the lead sign guy began bolting the bracket to the porch structure. "I can't believe I'm even saying this, but I don't know," she said softly. "I don't *think* so, but

I wouldn't bet my life savings on it, you know?"

"Why is that? Shouldn't we have a feeling, one way or the other?"

Becca glanced over at her. "I remember how he was when Rhonda told him to take a hike. He was *really* angry. If he had more guts he would have fought Gus Majewski, but Brock . . . he's a coward." She sighed and frowned, then glanced over at the Emporium. "I hate to even think it — for Valetta's sake, mainly — but that kind of guy might take it out on a girl, you know? Maybe if he did, Rhonda was his target."

"But then, why Delores too?"

She shrugged.

"Becca, I know you wanted to talk to me about the shop and show me around, but I've got a jam-packed day. Can we do this later?"

"Sure. Kevin is coming tomorrow morning. He's bringing his sister, Georgina, here for the shower. We've got her apartment ready in the back and she's anxious to see it, so she's going to stay in it while she's here. She's looking forward to the shower and getting to know all the ladies of Queensville."

Jaymie felt a trill of nerves that may have also been excitement. Sometimes it was hard to tell the difference. "I'm so *anxious*! In a way, I'll be glad when this is all over with and I'm living my life again."

Becca grabbed her shoulders and turned her around, staring straight up into her younger sister's eyes. Her glass lenses caught the sunlight and reflected the blue of the April sky. "Honey, don't you wish away this time. I *know* you. You'll only be doing this once in your life, so enjoy every minute of it. Be present. Relax. Don't worry about everything going perfectly; that's *my* department. You'll enjoy the memories even if there are screwups along the way."

Taking a deep breath, Jaymie held it for a minute, then let it out, slowly, and folded her sister into a hug. "You're right." She released her big sister. "I gotta go, but don't forget, Becca: you have to talk to the police chief about what you remember about that day."

"Oh. *Oh!* Jaymie, I *did* remember something. Not about that day, something else. Delores was angry at her aunt and uncle. She wanted to get her driver's permit, but she needed her birth certificate for it. They kept stalling, she told me. They wouldn't hand it over, not even to apply for a social security card. She started to believe they didn't have it."

That fit with Jaymie's suspicions that Delores was *not* their niece, and may even have been a stolen baby. She kept coming back to the central hypothesis: both girls had been murdered the same day by the same person or people. But if that was true, what was the motive that covered them both? The idea of Delores being kidnapped and Rhonda helping her figure out the truth was all she had, so far. And it was enough, if she were going to pin the blame on the Pagets. Stealing a child was an offense that could have landed them all in jail for life.

But now there was the added wrinkle of Brock's behavior; he was a point of contact for both girls too. If he had killed Rhonda and Delores found out, he would have had to kill her too to keep his secret. She shook her head. That was far-fetched, but it did make her quest to discover the truth more urgent. Valetta was suffering the anguish of suspecting her brother, who was a jerk but whom she loved. "I have to go, Becca. If you go back to the house let Hoppy out, but make sure both animals are back in before you lock up and leave."

Becca rolled her eyes. "You would think I was not the older, more responsible sister."

"Older, yes, but you've never had pets!" Jaymie laughed and trotted back to her van.

"I have to drop off a check at the florist in Wolverhampton," she said over her shoulder. "See you later."

"I'm going to take Valetta and Dee out for dinner while Kevin helps his sister set up house, so we might all be late."

"That's okay. I might go over to Jakob's this evening anyway."

She dropped the check off at the florist, then stopped at the bakery. Tami was taking care of a customer, so Jaymie waited.

"What can I do for you?" Tami asked as the customer left the shop.

"I'm going to have lunch with someone I don't know very well and I'm wondering what to take. Maybe some tarts or little cakes?"

"Oooh, is it a secret rendezvous?" she said, lifting her brows. "Cheating on your honey?"

Jaymie laughed politely, but didn't think it was a very funny joke. "No, actually — you'll find this interesting — I'm going to talk to Petty Welch. She's Rhonda's aunt. She has a lot of Rhonda's stuff tucked away and said I can have a look at it." Jaymie eyed the glass cases of pretty and tempting bakery goods. "Maybe I'll get a dozen of those pastel petit fours."

Tami grabbed a box. "I'm surprised you're wasting your time on all of that when you have a wedding to plan. You wouldn't find *me* doing that. Not with a guy as great as Jakob wanting to marry me." The woman eyed her critically. "Maybe they're right, after all," she said.

Jaymie paused. "Who is 'they'? And what are they right about?"

Tami shook her head. "Never mind." She filled the box and told Jaymie the price.

"Please, tell me what you mean," Jaymie said, fishing for the money in her wallet while still watching the baker.

Tami put her hand to her mouth, a stricken expression on her narrow, lined face. "Now I've offended you. I'm so *sorry*! It's just . . ." She sighed. "*Some* people — I shouldn't be listening to that kind of people I guess, but there are all kinds in the world — say you like being the center of attention. *Some* people are even saying that you get involved in all these murders because you like being part of a circus."

"That couldn't be less true," Jaymie said. As much as she was stung by it, she knew what Tami said was true; there were people who looked askance at her for having gotten mixed up in multiple murders. "I didn't choose this, but I won't shrink away from it either. *Especially* this time! This case directly affects friends and family who knew those two girls. Like your brother; he *loved* Rhonda. Don't you think he would like to know what happened?" *And to be out of suspicion himself,* Jaymie wanted to add but didn't.

Tami handed over her change. "Maybe you're right. How are you going to figure it out, though? I mean, it was so *long* ago. All the evidence is gone, right?"

"It wasn't *that* long ago. All their friends are still around, and even the detective in charge is still alive. I'm going to see him as well as Petty this afternoon."

"You know . . ." Tami looked thoughtful, but undecided, then seemed to make her mind up. "I still have my diaries from when I was a teenager. I wonder if there's anything in there that would help?"

Jaymie smiled. People soon got on board once they realized that it was not impossible to figure out. "I'd love to see it, or you can hand it over to the police, if you think it would help."

"I don't know," she said. "There's probably nothing there. I'd feel a fool handing it to the police. You'd probably be best to look it over first and see if there's anything there that would help."

"What kind of things did you write in your diary?"

"Geez, I don't remember. What was going on at school, I guess, when I went. What the family was up to. What Gus was doing. I went to all his football games."

"He was supposed to go on to college on a scholarship, right? Did he?"

Tami shook her head. "He wasted every opportunity that was given to him until he was washed up. *Now* look at him. Wife. Kid. Struggling to get by." She shook her head.

Not knowing what to say, Jaymie simply smiled and headed out, with Tami calling after her that she'd find her diary and give her a call.

Jaymie realized that the detective's home was on the way from Petty's cottage to Queensville, so when she pulled up the lane she paused and texted the police chief to say if it was all right, she'd be stopping around at Detective MacDonald's home that afternoon sometime. Then she picked up the bakery box and her camera and headed to Petty's front door. They greeted each other and Petty exclaimed over the box of petit fours and made a joke on her name, petit fours for Petty.

The morning sun streamed into the cottage, making it a pretty and inviting place to linger, but the hostess said, as they paused in her living room, "I have a sheltered back patio and it's actually quite warm with the sunshine. We'll have lunch out there. But I could show you my Pyrex collection first, if you don't mind?"

"I'm game if you are."

Petty led her into her sun-soaked kitchen and Jaymie caught her breath. It was *gorgeous*. A pastel pink paradise, as feminine a kitchen as one could ever hope or wish to see. The cupboards were painted ivory, but the sink was pink, as were the stove and fridge. The floor was a muted check done in white, pink, blue and butter yellow linoleum tiles. The table was robin's-egg blue arborite, which set off the piles of pastel Pyrex mixing bowls, refrigerator dishes, serving dishes and accoutrements to perfection.

"I'm . . . speechless. Overwhelmed. And I want to photograph it *all*!"

What wasn't Pyrex was melamine, or glass, or even plastic, but all pastel and mostly pink. There was a set of canisters, salt and pepper, egg cups, serving trays, a foil and plastic wrap dispenser and a hundred other "smalls," as small items are known in the vintage and antique business. It took time, but Jaymie eventually began to process it all and found angles to photograph it to highlight the Pyrex.

They talked about the allure of Pyrex — equal parts utility, beauty, durability and ease of acquisition — and how collectible it was. Petty, with excellent instincts and a vast knowledge of her collection, helped set up the shots. Jaymie found a collecting sister in the woman, and in the process a friendship began.

Finally it was time for lunch. The back patio was sheltered out of the breeze by the back wall of the cottage, a board-clad shed attached, and a copse of trees. They sat at a vintage wrought-iron patio set and chatted over a lunch of dainty crustless sandwiches, shrimp salad and tea, all served on Fire King Anniversary Rose snack sets, pretty milk-white oblong glass plates with a teacup inset in a depression, decorated with pink roses and trimmed in gold. It was a most civilized way to dine, and Jaymie vowed she'd get herself a snack set sometime.

Jaymie told her new friend all about her family's cottage on Heartbreak Island, and Petty asked about the wedding. Jaymie had to explain her unique function, where she and her sister had combined their weddings in deference to their older relatives. "Becca and I are closer now than we've ever been, in some ways," Jaymie mused, feeling a peace seep through her as she sat on the sunny back patio and sipped tea from the pretty Fire King teacup. "So it makes sense. I was hesitant at first, but now I'm happy."

"You're so lucky to have a sister," Petty said. "In some ways that's what Rhonda was to me. There was about the same age difference between me and Rhonda as there is between you and Becca."

"Did you know who her friends were? Who she liked, didn't like, that kind of thing?"

"Unfortunately I was kind of persona non grata with my brother, so I didn't get to see Rhonda that often the last year or so of her life. I was a woman living alone. To my brother's thinking I should have stayed at home until I was married, but I moved out and lived in a bachelorette apartment. I dated. I went to bars. I danced. I drank." She sighed. "Not to excess, but I enjoyed my life. He was afraid I'd infect Rhonda."

"What a waste," Jaymie murmured.

"I did get to know one of her friends, Sybil Thorndike. She spoke to me once; called me out of the blue for some reason a few months after Rhonda disappeared."

"What did she say?"

"I can't quite remember. I was in a fog a lot of that time, trying to understand what was happening. Maybe it will come back to me." Petty frowned, lines pinching between her eyebrows. "It was something to do with something Rhonda said to her. I don't know what. Let's go in," she said with a shiver. The sun was moving and they were now almost in shade. "I have Rhonda's stuff in the living room."

They retired to her pretty living room, where two cardboard boxes, dusty and battered, sat near a slip-covered chair. Jaymie sat in the chair, pulled the flap of the first box open, then looked up at Petty. "You don't mind if I dive in?"

"No, of course not, but . . . would you prefer to take them with you?"

Jaymie considered; she had so much stuff at home already: there was Valetta's box, and a couple of boxes of stuff on the summer porch from her most recent thrift store visit, among others. Becca was staying the weekend with Kevin. The two sisters' constant tussle over the cluttered nature of Jaymie's idea of homey was one brick in the wall that sometimes threatened to separate them.

But it was *her* home most of the time, and she needed to live as she wanted to live and not make choices based on her fear of what Becca would say. "If you don't mind, it might be helpful. I don't know if I'll find anything out but I might. Have you looked through them?"

She nodded, tears gleaming in her eyes. "After she disappeared I did read some of Rhonda's stuff they had at her school; I was hoping it would give me a clue as to where she had gone and why. But when my brother and sister-in-law came home they shut me out. They blamed me for Rhonda disappearing, especially my brother. Said if I hadn't encouraged her to be defiant of them, she would have stayed at Chance Houghton where she belonged." She sniffed back a tear.

"You know that's not true."

Petty nodded, tears glittering. "Rhonda was her own person. And now I know for *sure* it had nothing to do with me. The police finding her has given me peace. I think you're right; I believe Rhonda was going to enlist me to help Delores find out if she was adopted or abducted." She grabbed a tissue and blew her nose. "I opened these up when I got them down out of the attic and went through the stuff," she said, waving her hand at the boxes. "There's a journal in there you might find interesting. I hope it helps you figure out what happened. I can't go through it *all;* it hurts too bad."

She hugged herself and rocked. "I'm going out to see my sister-in-law this afternoon. I'm not sure she truly understands about the body being found, and I want to talk to her in person." She took in a long, shuddering breath, composing herself. "The retirement home has offered to have a memorial service for Rhonda. I want to help plan it." She blinked back the tears, then continued. "Would it be asking too much . . . if you find anything in there we could read at the service, or artwork or pictures . . . could you set it aside? I know I'm being a coward, but . . ." She shrugged, grabbed a tissue from the side table and sniffed.

"No, I understand," Jaymie said. She shifted the box and closed it. "I'll look through this stuff and if I see anything, I'll set it aside." She went over her calendar in her mind. Tomorrow was Friday, and Saturday was the wedding shower. "I may not be able to do it until after this weekend. Will that be okay?"

She nodded, her eyes still shining, her fingers restlessly plucking at the patchwork quilt over her chair arm. "Do you think it's possible to find out who killed Rhonda all these years later?"

Tami had asked pretty much the same thing. "I do. It's not *that* long ago, and there's lots of material. The police are being meticulous, starting from the beginning and working through it step by step, and I know the chief well enough to know he won't be satisfied until they get there. I'm going to try to help any way I can, Petty. I think it was probably Delores's aunt and uncle or cousin who did it, but there are a couple of more possibilities the police are interested in."

"I'll help you get these to the van," Petty said. Jaymie carried one box and Petty the other. "I have remembered one thing," she said as they went out to the front where the van was parked. "That evening, the evening she disappeared, the school said that another call came in for her early in the afternoon. It was urgent, the caller said — a young female, the secretary told me — but the caller wouldn't say *why* it was urgent. They went looking for Rhonda but she was gone by then, which is why they were kind of odd to me when I phoned them later that afternoon following up on Rhonda's call to me at work, the one I missed." She sighed as Jaymie unlocked the van. "If *only* I'd gotten that call. It may not have prevented her going missing, but I may have known more, been able to tell the police she was *not* running away! I did *try* to tell them that if she was going anywhere she would have at least told me, but they wouldn't listen."

"That's interesting." A call from a female saying it was urgent. Could that have been Delores trying to talk to Rhonda? Were they meeting somewhere? "If I figure out who it was from, I'll let you know."

Petty nodded.

As they slid the boxes into the back of the van, Jaymie turned to her new friend on an impulse and said, "If you're free on Saturday, would you care to come to my wedding shower? It's at the Queensville Historic Manor outside of Queensville."

The woman appeared taken aback.

"I mean, it's family and friends, yes, but that's a pretty broad group," Jaymie said, prompted by Petty's surprised expression. "You'd like them all. It's not your typical wedding shower; no gifts, no games, just tea and food and chat. You'd meet so many of the town ladies! And you could see my work in the vintage kitchen of the house. It's my own, top to bottom."

"If you're sure I wouldn't be in the way I'd love to come. You know, I moved here two years ago when I retired. Then my brother died shortly after and I was his executrix, so I had to help my sister-in-law move to the retirement home and close up and sell their house. I've been busy redoing this place, too. I don't have any friends, I'm afraid, not around here, anyway; I haven't had time to meet any until now. I was thinking I should take a course, or volunteer, just to meet people."

There was a haunting loneliness in Petty's voice, a wistfulness. The discovery of Rhonda's body had likely made it worse. Now she *knew* her niece wasn't out there somewhere in the world, ready to pop back up at any time. Jaymie reached out and hugged her new friend. "Come. It starts at two in the afternoon, everyone welcome."

As she drove away, she tooted the van horn and eyed the small figure in the rearview mirror. Somehow, some way, she would find justice for Rhonda Welch and Delores Paget.

Sixteen

Detective MacDonald lived on a rural gravel road. As was true of most country homes, there was a number signpost at the road for emergency vehicles to identify it. Jaymie drove up the lane and stared. It was an old farmhouse with stained white vinyl siding and a wrought-iron porch probably added in the seventies; unremarkable enough, but what stretched out around it was indeed extraordinary. The property had numerous outbuildings, and every single one had rusting farm machinery, old cars, and piles of tires and car parts around it.

Another collector, it appeared!

She climbed out of her van and noticed a man in overalls out by one of the buildings. When he turned, a machinery part in hand, she waved and called out, "Are you Detective Lenny MacDonald?"

"I am. Or used to be, anyway." He pushed his glasses up onto his seamed forehead and strode toward her, a trim man with very little reddish gray hair left in a fringe around his head, and a lean tanned face wreathed in a smile that was topped by a luxuriant reddish gray mustache. "You must be Jaymie Leighton. Ledbetter warned me you might visit." His gray eyes twinkled with humor and he smiled.

She smiled back and took his offered hand, greasy though it was. "Is all of this yours?" she asked, waving a hand at the groupings of machinery. As she looked, she began to see some semblance of order. Farm machinery was in one fenced-off area. Old cars were parked in a systematic fashion in a gravel lot to the right of a rusting steel Quonset building. The Quonset's sliding doors were open, and inside she could see rows of tables with machine parts on them stretching into the distance. "Oh, wait! I *know* who you are," she said, eyeing it all. "Do you know Jakob Müller?"

"I sure do. He comes by whenever they need a part for the Müller farm machinery. You know him?"

She felt a blush rise on her cheeks. "I do. We're getting married in a few weeks."

"You're *that* Jaymie? *You're* the gal he's always gushing about? Well I'll be."

He showed her around, and it was as

organized as it seemed. After he retired from the force ten or so years ago, he told her, he was able to indulge in his lifelong love of tinkering, and it had become something of a business. "If you don't mind, I gotta keep working while we talk. I have a lawn mower I need to fix for someone by dinner today 'cause they're coming to pick it up," he said, tossing what Jaymie recognized as a mower muffler up in the air and catching it.

"No problem. I'll follow you," Jaymie said.

He led her to a smaller outbuilding, a timber shed with barn doors open to the spring breeze. He had a workbench along both sides and one down the center upon which was an elderly Briggs & Stratton lawn mower. He pushed the pair of close-up glasses down onto his nose, turned on the pendant light and leaned over the lawn mower. "So, Ledbetter said you're kind of helping him on the case of those two girls who disappeared in November eighty-four." He paused and looked up. "Damnedest thing, you finding Delores Paget and then the MSP finding Rhonda Welch two days later."

"I know. That was a true coincidence, and without it we may never have connected the two incidences."

"Maybe, maybe not. The police would

have rediscovered the two girls missing on the same day, but without Rhonda's body . . ." He shrugged. "I hope Ledbetter and his people can figure it out."

"Finding the two bodies helped. You know, Chief Ledbetter doesn't mind me poking around, and anything I figure out I take back to him."

He smothered a smile and just nodded.

"Anyway, my sister and friends knew both girls, so I've uncovered some connections that weren't highlighted at the time. I'd love to tell you about them, if you don't mind, and then ask you some questions?"

"Shoot. I like to listen while I work." He pointed a wrench at an old wood-grain tape deck and two speakers on a shelf. "Sometimes I listen to books on tape . . . or CD. Listened to most of Dick Francis that way."

Jaymie hoisted herself up to sit on the bench opposite his work table, careful to keep her good slacks away from any potential grease spots, and filled him in on what they had learned about Rhonda and Delores being seen talking days before she was sent to the boarding school. "You worked the case at the time," she said. "What do you think was the biggest impediment to solving it?"

He glanced up. "Interesting question. One

problem is that we had no reason to think the two disappearances were connected. The Welch girl was unhappy at school; we knew that from something a friend of hers there said."

"What friend was that?" Jaymie asked, though she thought she knew.

"Girl named . . ." He frowned and stared down at the motor. "What was her name? Ah! I know . . . Sybil Thornley, or Thornton . . . Thorn-something."

"Thorndike."

"That's it!" he said, pointing the wrench. "She said Rhonda had no intention of finishing her school year at Chance Houghton, that she was leaving. And then the car was never discovered; that led us to believe it was most likely a case of a runaway."

"But what about Delores?"

He straightened and frowned. "Again, everyone kept saying she was a runaway. Even her teachers said she had been troubled lately over some boy, and that she said she should leave."

"Teenagers say that kind of thing all the time."

"Exactly what I told my chief at the time," he said dryly. "I had two teenage girls at home, and both of 'em were always threatening dire consequences. However . . ." He shrugged. "I tried to get more time on the case but there was a murder/suicide near Christmas that took everything we had. That poor kid's disappearance got put on the back burner. And Rhonda Welch's disappearance? That was in a whole different jurisdiction because she disappeared from her boarding school, not her home. We didn't get a lot of cooperation."

"Did you search the Paget home?"

"It *was* searched, not by me, but by other police officers. Evidently not thoroughly enough." He shook his head. "It's hard for me to believe her body was there the whole time. I feel like we let that little girl down. It's hard to look back at the mistakes made. We went back to the investigation over the years but never made much progress."

"Finding the bodies and the connections between the two girls makes a big difference." Jaymie looked up at the ceiling of the shed, raw wood with hooks from which hung chains and small engine parts. "Did anything strike you as . . . odd, about the Pagets?"

"Odd? *Every*thing!" he said promptly. "Every *damn* thing about them seemed odd. Clifford Paget was a ne'er-do-well if ever there was one."

"My sister said he bragged about stealing

from sheds and selling stuff for pot money."

"No doubt. And the aunt and uncle —"

"Who weren't, according to the most recent news, her aunt and uncle at all."

"Really?" He looked up, an expression of surprise on his lean face. His eyes went misty, he thought for a long moment, then nodded. "Yeah, that makes sense. I hadn't heard that. What's the story?"

She told him what she had learned, the connected story of Petty Welch's information about what Rhonda asked her, how to discover if a child had been abducted.

"I wish we'd known that then. It would have made a difference."

"You couldn't have known. Petty only thinks *now* that Rhonda was asking for help for Delores. At the time she thought that Rhonda was asking about herself, like she thought she might not be her parents' daughter. Some kids go through a phase of thinking they're adopted."

"True. As far as Rhonda Welch goes, I came to the conclusion she must have run off, given what little we could learn from the other police force. If we'd found her car . . . but the killer was smart. Or lucky. Kids run away every single day in this country. I met her dad when we were trying to figure out if there was a connection between the two girls' disappearance; he was a self-righteous bugger, pardon my French. Blamed his sister for putting ideas in her head about feminism." He shook his head and bent back down over the machine. "Like a perfect storm keeping us from solving it. There was no Amber Alert back then, but we got sightings from all over the country on both of them. Nothing credible on Delores, but there was a good report on Rhonda and her Ford Falcon."

"Which we now know is false. She never made it out of Michigan. How did her car get into the river, do you think?"

He straightened and paused, wrench in hand. "I'd need to look at the lay of the land and know exactly where the car was found. But I know that island pretty well. Back then there was a parkette on a rise above a deep part of the shipping lane. Kids used to go there to make out, and some got drunk and jumped off the cliff to swim. Daredevils, you know. Closed up in the nineties; couple of houses on that rise now."

Jaymie nodded. "I think I know where you mean, but I've always known it to be a cottage area. Do you think someone could have pushed the car off there?"

"I don't know, Jaymie. I'm sure the police

are trying to figure that out even as we speak."

"Detective, you said that there was *everything* odd about the Pagets. What were they like?"

"Jimbo Paget was one of those fellows who look sneaky no matter what they're saying or doing. And Mrs. Paget . . . she was a piece of work. Critical of Delores in every way. Called her ugly. Called her useless. Made my skin crawl. If I could have arrested someone on suspicion of being mean, I would have locked her up. But it contributed to me thinking that poor kid had every reason in the world to run away from home."

"Do you think one or both or all three of them are mostly likely to have killed Rhonda and Delores? The chief thinks Delores was killed in the Paget kitchen."

"Only fools speculate."

Jaymie bit her lip. She speculated all the time.

He looked up and winked. "But I'm getting to be an old fool myself. Given the way and place she died, I'd say Delores had an argument with Olga Paget and Olga picked up a cleaver and whanged her with it. I'd bet she then roped those two fellows in on it to help her hide the body."

"That makes sense."

"Just a guess, Jaymie, not worth more than two bits."

"What do you think happened to Clifford? Do you believe he drowned?"

He tightened a bolt and tossed his wrench aside. "Nope. Never did. But he was an adult and we did our duty concerning him. Divers looked for him, but he was gone. Pronounced dead. If you ask me he's somewhere living as best he can with no documents. Look for someone who doesn't drive and only works under the table."

"Why would he disappear, though, if you don't think he killed Delores?"

He shook his head. "You're asking me to speculate even more. Just want to say . . . I don't *know* anything. Learning about Rhonda Welch being dead and about the two cases being connected, likely, changes everything and I haven't adjusted yet. It's important not to get hung up on one explanation when the next piece of information you discover could change *everything,* make you see it from a whole different angle. I only know in my gut, I never thought Clifford Paget was dead, which means Henk Hofwegen was probably lying through his teeth. Ask *him.*"

"As a matter of fact, the chief is going to

be doing that exact thing."

He told her to come back any time she had another question, and he was sorry he wasn't more help. He'd think on it. She gave him her number.

Back in her van, Jaymie texted Jakob and asked if she could come over and fix dinner for them. She started toward home but her phone pinged, so she parked on the side of the country road. *Better yet,* he texted back, *meet me to pick up Jocie from school.* He had to speak with the principal for some reason, and then he was going to take his daughter over to her oma and opa's to stay the night. He had an early appointment the next morning, so his mother was taking Jocie to school.

What R U Saying? she asked.

Dinner & evening alone?

Starry-eyed emoji back.

She had a million things to do, but nothing took precedence over spending time with Jakob. Becca was home when she got back, and Jaymie explained the rest of her day after leaving the antique store that morning and her plans for the evening.

"Can you look after Denver and Hoppy?" she asked her older sister.

Becca agreed, so Jaymie took Hoppy for a long walk, knowing he'd be content to use the backyard that evening for his ablutions. Becca was gone to dinner with Valetta and Dee when Jaymie got back, so she left a note explaining the animals' nighttime ritual, and said both animals could sleep in her room, but Hoppy would require help up the stairs. Then she packed an overnight bag. She didn't know if she was spending the night with Jakob, but better to be prepared than not.

The elementary school was a 1960s low building constructed of glossy red brick and surrounded by a grassy playground and paved parking lot. It was the school Jaymie had attended, though Becca and the others had gone to an older school that was now light industrial space. She parked in a visitor's spot and headed directly to the principal's office, which had a waiting room outside of the actual office. Jakob, who was thumbing through a magazine while sitting in one of the hard vinyl chairs, stood when he saw her.

"Hey, what's up?" she asked after sharing a brief kiss.

"I'm not sure," he said, a worried frown on his face. "I have to meet with the principal."

Sybil Thorndike ducked out of her office,

motioned to Jakob, and led them back in. She was an energetic woman about Becca's age with graying, neatly curled short hair and glasses on a long chain around her neck. She wore sensible loafers and a skirt suit and had a file in her hand. "Mr. Müller," she said by way of greeting, and she pointedly looked at Jaymie as she sat down.

"This is Jaymie Leighton, my fiancée. We're getting married in June. She'll be Jocie's mom." He smiled at Jaymie and took her hand.

"Interesting," she said, and laid the file open on her desk, then folded her hands on top. "Mr. Müller, there was an incident on the playground today. Jocie pushed a boy."

"That doesn't sound like my daughter," he said.

"Nevertheless, one of the parent volunteers saw it happen."

"What does Jocie say?"

"That's the problem. She won't say anything." A bell rang out in the hall and Sybil glanced up at the clock. "She'll be meeting us here, along with the parent volunteer."

Two minutes later Jocie entered, a mulish expression on her round face, her rosebud lips set in a frown. She was guided by a young woman in yoga pants and a brightly colored tunic top, her blonde hair up in a high ponytail. Jocie's eyes lit up when she saw Jakob and Jaymie, but she didn't say anything, just moved to stand between their chairs.

Introductions were made and the mom, Dina, explained what she saw. Jocie apparently had a conflict with the boy, one of her classmates, and she ran at him and pushed him into a puddle.

"What had he done to her?" Jakob asked, his gaze slicing back and forth between the mother and the principal.

The young mom bridled. "Not a *thing*! I don't tolerate bullying on the playground. He likes her. She's one of his favorite people."

Something wasn't right, Jaymie thought, as she watched the young woman's face. There was something she wasn't saying.

"What's going on, Jocie?" Jakob asked his daughter, pulling her close. He ducked his head and looked into her eyes as she stared down at her pink running shoes. "Did you push that boy down?" She nodded. "Is it true? Does he like you?"

She shrugged.

"Is it okay if I step in, Jakob?" Jaymie asked, and he nodded. She turned and asked Dina, "Why do you say he likes her?"

Her expression was full of uncertainty;

she looked back to the principal.

"Go ahead, Dina," Principal Thorndike said.

"You can tell when a little boy likes a little girl," Dina said.

"How?" Jaymie asked.

"Jaymie's not Jocie's mother," the principal explained to Dina. "But she's marrying Mr. Müller and will be Jocie's stepmom soon. She doesn't have kids of her own yet."

Jaymie took a deep breath to keep from retorting. There would be time for that later. Right now . . . "So, Dina, how can you tell the boy likes Jocie?"

"He shows it in little-boy ways, you know?"

"And that is . . . ?" Jaymie had a feeling where this was heading.

"He pulled her hair," Dina said, looking away and shifting in her chair.

The principal's eyes widened but she clamped her lips together in a tight line. This was clearly news to her.

"What did you do about that?" Jaymie asked.

"I told him he shouldn't do it."

"Did Jocie say something to you?"

"She told me what happened. I told her that he pulled her hair because he likes her." She gave a nervous laugh. "It's what little boys do."

Jakob took in a deep breath, but Jaymie had it covered and took his hand, squeezing it. "And I'll bet he pushed her, too?"

Dina shrugged. "I didn't see it."

"But she *told* you it happened?"

She nodded.

"And did you then tell her again that he did that because he likes her?"

"It's true! That's how little boys are," Dina said, her tone defensive, arms crossed over her chest. Her gaze slewed among the principal, Jakob and Jaymie, but she didn't have any support. "I *have* little boys. If you don't have kids, you don't know. That's what little boys do. They're more . . . you know . . . *physical* than little girls. It's their *way*."

The principal was still silent, just watching and listening.

Jaymie considered what to say, how to not over- or under-react. "Dina, what I'm hearing is what has been told to girls for a long time, that boys will pinch and push them and pull their hair because they *like* them. Maybe I haven't had children until now, but isn't that *exactly* when little boys need to be told . . . *no* one pinches or pushes or pulls hair? It's not nice and it's not how we show people we like them. I think that boy owes

Jocie an apology."

Jocie was grinning and hopping on one foot in her dad's arms.

"And I think Jocie owes *him* an apology too." Jaymie caught the principal's eye. "Do you think that's fair, Ms. Thorndike?"

"I do." She stood and circled the desk, opening the door out into the anteroom. "I'll talk to the little fellow's parents, see if we can get them on board with modeling more appropriate behavior. Dina, I'll be having another parent with you in the school yard for a while until we see if you understand acceptable behavior. You can head out."

Dina left in a huff. Jakob squeezed Jaymie's hand. She had been worried that she was taking the lead when she still wasn't married to him and legally had no right, but he looked satisfied.

"That was productive," the principal said and smiled at Jaymie. She had circled back behind her desk and shuffled her papers together. "Jocie, do you understand what we've been talking about? That what the boy did was wrong and that Miss Dina should have listened to you?" Jocie nodded. "But that *you* can't push either, that that wasn't right?"

Jocie nodded. "I'll apologize. If he apologizes first. Because he *pushed* first."

"Okay, I think that's fair, Jocie. That's good enough for this time, Mr. Müller, unless you have any questions?"

"I think we need to talk at the next parent-teacher evening about parent volunteers . . . maybe some training in school yard etiquette. And maybe a code of conduct for the kids?"

"We do have something in place, but it may be time to revisit it. Perhaps you can raise the topic." She turned to Jaymie and held out her hand. "Welcome aboard, Jaymie. It seems like you'll fit in just fine here as a parent." She and Jaymie shook hands.

Jakob took Jocie's hand and led her to the door.

"I'll follow you in a moment, Jakob, if you don't mind," Jaymie said. "I have an off-topic question for Ms. Thorndike."

Once they were alone, Jaymie sat back down, and the principal, looking mystified, did the same. "Do you have some questions for me?"

"Yes, but not about the school, or Jocie, or anything like that." She paused, wondering where to start, then made up her mind. "If you've been watching the news, you'll know that the bodies of two teenagers missing since 1984 have been found. I found the first one, Delores Paget, and the MSP found the second . . . Rhonda Welch."

The woman took in a deep breath and sat back, folding her hands over her stomach and pressing. "I knew I'd seen your name in the paper. You're wondering about Rhonda Welch. I was a schoolmate of hers briefly — very briefly; a few days — at Chance Houghton Christian Academy."

"And gave them a statement at the time. Rhonda apparently said something to you about not finishing her school year at Chance Houghton."

"She was dead set on getting away from CHCA."

"But did she actually *say* she was running away? Do you remember *exactly* what she said?"

"After over thirty years? Not likely."

"Please try."

"Why is this important?" she asked, fiddling with the string on her glasses. "And why are you asking me?"

"The police chief knows I'm asking around. He's okay with it," Jaymie said to reassure her. "I know many of the people involved. In fact, my older sister was friends with poor Delores."

"I see." She turned her thoughts inward, staring down at her hands. "I'm trying to remember that day. It was . . . the beginning of November, a Thursday, I think?"

"I believe so. November first."

"I liked Rhonda. I'd only known her a couple of days, but . . . I really *liked* her. She was so beautiful, that thick black straight hair, the most lovely skin. And she was nice to me. I already had a mad pash on her," she said, a watchful look in her eyes as she met Jaymie's gaze.

"Pash?"

"Sorry . . . my Aussie roots are showing. I was infatuated with her."

"Her aunt said she was a lovely person," Jaymie said softly. "I can understand you having a crush on her."

The principal nodded, sadness softening her regal expression. "She was . . . *she* was when I knew. She was so kind to me. I believe she knew how I felt but she didn't make a big deal out of it, or try to avoid me."

Jaymie understood what she was saying.

"I don't remember *exactly* what she said to me that day, but I took from it that she was leaving."

"Could it have been something slightly different? Like . . . maybe she wasn't running away, maybe she intended to go stay with her aunt? With her parents gone over-

287

seas, perhaps she thought she could talk her aunt into taking her in."

"It's possible. Does it matter?"

Jaymie held back what she felt, that what Sybil said back then had misled the police to not consider her a missing person so much as a runaway. She didn't think Rhonda had any intention of leaving for good. With the optimism of youth she probably thought that while trying to enlist Petty's help to discover Delores's origin, she could talk her aunt into letting her stay with her and finish out her senior year at a public school near Petty's home. It was immaterial now. "Did she talk about her boyfriend much?"

"Gus? She sure did. It depressed me, and I guess I knew then that I had no chance with her, but still . . . I wanted to be close to her so I listened. She *really* liked him. They had had sex. I think he was her first." She paused and her eyes clouded. "Her only, I guess I should say now. But she wasn't sure she was ready to get serious. Her parents wanted her to join them wherever they were after her school year was done, but she intended to stay here and go to college. Being away from Gus for a few days gave her some . . . perspective, I think she said? Yes; perspective."

"Did she mention thinking she was pregnant?"

Sybil smiled for the first time. "She was so *relieved* when she got her period! She was going to meet up with Gus and tell him the good news, that he didn't have to quit football. He was so into her that he wanted to give up his college scholarship, get a job, get married. But she didn't want that for either of them. She had dreams, and they didn't include quitting school and being a mom at seventeen."

"Did she call him? Do you know if she was going that day to talk to him?" Jaymie wondered, did Rhonda actually meet up with Gus and tell him she didn't want to see him anymore? Was this a simple case of a rejected boy going off the deep end?

"I don't know. I do know she made some calls. You had to get special permission at CHCA, and there were only phones in the office that were made available for students to use. I helped her figure out the school bureaucracy, because she'd never had to deal with it before."

"Did you stick around while she made the calls?"

She paused before answering, and her gaze seemed to be looking inward. Maybe she was trying to remember. "I did. I'm trying to recall if I know what she said, or if I had an impression . . . I'm starting to realize what you've been too kind to say, that what I said may have misled the police and ensured that they weren't taking the threat to Rhonda seriously." She met Jaymie's gaze and her expression was sad. "I'm sorry for that. I told them what I thought I knew."

"Ms. Thorndike —"

"Sybil, please . . . call me Sybil. I was named for a great actress." She paused and sighed, looking toward the window that overlooked the parking lot. "I know what you were about to say; I was a teenager and can't be held responsible for a failed police investigation. No one should assume a teen has run away. But still . . . Thoreau said to make the most of our regrets. To cherish them, because *to regret deeply is to live afresh.*

"This is going to sound silly, but all these years I've thought of Rhonda, and I pictured her in California maybe, driving down the PCH, wind in her hair. To hear about her body being found . . . it was like a dagger to my heart." She looked back to Jaymie, her eyes misted with tears. She reached for a tissue. "Isn't it silly?"

"No, it's not silly. You cared about her; all we have after we're gone is the people we've touched, the people who care about us. Rhonda had her mother, her aunt and you, at the very least." She waited a moment, then said, "Sybil, I have to go, but if you think of anything, remember anything, give me a call." Jaymie reached into her purse and got out a scrap of paper, scribbling her name and number on it. "Or if you need to talk, call me."

Seventeen

The conversation left her melancholy but she put on a happy face as she joined Jakob and Jocie in the parking lot. She gave Jocie a big hug and kiss, then told Jakob she'd meet him at the cabin, as he was taking Jocie directly to his parents' place.

She was actually grateful to be at the cabin alone. It was a peaceful place, with the spirits of Jakob and Jocie filling it with love. She picked up Little Bit and snuggled him, while he played with her hair and tugged it out of the band she used to hold it back. She did the dishes left from their breakfast — pancakes with sticky syrup — started dinner, and made a pot of tea. As the sauce simmered she took her cup out to the porch, sat in the big Adirondack chair and gazed out to the road. Tears filled her eyes. She was so lucky, and the deaths of those two girls so many years ago had brought it all sharply into focus. What would they have done? Succeeded in careers? Raised great kids? Been happy, been sad, loved and lost and loved again? Someone took all of that away from them, and from the world.

Her heart flooded with peace as she listened to a red-winged blackbird chirr brightly, and watched goldfinches flit from bush to bush by the porch. She had been getting more and more nervous for the wedding shower in two days and the wedding in six weeks. She'd be the center of attention. She'd be hurried and rushed and watched and applauded. None of that made her comfortable. But it was all love flowing to her and Jakob, love in waves and waves, a whole *tidal* rush of love. She must not let shyness ruin the experience. She had to relax into it all, let the love bathe her.

When Jakob pulled up in his beat-up white pickup and parked it next to her beat-up white van, she set her tea aside and went to meet him. He encircled her in his arms and they stood, staring into each other's eyes for a long time. His were brown and warm, with gold flecks. When he finally kissed her he literally lifted her off her feet and she laughed.

"You were a rock star at the school," he said as they entered the cabin, arms still around each other. He paused and sniffed.

"Something smells good."

"Spaghetti sauce. There will be enough to freeze for an easy dinner for you and Jocie another day."

It was a lovely evening, and an even better night.

Between kisses and cuddling on the sofa in front of the fire that evening, with a lonely Little Bit cuddled between them, Jaymie and Jakob had talked extensively about what she was looking into. She told him about Petty, Detective MacDonald, and what she spoke to Sybil about. He made a comment that had her thinking. He said that whoever drove or pushed the car into the river on the island had to not only take it over on the ferry, but drive it into the river after dark, and most likely return on the ferry as a walk-on. The time of year was in favor of the car not being discovered, he theorized. Shipping on the St. Clair went to December, but it was slower, not many people to observe. If the winter was cold and ice floes jammed up, as they often did, it might be enough to move the car into deeper water, ensuring it never became visible.

It gave her a lot of food for thought and ideas to share with the chief. One of the many things she loved about Jakob Müller was that he never tried to tell her what to do, or questioned her need to investigate. He accepted it as a part of her.

The next morning she called Becca to check on Hoppy and Denver, and to remind her sister it was garbage day. Could she please put the garbage can and recycling out in the back alley, since Jaymie was running late? Becca agreed. Jaymie then rushed around the cabin to feed Little Bit and play with him, make breakfast, wash dishes and tidy. Jakob was out chopping wood for the fireplace and came in smelling of fresh pine and sawdust. He had to leave in moments to rush off to a pre-sale viewing of a liquidation lot from a home décor store a few towns away.

"So what are you up to today?" he asked, hugging her from behind as she finished drying the mugs.

She leaned back against him, relishing the feel of his whiskers on her neck. "I'm not sure. I have some tasks to do, but I'm confused about Rhonda and Delores. I still don't even know who was the real target, and who was collateral damage, if that's even how it worked. I think I need to go through all the stuff I've gathered from Valetta, Petty and Nan."

"*And* the stuff from the dressing table

from the Pagets' barn," he said, releasing her.

"What?" She turned to face him, her mind racing.

"You told me Heidi gave you a plastic shopping bag of stuff from the dressing table at the Pagets'. Isn't it possible that piece of furniture was from Delores's room?"

Oh. *Oh!* Jaymie stood stock-still for a moment; what if . . . "Jakob Müller, thank goodness you listen to me!" She kissed his cheek. "I have to go." She grabbed her purse and sweater and headed to the door.

"Wait!" He followed her and took her in his arms. "You've got time for a proper kiss."

Five minutes later she started up the van with a grin on her whisker-rubbed face, and tooted the van horn as he climbed into his truck. Anxious to look into the bag, she took off with a spray of gravel that rattled on the underbelly of the van.

Garbage day was always a tangle in Queensville, which had narrow streets. Many, like Jaymie's, did not have driveways, but parking lanes that ran behind houses. Jaymie scooted down her lane before the garbage truck and pulled in by her garage. She locked the van and raced to the house. When she opened the back door Hoppy belted out through her feet, as did Denver, both choosing a private place in the yard to piddle. Hadn't Becca let the poor critters out at all that morning? Dang.

She stopped and looked around; the kitchen positively *sparkled.* All her paper-work was gone from the counter. Pray to heaven it wasn't all in the recycling. She draped her sweater over a chair and called out, "Becca? Kevin?" There was a note on the table from Becca: *Jaymie . . . gone to grocery store. You're out of milk. How could you be out of milk???????*

"I'm not out of milk," she grumbled. "I'm out of *skim* milk."

Now, where was that bag of stuff from the dressing table? Hoppy, as usual, barked frantically through the fence at the garbage truck as it clattered its way down the alley. She stepped down into the summer porch and to the back door. "Hoppy, stop it! Come in, right now!"

Her little dog listened as well as he always did, which meant he kept barking. Oh, right, she thought; she had slung the bag onto the sofa of the summer porch, worried it had vermin from years in the barn at the Paget home. She turned and looked but it wasn't there. The garbage truck clanked and banged closer. Hoppy's barking got more frantic.

Her sister had cleaned.

"Crap!" She slid her feet back into her loafers and raced out the back door, almost slipping on the dew-damp flagstone path. She wrenched open the gate and stumbled to the back alley as the garbage truck clattered to a halt directly between her backyard and that of Trip Findley, her behind-most neighbor. He waved from his back porch and she gave a distracted flap of her hand in return as she found the garbage can and ripped the lid off. There was the bag, atop — thank goodness — the other garbage. She snatched it just as the buff young guy approached in search of her garbage can.

"Anything else you want to rescue, ma'am?" he asked with a grin and a wink.

"No, no, this is all. Stuff put out by mistake . . . valuable research," she babbled, turning crimson. His laughter followed her as she checked the recycling bin — nothing untoward in there — closed her gate and returned to the summer porch. Of course, this was going to be a wild-goose chase. It was likely moth-eaten recipes or receipts.

She sat down on the summer porch sofa and dumped the bag contents on the floor. There was a bundle of newspaper clippings, a few tattered notebooks, a tiny address book journal with glittery heart stickers on it, some dirty combs and brushes, a dried-out and brittle bottle of VO5 shampoo, and an empty old bottle of Love's Baby Soft. There were hair scrunchies with a tangle of dark curly hair, and photos. Jaymie got a prickle that started at her hairline and trailed down her back. This was, indeed, Delores's stuff.

And if not for Jakob, it would have been in the dump. It might not reveal anything, but still . . . Hoppy nosed at the pile and yapped.

"Okay, all right, breakfast first. I doubt if Becca even realizes animals need breakfast and clean water."

Ten minutes later she had all the stuff laid out, including the photos and pictures, one of Delores and others in a familiar place, her front living room. It must have been Becca's sweet sixteen birthday party, Jaymie thought, peering at the curled and mildewed photo up close, in September of 1984. *This* was where Delores started going with Brock, and yes, there she was beside the teenage boy staring at him with fascination. Jaymie recognized Delores from descriptions and photos in the *Wolverhampton Howler*. She was sporting a couple of pimples, her curly hair held back with a stretchy headband, and wearing an ill-fitting jean jacket. Brock was staring straight at the camera with a smug smirk on his face, knees spread wide, arms flung out over Delores's shoulders on one side and Becca on the other. Valetta was in a corner looking fed up, Dee was whispering to Johnny Stubbs. Becca looked miserable. A couple of others huddled together in bored misery.

Jaymie touched the picture; she, herself, was somewhere in the house that night, a few months old: crying, colicky, a burden to her mother, who had never bonded with Jaymie in the same way she bonded with Becca. It was to Becca's credit that Jaymie had such a happy childhood, because she filled in so many of the spots that Jaymie knew her mother would have if she had felt better. Thank goodness for Becca, despite her occasionally annoying big-sister know-it-all moments, and their Grandma Leighton, who provided many more of her youthful good memories. Jaymie smiled and set the photo aside.

But back to the problem at hand. She sorted through the newspaper clippings. There were some of music and movie stars, but there were also several to do with infant abductions. They were on the right track;

Delores thought she had been abducted as a baby, and it was possible she was right. She'd have to call the chief to see if they had made any progress on that part of the investigation.

She picked up the address book, which was sectioned off with a journal of sorts at the beginning and an alphabetized phone listing at the back. There was some scribbling in the journal, flowers, arrows, and Brock Nibley's name with a heart around it. It was funny that even though she thought Rhonda had stolen Brock's affections, she had enlisted Rhonda's help to figure out the truth of her past. Maybe Rhonda, being the kind girl she seemed to have been, had felt regretful when she realized Delores was hung up on Brock and she had inadvertently interfered in their romance, such as it was. Perhaps she decided to help Delores find her real family to make up for it. It made a kind of twisted teenage logic, but a tragic end for both was the result. Somehow, some way, they were tied together in death.

The phone listing had very few numbers, but Becca's name was in there as BL; Jaymie recognized the home phone number because it was still the same one for the landline, all these years later. Otherwise, the listings weren't going to help Jaymie at all

301

because they were just initials: BN, GM, CH, and RW. RW! That *must* be Rhonda Welch. Maybe the police could confirm the number. All it would prove was the possibility of contact.

Jaymie retrieved the boxes of Rhonda's stuff from her van and started sorting that, too, being careful to keep the two girls' belongings separate. Rhonda didn't keep a diary like Valetta did — or at least there wasn't one among her things — but she did have a journal where she scribbled snatches of poetry, sayings, and questions about life. *Do I know what love feels like? What do I want to be doing ten years from now?* Interesting thoughts. There was also a list of goals: *Be kinder! Be smarter! Don't let my heart lead my head. Help and encourage others.*

Jaymie stuck a piece of paper in that section to point it out to Petty; it would make a poignant moment in the memorial that would show what kind of girl she was. There were a few lyrics written in from Cyndi Lauper's "Time After Time," which most notably said that if the listener was lost, they could look and they'd find her. That was a good song for the memorial service, Jaymie thought, reading through, a whisper of hope and comfort, an assurance that she'd try and help, no matter what.

As Petty Welch had said, Rhonda was the kind of girl who would help another human in need. The world had lost all that potential because someone wanted her gone for some reason. But *why*? It didn't make any sense. How could she, at seventeen, be such a threat that she needed to be removed? Or who had she hurt, even inadvertently? Whose life was made better by her death?

There was no money to inherit, nothing material to gain by her absence. The motive was locked firmly in the past, so far back that memory blurred the edges of the pain for those involved with both girls. Except for Petty, and Rhonda's mother; they still felt the pain as sharply as when she disappeared. Sadly, the most likely explanation was that Rhonda was killed because she was a good person and had tried to help Delores.

In a mystery movie of the week this is *exactly* when she would discover something that would make all the puzzle pieces fall into place, Jaymie thought, sighing in frustration. If only she was a heroine in one of those. The phone rang and Jaymie answered it. There was only some breathing. "Who is this?" she asked sharply. Still no one. Just as Jaymie was about to hang up, a voice.

"Jaymie, can we talk?"

The voice sounded familiar. "Who *is* this?"

"It's Brock Nibley."

"Brock?" Jaymie held the receiver away and stared at it, her mind spinning through possibilities, then brought it back up to her ear. "Okay. When?"

"Right now. Can I come over?"

She didn't completely trust him. But for heaven's sake, this was her best friend's brother. She had been in his company hundreds of times; had sat with him at Valetta's dinner table, gone to the same events, laughed at his children's antics. He wasn't going to do anything to her. "Come to the back door, Brock. We can have a coffee."

"Thanks."

Just as she hung up the phone rang again.

"Jaymie, Ledbetter here. Got news I want to tell you."

"Can you come here? I have someone coming for coffee and can't leave."

Jaymie tided up the mess she had created with the piles of teen detritus and put on a fresh pot of coffee. Though she was curious about the police chief's news, her mind kept returning to Brock. Why call *her*? What did he want? Even though she had known him her whole life, they were not friends. She didn't even like him. The only reason he'd seek her out was if he was trying to find out about the investigation into Rhonda's and Delores's deaths. But what did it have to do with him, beyond him dating both girls?

The more she thought about it, the more uneasy she felt.

For once the police chief drove his own Queensville Township PD car. He often relied on Bernice to drive him places. Bernice had confided that though it was not an actual position, driving the chief places had definite advantages. It certainly seemed that Chief Ledbetter was mentoring her, in a way. Jaymie felt the same; he clearly liked Bernice and had often commented that she showed great potential to move up the ranks.

But this time he was driving and pulled into the only free space beside Jaymie's van. He heaved himself out of the driver's seat and lumbered through the back gate and up the path. She opened the door for him and he entered, then took a seat at the table with a groan. Jaymie looked out the back door as she closed it behind him. A car pulled slowly past but kept going, so, not Brock. Maybe he'd walk over. Or maybe he'd come to the front door; many did.

She poured the chief a cup of coffee while he caught his breath. "Can I get you a slice of banana bread?"

He sighed and shook his head. "Nah, I'd better not. The wife is right. I need to lose some of this," he said, rubbing his belly. "She's got all kinds of plans and I don't want to disappoint her."

"Have you been married a long time?"

"Long enough," he said with a wink. "Not my first marriage; the first one only lasted a few years. I was a young cop; that's hard for the spouse, you know. This one stuck, though. Twenty-three years this June."

"So you said you had news?" Jaymie watched as Hoppy wiggled over to the chief and waited for a head pat. Denver sauntered through the kitchen, eyed the chief, and disappeared to the front of the house.

"Yup." He paused and eyed her, watching her expression as he continued. "We found Clifford Paget."

"You found his body?"

"Nope. We found him alive and well and living in the next township over."

EIGHTEEN

After her initial shock, he explained what had happened. "As you know, Henk Hofwegen was in the hospital after being hit by a car. He was drunk as a skunk, stumbled right into traffic. The driver didn't have a chance in heck of avoiding him. He was banged up pretty bad, but he'll be okay. When the officer went to talk to him there and ask him about the accident, he said he had something to say.

"Told the officer that back in 1990 or thereabouts — he couldn't remember the year; he's a fellow who drinks most days and loses whole months — Clifford Paget told him he needed to disappear because he'd done something awful a few years back. Henk was a little hazy on what exactly he'd done but they were buddies, so he helped Clifford. They went out in his rickety boat and Clifford 'went for a swim,' as Henk put it. Clifford then changed his name, moved to another town, and started working under the table for whoever would pay him. He lived with a woman for a while but she kicked him out a month ago and he wound up back on Henk's sofa. Henk had been sober for a while, I guess, but Clifford being around made him fall off the wagon, and so he blamed him for getting hit by the car. He wants him out of his life and thought turning him in was the best way."

Jaymie sat back and digested it all. It was hearsay, she supposed, in a legal sense, what Clifford had told Henk, but it was certainly revelatory that he said he'd "done something awful a few years back." "Henk doesn't realize that he's left himself open for prosecution too? That he filed a false police report, and maybe helped a criminal escape justice?"

The chief laughed, his chins waggling. "He's scared to death but sticking by his story, which I think kinda speaks to it being legit. And made voluntarily, I might add, after the warning."

"This may be the solution, Chief."

"We'll see when we get Clifford's statement."

"It looks bad that he faked his death." Jaymie looked up at the clock. Why wasn't Brock there yet? He should have arrived about the same time as the chief.

"Yup, but I'm not jumping to conclusions."

"I have some things I've been thinking of, Chief." She hesitated; she didn't want to talk about Brock until she'd seen him.

But the chief heaved himself up. "I'd love to hear what all you've been looking into, but right now I gotta get back to the station. Can it wait?"

"Actually, yes, it can wait. I'd like to think on everything, but my mind is so scattered right now with the shower coming up tomorrow."

"Maybe we can get together Monday or Tuesday. Gimme a call." He headed toward the door but then turned back again and eyed her. "You waiting for someone? Is something going on, Jaymie?"

"Nothing, Chief. I'm nervous today, I guess. About tomorrow."

"I know you don't like being the center of attention, kid, but your sister will be there too, and if I'm right she's one who deals well with the spotlight."

Jaymie smiled as the police chief left. He knew her better than she would have expected.

Even without having anything specific planned, the day was full. Becca had arranged for a facial and then a hair appointment for both of them in Wolverhampton, which she chose to tell Jaymie about a half hour before the first scheduled time. Then she was aghast when Jaymie confessed that she was going to go with the vintage wedding dress option Heidi had provided, so after their facial she dragged Jaymie to three different clothing stores in the faint hope that something — *anything,* it seemed at times — would please her sister better. She even tried to bribe her by saying she'd buy it, no price too high.

There was nothing. Every dress was either too tight, too fancy, too long, too white, too . . . something. And shimmying in and out of unflattering dresses for hours at a time was exhausting, as was the attitude of one of the shop associates (only one; the other two were very nice!), who was bored and blasé, needing to be asked several times to take away the discarded gowns. After three shops in as many hours and then their hair appointment — which hadn't gone well because the hairdresser tried to coil Jaymie's hair up in a tight French roll, giving her a headache — they were finally back in Becca's comfortable car on the way home from Wolverhampton. Both of them were grumpy and tired.

"You're going to regret it, Jaymie. Honestly," Becca said, for maybe the fourth time. "This is your *one* wedding. Can't you at least consider that you may be going wrong about the dress?"

"Becca, no! For the last time, I am completely and *utterly* happy with the dress Heidi found for me. Nothing I've tried on comes even close. I didn't expect to like it, but I do and it fits beautifully. You haven't even seen it, so how can you say you won't like it?"

"I didn't say I wouldn't like it." There was silence for a moment, but irritation shimmered from Becca in waves, and finally she burst out with, "But you said it's from the seventies, *not* a decade that inspires confidence in bridal fashion design."

Jaymie stayed silent, unwilling to mention that she didn't think the dress was intended as a wedding dress when it started its life. Resentment at her older sister's usual high-handed bossiness started to creep into her.

Becca glanced over at Jaymie in the passenger seat. "I want the best for my sister," she said, her tone softer, almost pleading.

Taking a deep breath and rejecting anger, Jaymie said, "I've made up my mind and that's my final word on the subject. Please, no more!" She decided to change the subject and told Becca about the bag she had retrieved from the garbage, making her laugh by relating her exchange with the garbage collector. "It did turn out to be Delores's belongings, and must have been from the months before her death. There's a picture from your sixteenth birthday party that fall."

"I remember now! Dad had copies of the photo made and told me to give one to each of the kids who were there. It was all girls except for Johnny Stubbs and Brock Nibley; there were Val and Dee, of course, as well as Delores, Tami, and some other girl . . . can't remember her name." Becca was silent for a few miles. As they entered Queensville, she said, "It's all so sad. I know we're coming up on happy times for us, but I keep thinking of Rhonda and Delores, how they were cheated out of all this."

"Me too. Becca, tell me more about what Brock was like back then."

"Why?" Her older sister glanced over at her. "You don't suspect he had anything to do with it, do you?"

"I don't know. But tell me what he was like anyway."

Brock, Becca told her, as they arrived home, unpacked the few things they had bought in Wolverhampton and made a very late lunch, was one of those people who always seem out of step with everyone else. "I guess nowadays you'd say he has social issues. He's not very intuitive, you know? Even less so than most men I know. Weird for a real estate agent, but I think he makes it work for him. I've seen him in action when we bought the property for the store; he manages to sell homes fairly effectively and he won't take no for an answer, which is good when he's negotiating *for* you. His real weakness is that he can't see himself as others see him."

"But he's never been violent, as far as you know?"

Becca paused with a forkful of salad midway to her mouth and stared across the table at her younger sister. "Not in the least. What would make you ask that?"

"Just curious."

"He's kind of a wimp, I think. At least he was back in high school."

That didn't comfort Jaymie as much as it should. She kept thinking that even small creatures, like rats, if cornered, will turn and bite viciously.

Becca headed over to the antique store to do some work arranging stock. Using some less-expensive tinned pink salmon, Jaymie worked on the loaf recipe and came up with something that was actually pretty good *and* budget-friendly, tasty served with a creamy mushroom sauce. She took pictures, then retreated with her laptop to her bedroom and wrote the "Vintage Eats" column. Just as she hit Send on the email to Nan with the article attached, the phone rang. It was almost dark. Maybe it was Jakob, she thought, picking it up.

"Hey, Jaymie? This is Sybil Thorndike. I hope you don't mind me calling?"

"Not at all. What's up?"

"I've been thinking of nothing but Rhonda since we talked yesterday. I went back through, in my mind, a typical Thursday. Our day was regimented at Chance Houghton, so much so that any time of the day I could tell you where I'd be. Thursday in my senior year was math, Spanish, physics, and then lunch. I had a study period after lunch, and that's when I helped Rhonda get some time on the student phones. You were supposed to sign up ahead of time, but she didn't know that so I helped her bribe two kids to use their call time."

"And you heard some of what she said?" Even if it turned out that Clifford Paget was the killer, it would still be helpful to reconstruct the two girls' last few hours, to sup-

314

port whatever conclusion was reached. If he did murder Rhonda there was still the question of how he came to do so, where she was and why she died.

"Yes, I remember now. You know, I had a dream last night about Rhonda. She was standing there with the phone in her hand — it was one of those old heavy black handsets with the coiled cord; you're younger and probably don't remember — and saying, 'Sybs, I can't get through to him!' "

"Is that what she actually said?"

"Something pretty close. She was going to pick up some friend —"

"Delores Paget?"

"Maybe. She didn't say her name. But first she was going to go see Gus."

Jaymie's heart thudded. Gus had dropped from her radar, but given their relationship he was still a suspect in Rhonda's murder. "You're sure of that?"

"I'm positive that was her intention, anyway."

"So she called him?"

There was silence for a moment as Sybil pondered. "Wait a moment . . . I'm trying to get it straight. It was so long ago. She made a few calls, but not all of them connected. The *first* one was to her aunt at work."

"Petty Welch," Jaymie said.

"I guess. It was her work number. Rhonda left a message, but I don't know what it was and I don't know why she was calling her."

"She likely *did* intend to go see her. I've found out that Petty intended to visit Rhonda at school, but maybe that didn't suit the two teenagers' purpose. We think she was going to pick up Delores and go to Detroit, enlist her aunt's research skills to help her new friend find out what happened to her parents. Who were the other calls to?"

"I don't know for sure, but she said she was going to go see Gus."

"You're sure she intended to see him that afternoon?"

Sybil was silent for a moment. "I can't *swear* to that. I'm *not* sure. All I heard her say was, *'we have to talk.'* She could have said that to anyone."

"But you said she also told you that she couldn't get through to him."

"I've been thinking about that . . . it could have meant she literally couldn't get through to him — meaning connect on the phone — or . . . she couldn't get through to him, meaning he wasn't listening to her, or wasn't getting what she was trying to say."

"True."

"But I will say, she sounded so *cold.* At the time I didn't think she was talking to Gus. Wouldn't she have been nicer to her boyfriend?"

Not if she intended to break up with him, or if she thought they needed to slow down their relationship. Jaymie chewed on her lip, thinking. Given how Gus apparently felt about her, breaking up with him may have led to a violent argument. Maybe he killed her for it. But how did that fit with Delores being murdered in her own kitchen? Was this two separate crimes after all? Gus killed Rhonda and Clifford killed Delores? It would be a gargantuan coincidence, but it was possible. "I don't know, Sybil. Is that all you heard?"

"Unfortunately, yes. When she got off the phone she was in a hurry to go. She had a car — her parents' old Ford Falcon — and she was leaving."

"Did she say she'd be back?"

"The police asked me that at the time. She never did *say* she'd be back. I'd have remembered that." Sybil was quiet for a moment. "I've been beating myself up pretty badly over this. If only I hadn't said all I said maybe they would have looked for her more diligently."

"Sybil, I know how you're feeling but you didn't do or say anything wrong. It's likely that even if they were looking for her as a victim of some crime they wouldn't have found her car." Although, if there had been more of a fuss made about the Ford Falcon, the pilot of the Heartbreak Island ferry that night may have remembered the car and come forward. But what point would be served now to make Sybil feel worse than she already did?

Becca and Kevin had been at the antique store getting Georgina, his sister, settled into her apartment. They came in moments after Jaymie hung up the phone, as she let Hoppy out for his last piddle and summoned Denver from under the holly bushes.

Kevin looked gray and weary, showing every year of his age, a decade or so more than Becca. He hugged Jaymie and said good night; he was dog tired and going to bed. Jaymie got the feeling from what he *didn't* say that Georgina was extremely particular and not completely pleased by her new digs.

But Becca lingered to share a pot of tea. Jaymie recounted what she hadn't told her sister yet, about her odd morning call from Brock and how he didn't turn up. Hesitantly, she shared her theory about him not wanting to come see her while the police chief was there.

Becca fluffed her curly hair and adjusted her glasses, as she did when thinking deep thoughts. Jaymie expected her to dismiss her younger sister's concerns as absurd, but she shook her head. "I don't know. We'll see Valetta tomorrow at the shower. Maybe she'll say something about Brock."

Jaymie didn't answer; she already knew Valetta was worried about Brock lying about that day. They both retreated to their bedrooms, Jaymie with her animals. She called Jakob and they shared their day with each other.

"Something is up with Gus," Jakob said with a sigh. He was doing dishes; she could hear him clanking around. She could picture him, tea towel over his shoulder, phone wedged against it and head tipped, while he washed and set the dishes in the drainboard. She'd be happy when she would be clanking right alongside of him.

"What's up with him?"

"He went off on a customer today. He's been cranky as all get-out and today he stormed out after a customer who mouthed off at him and practically got in a fistfight in the parking lot."

"That doesn't sound like Gus," Jaymie said. He was always even-tempered. Her stomach churned and she wondered if the past was catching up with him. "Is something bothering him?"

"I wish I knew."

Jaymie didn't answer and changed the subject. It concerned her. There was a very real possibility that what was on his mind was what he had done to Rhonda over thirty years ago. But Jakob didn't need that worry on his hands, especially when there was no proof yet to back it up.

He promised that his sister-in-law was going to bring his mother and Jocie to the shower — the little girl was extremely excited to be attending a grown-up girl tea party — and they went through their nighttime ritual of whispers and kisses. She finally hung up, turned off the light and curled up with her dog and cat to try to sleep, but slumber was elusive.

November 1, 1984

It was late and quiet and Valetta was ensconced in her bedroom, sitting on her bed propped up with cushions. It smelled far too strongly of Love's Baby Soft perfume. She couldn't figure out why, since she was real careful about using too much of the stuff her older brother had sent to her from Canada for her sixteenth birthday. He worked in a mine, some place in Ontario called Sudbury. She had her diary — a birthday gift from Becca Leighton, her best friend in the world — open on her lap and was writing about her day.

Dear Diary,

Today was super weird. I don't know what's up with Brock, but he left school after lunch period. I was out on the track for PE and I saw him. I yelled, but I guess he didn't hear me.

I wish I could have stayed late. There was a football game and I could have caught a ride home with Dee after it. But Mom was working at Mrs. Stubbs's today and it was my day to cook dinner. So I came home, and Brock wasn't even here. That meant I had to do my chores *and* his chores. It's not fair. He always ducks out on chores and I get stuck doing them. He's *such* a jerk.

I know my friends think he is too, so I always have to stick up for him.

But he **is** a jerk.

He even has the car without permission tonight and Mom didn't say a word! It sucks.

Anyway, I made dinner, tuna casserole. Mom came home real tired, so I made her a cup of tea and told her to it on the sofa, that I'd bring her dinner on a tray so she could watch the news. We ate and watched together. Yesterday Indira Gandhi, the Prime Minister of India, was assassinated. It's horrible. She was killed by her own bodyguards!!!! I don't understand what's going on over there, but it's scary.

Next week is the presidential election. The Democrats have a woman, Geraldine Ferraro, on the ticket . . . *finally!!!* When I asked in history class why there has never been a woman or a black person as president or vice president of the country, I got basically zero answers. *Something* is wrong. You mean there's never been a woman or black person good enough to be president?? That's just stupid. Maybe this time will be different. And maybe someday we'll have a black or Asian or Indian or a *woman* as president, even. I hope so. Would that be *cool*? I was hoping last year when the Reverend Jesse Jackson decided to run we'd maybe have a black man as president but it didn't work out.

I hope it happens someday. Michael

Jackson in '88! I'll be able to vote by then.

The Cosby Show was on tonight, but Mom wanted to watch *Magnum PI,* so we watched that instead. It's okay . . . *Dukes of Hazzard* is on tomorrow night and I get to see John Schneider!!! Yum.

Anyway . . . Mom didn't say anything, but I know she's worried about Brock. Why can't he see how much he upsets her when he acts like a giant jerk? She shouldn't work so hard, but I know Mom never misses the day working for Mrs. Stubbs because she pays well . . .

Valetta paused and looked around her room. Her curtains were pretty, dotted Swiss, and her bedspread was nice, a rose pink chenille; both originally came from Mrs. Stubbs's home. Mom's favorite clothes came from her too, and so did some of their best furniture.

. . . she pays well and she's always giving Mom stuff: clothes, curtains, towels, furniture. She buys such good stuff, she always says, that she gets tired of them before they're worn out and wants to change them, so someone may as well have the use of them. Mom says that

Mrs. Stubbs only says that because she's afraid Mom will be too proud to take hand-me-downs, but little does she know, Mom's got no pride, or at least not *that* kind. Mom always laughs when she says it, but I don't think it's funny.

Someday I'll make enough that Mom won't have to take hand-me-downs anymore. I'll get a job that pays well and look after her. If Brock's not going to try at school then the least he could do is get a job and help out around here. I work. Why shouldn't he? I know he does some stuff for Mr. Waterman, but not much and not often. Mom always makes excuses for him, like, a boy needs a father, and if Dad hadn't died . . . blah, blah, blah. He gets away with murder, while I do everything.

Valetta heard a noise in the kitchen and tiptoed out to see what was going on. Brock was home and he smelled of booze and other odors. She wrinkled her nose. "You've been smoking and drinking," she accused, keeping her voice low and glancing toward her mother's closed bedroom door.

He glared at her, bleary-eyed and blinking. "What's it to you?"

"Shut up!" she hissed. "Don't talk so

loud. Mom's tired and she's in bed. No thanks to you, I had to do your chores *and* my own, and then get Mom to bed with a cup of tea. She's worried sick about you. What's wrong? Why did you leave school today? And why did you have the car? You're not supposed to take it without permission, you know."

"None of your business. I'm going to bed."

Valetta watched him grab the last Coke out of the fridge and head downstairs to his room in the basement. She raced to the railing and bent over it. "Next time it's *your* turn to do everything while I stay at school and watch the game!" she hissed down the stairs after him.

. . . so Brock just came in and didn't even care that I had to do his chores as well as mine. What a *jerk*! He makes me so mad. I feel like I say that a lot, but you, Dear Diary, are the only one I can say it to. I told him next time there was a football game at school he was coming home early and doing the chores and I was going to stay to watch. Right, like that'll ever happen.

Anyway, good night, Dear Diary. Tomorrow is another day, but at least it's Friday!

Valetta shut the diary, set it on her side table and turned out the light. Someday her brother was going to get himself in a whole lot of trouble, something he couldn't get out of, and when that happened, she would gloat!

NINETEEN

It was finally here, the day of Becca and Jaymie's joint wedding shower. They had been told to not worry about it, that their friends would take care of everything from the organization to the guest list, so Jaymie did her best to obey. Becca, who of the two of them was the control freak, kept busy with working on the antique shop with Kevin. Jaymie couldn't settle to anything, so she spent the morning reading Valetta's diary, finally coming to the Thursday of the murders.

There was some interesting information. Brock, Valetta complained, had skipped school for the whole afternoon and wasn't home when she returned on the schoolbus. She went into detail about how she had to do Brock's chores, what she made for dinner, and then television. She complained that Brock had the car without permission . . . interesting.

After that she made some tea for her mom, who seemed down and was worrying about Brock, and helped her get to bed. Her mom wasn't well, but still . . . she worked hard for what money she could get. She never complained about Mrs. Stubbs because although the woman was demanding, she also paid well and always gave Valetta's mom lots of used goods, which were all excellent quality because the woman only ever bought the best.

Jaymie's eyes were filled with tears by the time she was done reading that section. It confirmed to her that her two best friends, Valetta and Mrs. Stubbs, were both the most worthy of women, loving and giving. She saw through Mrs. Stubbs's attempt to give Mrs. Nibley stuff for her home and yet not make her feel bad about taking it. It seemed from the diary entry that Mrs. Nibley saw through it too, but didn't mind.

Maybe the tears were the result of weariness. She had tossed and turned all night worrying about today. Being the center of attention was never easy. As long as she had something to do, like when she was working in the historic home kitchen, it was fine, but at the shower she would be expected to smile and receive all the outpouring of affection. She'd get fidgety and try to help and her friends would make her stop. It would not be easy.

But there was more to her melancholy; she was getting a peek at years gone by, and it left her feeling like she had missed what the others had experienced together. She had had friends growing up but not many, not like Becca had. Valetta, Dee and Becca had been a tight group, though they had their individual trials. Dee had been going steady with Johnny even then, and spent all her free time with him. Valetta clearly had her worries, with no father — he had died several years before — and Brock such a pain and her mother working and worrying herself to a nub. Valetta worked too, Jaymie knew, at the Emporium, and put herself through school to become a pharmacist with work and scholarships. And Becca . . . poor kid was saddled with a baby sister who was foisted on her more often than she should have been on a sixteen-year-old.

It was odd seeing it through Valetta's eyes.

Her mind returned to the day of the crimes. Brock skipped school that afternoon but had not come home with the car until late, Valetta said, and then wouldn't tell her where he'd been, though he told the police he had briefly seen Delores in Queensville, when she told him she was leaving town.

329

He'd also told the chief that he had hitch-hiked back to school, but Valetta's diary proved that was untrue.

Valetta said she had wanted to stay at school that afternoon and watch the football game. Football game . . . Jaymie reread that passage. Did that mean Gus would have been in school and busy that afternoon? No opportunity to see and kill Rhonda? Or had he skipped the game and gone somewhere with his girlfriend? Jaymie jotted a note.

Maybe there was a reason Gus was so cranky: a guilty conscience.

Or maybe Brock had not come home until late for a nefarious reason, and that's why *he* was acting so weird.

She sighed and put her head in her hands. This time the crime was so long ago there didn't seem to be a whole lot of ways to figure it out. She closed up her notes and Valetta's diary. She had other things to do, and the first was bathe the dog. "Come on, Hoppy; if you're coming to this wedding shower — and you *are* coming to this wedding shower — you are going to look and *smell* pretty."

Jaymie was too nervous to eat all day, but there would be food aplenty at any shower that involved the Leighton sisters. Though she was supposed to keep her nose out of the plans, Jaymie knew that many of the ladies were bringing food, but that Heidi was having Tami Majewski deliver trays from the bakery, too, as well as food Tami made in her own kitchen. She catered on the side, a lucrative business for someone as talented as she was.

Becca drove, of course, and Jaymie fidgeted as Hoppy quivered with excitement in the backseat on a carefully folded doggie blanket. Two hours. She only had to last two hours, and it would all be done. Then there would be the wedding to worry about. But first . . . the wedding shower.

Becca wore a pale blue skirt suit, her dark (dyed to conceal the threads of gray) hair beautifully curled and fluffed, with discreet diamond studs in her lobes. Jaymie had always teased her about having old-lady style sensibility but that wasn't true, especially not in her business or dressy clothes. Becca was always well turned out. "So, how painful is this for you?" she asked, glancing over at Jaymie.

"Painful?" Jaymie sighed and fiddled with her clutch purse, opening and snapping closed the clasp. She had struggled with what to wear. She liked dresses but she was on the full-figured side and sometimes felt like she'd look foolish in a dress, as if she was trying too hard. But this time she had taken Heidi's advice and bought a pretty cerise dress with a handkerchief hem from a store online. She loved it, fortunately, and how it went nicely with her long hair up in a pony with a vintage clip. "I wouldn't say it's painful, but I'm glad it's both of us in this." She glanced over at her sister. "I'm happy I'm not going to be the whole center of attention."

"Honestly, you'd think you were going to your execution. This will be fun, you'll see."

Jaymie wasn't going to be a downer on a special day and nodded. "I'll have fun," she said, injecting all the vivacity she could into her tone. She paused, then said, "You know, it's been weird, reading Valetta's diary, seeing you and all of your friends' daily lives from when you were a teenager. I never think about that with Valetta because she's just my friend. But she was *your* friend first."

"She always wished she'd had a sister." Becca glanced over at Jaymie. "With having their older brother and Brock, she always felt like she missed out on the sisterhood thing. You were her little sister from the day you were born. She was the only one of my friends I'd trust you with."

Jaymie nodded. Many of her first memories as a child were of Valetta looking after her, taking her for walks, doing special things for her. "I just realized . . . you know, you can probably blame Valetta for my mania for collecting vintage. She was the first person to take me to a thrift store. She bought me a kitten figurine that I still have."

"Curses on you, Valetta," Becca said, shaking her fist and laughing.

They pulled up in front of the Queensville Historic Manor, a huge two-and-a-half-story Queen Anne with clapboard siding and gingerbread trim. The parking area was crowded with cars. Jaymie shuddered. These were all friends; she had to keep reminding herself of that. There was a hand-drawn sign with balloons and streamers that said *Leighton-Burke Wedding Shower,* and there was another sign with balloons attached where they, as the guests of honor, were supposed to park. Jaymie got out, patted down her dress, brushed off some cat and dog hairs, then picked up Hoppy and trotted to catch up with Becca, who was eagerly climbing the steps up to the porch and already had her hand on the doorknob.

The first half hour was a tumult of noise, chatter, congratulations, hugs, kisses, and laughter, all accompanied by Hoppy's enthusiastic participation. It wasn't so bad, Jaymie decided, feeling her cheeks burn and a frantic giddiness well up in her, as long as she kept moving and talking and smiling. She desperately tried to keep her expression from becoming manic when her shyness overwhelmed her. Heidi and Bernie had done most of the planning, but Heidi confided that Dee, but more especially Valetta, had insisted on doing a lot, too, as well as footing some of the bill. Valetta had been there all morning helping decorate and had insisted on contributing vintage touches here and there from her own collection.

The theme was a Very Vintage Wedding Shower, so there was a retro feel everywhere, from the crepe wedding bells that hung in the middle of the big parlor to the pretty vintage parasols hanging upside down from the ceiling. There were fifties and sixties knickknacks tucked in spots, and vintage china serving pieces being used for the food table. Everything was lovely and Jaymie appreciated the efforts of their friends.

There were lots of chairs in the long parlor/sitting room, with the pocket doors thrown open for extra space. It was a diverse group of thirty or forty, with everyone from eight-year-old Jocie, who was giddy with excitement, laughing and running with her two cousins and Hoppy, to ninety-plus-year-old Mrs. Stubbs, who was catered to by Dee and talked to by everyone. Even Mrs. Klausner was there, sitting alone and knitting while eyeing the children. Mrs. Bellwood, Imogene Frump, and Mabel Bloombury were in attendance. Nan Goodenough circulated, introducing herself and talking to everyone. Cynthia Turbridge and Jewel Dandridge drifted from group to group. Jakob's mother, Mrs. Müller, was looked after by Sonya, Jakob's sister-in-law, and indulgently watched the children run around and play as Valetta sat and chatted with her for a while. Kevin Brevard's sister, Georgina, trailed after Becca, who introduced her to everyone as they chatted about the new antique store. Locals, especially Cynthia and Jewel, tried to make Georgina, a petite blonde Englishwoman, feel comfortable.

There were, Jaymie was grateful to find, no games planned. She heartily loathed wedding shower games, though she knew some folks enjoyed them. At one point Bernie wheeled in a cart with a television on it and Jaymie thought, *Oh, no . . . embarrassing video footage.* There was some of her singing karaoke at Bernie's last Thanksgiving — she was belting out "Girl's Just

Want to Have Fun" — that she didn't want anyone to see since she had had too much wine.

But instead, there were video messages for Jaymie and Becca from their mother, in Florida, and their grandmother, in London, Ontario. Then, thanks to Bernice's technical genius and tech help from both London (the recreation director of the retirement home) and Florida (from Jaymie and Becca's dad, Alan), there was a live feed of both women, split screen, so they could take part in the shower from a distance. Tears flowing freely, Jaymie hugged her police officer friend and babbled an emotional thanks, then sat by the video with her mother and grandmother, telling them all about what was going on.

After another half hour the video was shut down and food was served buffet-style in the dining room. First to be served were those who were fetching for the older folks, then everyone else. Jaymie hung back, and as she waited she noticed Petty Welch, beautifully dressed in a vintage-looking sheath dress, hesitantly coming through the door from the front hall. She saw Jaymie and smiled, but didn't wave — her hands were full, since she carried a box with an elaborate deluxe ribbon on it — and rushed over to Jaymie.

"You came after all! I had given up on you," Jaymie said, getting up and giving her a brief, one-armed hug.

"I wasn't sure . . . I mean, I don't know anyone —"

"I can remedy that, trust me."

"This is for you," Petty said, thrusting the box at her. "I know there weren't supposed to be gifts, but this is out of my stock of vintage stuff. I thought you'd enjoy it more than I."

Jaymie sat down — Petty took the chair beside her — and tore the pretty paper off to find a vintage box with a full new-in-box set of Fire King snack plates and cups in the Primrose pattern.

"I thought you and your new stepdaughter would enjoy them for tea," Petty said, her eyes watering. She sniffed. "I'm so grateful you sought me out and it's wonderful to have someone to talk to about Rhonda!"

Jaymie set the box down and impulsively jumped up, leaning over the other woman and giving her a bigger hug. "How is your sister-in-law? Is she okay?"

Petty nodded. "She has her Bible and her pastor, who has been very good to her. He's helping her through it. It's the one time I envy people who have religion; it must be a comfort."

Jaymie stood, grabbed the other woman's hand and said, "Well, you are now going to meet everyone I know, all in one fell swoop." She introduced her to Valetta — their common love of vintage pastel kitchenware and kitsch making them instant soul mates — who took her under her wing. Petty was never alone for more than a second.

At long last the event was quieting down, with most guests eating and chatting. There were occasional bursts of feminine laughter, and the clop-clop of heels on wooden floors, along with the sound of cutlery scraping on china. Hoppy was curled up under Jaymie's chair. Dee, who enjoyed vintage everything and actually sold it online, also had taken Petty under her wing and was making sure the woman felt comfortable with them all. Jaymie finally entered the dining room for a plate of goodies, hoping her stomach had settled down from her nervousness earlier. Tami Majewski was refilling a platter of macarons glacés in lovely pastels, and Jaymie stopped to admire them as Jocie joined her. She hugged the child to her knees. "Jocie, have you met Ms. Majewski before?"

She shook her head.

"Then say hello; Tami, this is Jakob's little

girl, Jocie."

Jocie looked up at the woman and smiled. "Hello, Ms. . . ." She stumbled over the last name but did pretty well.

"She's your daddy's partner, Mr. Gus's, sister; did you know that?"

She shook her head.

"How are you, Tami?" Jaymie asked, beginning to fill her pretty china plate with some chicken salad sandwiches and thick-sliced homemade yum yum pickles. She looked up.

The woman shrugged. "I'm okay, I guess. Busy. Busy is good."

"Remember you said you had your old diary from 1984? Could you dig it out for me? I'm trying to get a mental picture of that . . ." She looked down at Jocie, who was reaching for a pink macaron. "That *time.*"

"Come into the bakery on Monday. I have some more cake ideas to fill you in on. I'll have it with me."

"That would be great."

"Hey, I also have some chocolate cake for you to try," she said, her eyes lighting up. "*Just* for you. Take it home, try it later — I want your full attention on it — and let me know if you like it. I *know* how you feel about chocolate." She retrieved a plastic container with some cake.

Jaymie smiled and returned to the parlor to eat, tucking the cake container in a bag under her chair (next to Hoppy) with the snack set Petty had given her. People drifted by, sat and chatted a moment, then moved on. Some were leaving, stopping to talk to both her and Becca before going. Both sisters had specified no gifts; they had all they could ever need. But people still brought cards, and some hard-liners did bring gifts, which were piled on a table in the entry hall.

Finally Dee Stubbs plunked down beside her and slipped her shoes off surreptitiously. "Lord, you'd think an ER nurse would have better feet. Or maybe it's the years of work that have *ruined* my feet."

"I have to thank you all for taking care of Petty; she doesn't have many friends. She moved back here when she retired after living for years in Detroit."

"You know me; never let *anyone* be lonely. Valetta is taking her to an auction while you're on your honeymoon and I've already got her signed up for line dancing and crochet club at the Wolverhampton community center. She'll be so busy she'll forget she's retired." Dee glanced over at Jaymie. "How *you* doing, kiddo? Becca's in her element, of course, belle of the ball, but I know how all this stuff traumatizes you."

Jaymie smiled and set her empty plate aside. "I have endured, and — don't tell anyone — actually enjoyed. You all did such a perfect job: no mortifying pictures or videos, nothing left undone."

"Have to say, it was *mostly* Heidi and Valetta. Those two work together pretty darn well."

"Agreed. But I know you all pitched in and we appreciate it. It's what Queensvillians do, I guess." She paused, her thoughts never far from the puzzle she was untangling. "Dee, with all this stuff about Rhonda Welch and Delores Paget, I've been delving into small-town life from the 1980s."

"Oh, *horrors*. Hope you haven't seen pictures of my big hair. I did love a perm, and lots of hairspray."

"Oh, I've *seen* pictures." She fished the curling mildewed birthday photo out of her purse. "This one in particular."

Dee took it and stared at it, a smile on her face. "Look at my Johnny! How cute is he?"

"You don't look like you had eyes for anyone but him."

"Not fair! I can name everyone in the picture. There is Val, and me and Johnny, and Becca and Brock and Delores — poor

Delores! — and Tami Majewski and . . . jeez, I guess there is another girl in the corner and I don't know who it is. So I lied about knowing who everyone was."

"Why was Tami there?"

She shrugged. "Just got invited, I guess. Look at the smirk on Brock's face. He moved in on Delores that night, I remember that."

"Why?"

She shrugged. "Brock was like that; he was a hound dog, but not a particularly successful hound dog." Her round, lightly lined face melted into a sad expression. "I've been shocked at the bodies found. Rhonda Welch and Delores Paget, both dead the same day; who knew?"

"It probably seemed like a school day like any other. But it was the day after Halloween, there was a football game that day and it was a few weeks before Thanksgiving. Would you or any of the others have stayed for the game? I know Valetta didn't, but did you?" Valetta's diary had hinted Dee had, but would their friend remember?

"I guess I would have because Johnny was the school mascot. He was the Wolverhampton Howling Wolf . . . so cute! He wore this papier-mâché wolf's head and a gray track suit to every game. I was always there to cheer him on."

Jaymie glanced around and leaned slightly forward, whispering, "I don't want this to get around, but do you know if there is any way of finding out if Gus Majewski played in that game that day?"

Dee looked puzzled for a moment, then understanding dawned on her face. "Oh, I see. Yes, I can understand how that might make a difference. *And* why you can't ask him. Is there any way to ask his sister?"

Jaymie shook her head. "I don't want to tip her off and I don't want to upset her, if there's nothing to it. She *is* going to give me her diary from that year, though, and I may find out from that."

"I'll see if Johnny remembers. But one game, over thirty years ago . . ." She shook her head. "A lot has happened since then."

"I know. I wonder if newspapers reported on high school games back then?" Jaymie felt a thump of excitement. "Or was there a school newspaper? They'd be sure to report on a football game and the star player's presence or lack thereof!"

"Good thought! I think there was a school paper but I didn't pay much attention to it. I wasn't much into school spirit. That was Johnny's thing. I'll ask him, and ask Becca, too. She's the one with the great memory."

"And Valetta. But here and now is not the place and time," Jaymie said with a smile. "I think I'd better circulate some more."

At long last the shower was done and Jaymie, despite rigorous objections from her friends, pitched in to return the historic house to its semblance of normalcy. The house was important to her and she felt a great deal of responsibility for its success as a historical living museum, as it was partly due to her finding of a historic letter that the historic society had been able to buy, renovate, and furnish the place. It had been closed today for the shower, but would open back up on Sunday for tours.

Afterward, Dee invited everyone back to her place — Johnny was going to pick up Chinese food from a place in Wolverhampton — and the fellows (Kevin, Jakob, and Johnny) joined them. Heidi was strangely silent about Joel's whereabouts. It was lovely seeing Jakob, and they had a few minutes alone before he finally took his sleepy little girl home.

Returning home after such a long, fretful, enervating day, Jaymie could *not* go to sleep. Hoppy was the same, overexcited by a long day among people. Becca and Kevin had retired immediately and Jaymie could hear Kevin's snores rattle the windows. But even a book wouldn't calm her. She wandered the house, ate the chocolate cake Tami had given her, read some more, watched TV. Let Hoppy out to piddle again . . . and *still* no sleep. She felt nauseated — probably the Chinese food, which often gave her tummy troubles — and nervous.

Looking back made her sad — the deaths of the two teens were weighing on her — and looking forward scared her. Could she truly be a mother to Jocie? She loved the little girl fiercely, and participating in the school problem had boosted her confidence, but having a child was a huge responsibility. Jocie was special and deserved only the best.

Worrying and fretting and being exhausted was making her feel even more ill and the rest of the night passed with symptoms that could only be described by saying they required hours spent in the bathroom with a book. By morning she was wonky, weary and feeling empty and dizzy. Becca, like the mother figure she had been for so long, made her have a hot bath, drink eggnog and go back to bed. She promised to let Denver out, Kevin would take Hoppy for a long walk, they'd feed them both, but Jaymie was to stay in bed. Becca would call Jakob and tell him she was under the weather.

TWENTY

The problem with being an introvert was that one needed to mingle from time to time. Add mingling to being the center of attention, a long, nervous day, too much rich food topped with more socializing and Chinese food, and you have a full day of sickness that only sleep and water could erase. Jakob had called a couple of times Sunday but she hadn't felt like company or even like talking much.

Monday dawned bright and cheery and it was May Day! May first. After many hours sleeping and a lot of water, Jaymie felt better. She and Jakob finally had a long chat very early Monday morning. Then, since Becca and Kevin were going back to London for a few days, Jaymie had breakfast with them and sent them off. It was a lovely spring day, with birds chirping and leaves showing brilliant new green, so she took her dog for a long, *long* walk, all the way to the

346

river and along the boardwalk in both directions, then home. Hoppy was so tired all he did when they reentered the kitchen was lap some water and go curl up in the bed he sometimes shared with Denver, which was beside the stove, warmed by the pilot light. The cat was enjoying a day with no Becca by sleeping on the summer porch sofa, sprawled out in a patch of sunshine.

But Jaymie was full of ambition. First, she needed to talk to Valetta. She walked over to the Emporium in time to catch her friend on tea break, at eleven. They sat on the steps in the sunshine and drank their tea. Valetta had commiserated with how ill Jaymie had been, and they chatted about Valetta's diary.

"Val, I have to ask you something," Jaymie said, sliding a glance over at her friend.

"Shoot."

"Brock called me the other day and wanted to come over and talk to me. The police chief called about the same time and dropped by. I think I saw Brock drive down my alley, but then keep going, like he was . . ." She hesitated. "Like he didn't want to visit me while the police chief was there."

Valetta was silent for a long moment and sipped her tea. Her face was turned away, but Jaymie knew she was upset. "Val, I'm sorry. I didn't mean to imply —"

"Jaymie, it's okay. I'm feeling bad because . . ." She shook her head. "I don't know. I'm so *scared.* Brock was a real jerk growing up. He still is, sometimes, though he's a lot better than he was as a teenager." She turned to look Jaymie in the eye. "But he has never, to my knowledge, raised a hand to a *single* person, man, woman or child. And he does the very best he can by his two kids. I don't want to think he could have done anything."

She shook her head, took a deep breath and sat up straighter. "No, strike that; it's not that I don't *want* to think it, it's that I truly, bone-deep, do not believe he did anything. But he's acted so weird lately, ever since Delores's body was found. What if I'm wrong? What if in a moment of . . ." She shook her head and slumped again.

Jaymie threw her arms about her friend and hugged. "Honey, he has to talk to me. He was ready to; I want to know whatever it is he has to say."

"I feel like the worst sister on the face of the planet," Valetta said, taking her glasses off and wiping her eyes with the back of her hand. She picked her mug up; today it was a plain one, with none of the funny pharmacist sayings she usually had.

It was indicative of her sober and frightened mood, Jaymie supposed. "You know Brock better than anyone on the planet. If you say he didn't do anything, I believe you."

Valetta looked over at Jaymie, tears rolling down her cheeks and her nose running. "Thank you. It's a relief hearing you say that. Lately I've been doubting everything I remember about that day."

"But he *did* come home late that night with the car and he wouldn't tell you where he'd been."

"You've read the diary."

Jaymie nodded. "Maybe he has something else to say about that day, maybe even something he's ashamed of, but whatever it is, I need to hear it." Maybe she was being presumptuous, but she had been emboldened by the chief's trust in her. However . . . what if he told her something she wasn't ready to hear? She took in a deep breath. She'd cross that bridge if she came to it.

Valetta nodded and said *Okay,* in a small voice.

Jaymie returned home to a flurry of missed phone calls and emails. Her mother called with wedding questions, her grandmother called to say how much she enjoyed being a virtual part of the shower; it had made her a hip hit among the folks of her retirement home. Dee called and left a cryptic message: *It was the wolf call.*

"Dee, what the heck did your message mean?" she asked. She held the receiver in one hand while sitting at the kitchen table, discarding spam emails and putting her laptop through a virus scanner.

"The *Wolf Call,*" Dee said. "That was the name of the school paper! How could you not understand what I was saying?"

Jaymie laughed. "You've always talked shorthand, like you just left the person two minutes ago and are answering the questions from then. That was Saturday, and I've been under the weather since."

"Oh, right! Becca told me. Anyway, Johnny doesn't remember if we were at that game or not, and he sure as heck doesn't know if Gus was."

She then launched into a dozen questions about Jaymie's health in dirty detail until Jaymie felt slightly queasy. "Dee, enough about that. Let's get back to the eighties. Even if Johnny can't remember that particular football game, do you know anyone who would?"

There was silence for a moment. "I think I may. Let me get back to you." She hung up as abruptly as she did everything.

Jaymie then read an email from Nan, who had a few questions about her column before it went to print. That reminded Jaymie of the information her editor had given her from the newspaper archives, and also that Clifford Paget had been found alive and well. She wondered, what would he have to say? It was quite possible — she hoped probable — that the murders would be solved by a confession from a man who had, after all, run away. She emailed answers to Nan.

She was finishing up when the phone rang, Dee again. She had a contact; an old friend of Johnny's was the school photographer for the newspaper, and took pictures of every single sports game, football included. He was also fanatically well organized. This very minute he was searching his archives, which he had digitized in the last ten years, and was going to send her the November first, 1984, football game photos. That would tell her exactly what she needed to know. Jaymie thanked her and hung up, but she could not wait for the photos. She had promised Tami she'd be in to the bakery to pick up the diary and talk about the wedding cake, and she was going to do it.

She was about to grab her purse when the

phone rang yet again.

"Ledbetter here. Jaymie, got some news. Want to tell you in person."

She paused and looked at her watch. "I'm heading into Wolverhampton right now, Chief. Can I meet you somewhere?"

"Coffee shop. Fifteen minutes." He sounded tense and hung up immediately.

She hit the gas on the highway to town and pulled into the parking lot of the coffee shop in seventeen minutes. The police chief was at a booth on the back wall. She entered, sniffing the smell of good coffee with appreciation. She usually drank tea, but coffee shop coffee was usually excellent, so she got a cup from the lunch counter, fixed it up with milk and joined him, sliding into the booth opposite him.

"What's up?" she asked after they greeted each other.

"You okay?" He drained the last of his cup. "You look a little pale."

"I've been under the weather the last couple of days. I'm fine. Now . . . what's up?"

"Told you we got Clifford Paget. He's given us a whole lot of information, and some of it we've confirmed."

"Okay." The chief looked deeply worried, his sagging face jowly, and she would swear he had lost weight in the last few days. "Tell me. Is there something . . . is it bad?"

"What? Oh, no, Jaymie, sorry if I'm acting vague. Trying to figure things out. First off . . . Delores Paget is not Delores Paget."

Jaymie sat back and blinked. "You'll have to be more clear; do you mean the body is not the girl known as Delores Paget, or —"

"No, no, I mean just as she apparently suspected, she was not the Pagets' natural niece. Clifford wasn't their nephew, either. Clifford Paget was Jimbo Paget's natural-born son. Those two — father and son — murdered Jimbo's wife — Clifford's mother — and took off with Olga, who stole a baby she was babysitting. Clifford said Olga couldn't have children and wanted one, so she just . . . took Delores."

Like stealing a chocolate bar from a candy store, it was that easy. How could she justify it to herself? Jaymie's heart thudded and her stomach churned. "That poor *girl*! She suspected it, and she was right." Her mind raced. So Delores was getting close to the truth, with Rhonda's help. Not only kidnapping, but murder! That alone — that frightening and dangerous knowledge — would have been enough of a reason for the Pagets, including Clifford, to kill both girls. "So what about Delores? What was her real name?"

"Cindy Lynn Walker, abducted on or around August third, 1968, the same day Clifford and Jimbo Paget killed Jimbo's wife. Not their real names, but that's neither here nor there. Father was having an affair with Olga, and they all took off. Clifford says the baby was not Jimbo's idea and he was plenty mad. Meant they had to run farther. They came all the way from Idaho and responded to an ad in the paper looking for farm help, with a house to live in as partial payment. It was work that paid under the table. That farm was owned by a real old lady, last of her family, who had to move into a nursing home. She was happy to have the help. Several years later when she died she left them the farm. They had their fake paperwork in line by then, and had established themselves with bank accounts and such."

Jaymie barely registered what he was saying, her mind still whirling. Poor Delores; just as she was about to get at the truth, she was killed.

"Jaymie, listen to me. Pay attention. Clifford swears up, down and sideways that he *didn't* kill those two girls."

354

Twenty-One

"What?"

"You heard me."

"Do you believe him?"

The chief held his mug up, signaling the waitress for a refill. "I don't know."

Jaymie took a long, deep breath. She trusted the chief. Should she tell him about Brock? It was tempting, but she couldn't. It would feel like betraying Valetta, and without any justification because she had no real reason to think Brock killed Delores. It could wait until after she talked to him. "One thing I'm thinking is, maybe the two murders are by two different killers."

"That's a helluva coincidence."

"I know. But it could happen, right?" She paused while the waitress refilled his coffee, then trotted away. "There is every possibility that the two girls intended to meet up to go see Petty but never found each other."

"You got any proof?"

"Not a bit," she said. "But I may, soon."

He watched her for a long moment. "You know or suspect something. You're not hiding anything from me, are you?"

She thought for a moment, then shook her head. "No, Chief, I don't *know* a thing. The minute I do, I'll tell you. I promise."

"You'd better do that. I'm going way out on a limb here, Jaymie, keeping you in the loop. *Way* out. Vestry is doing the best she can on this investigation — she thinks Paget is the culprit, and on paper he looks pretty damn good, but she's keeping her mind open — but if you've got anything that would help, you better hand it over."

"I know, Chief, I know. I don't have anything but some teenagers' diaries that talk about football games and petty rivalries." She drank the last of her coffee, then stood and hefted her purse on her shoulder. "I have to go. I'll call you."

The bakery was nearby so she walked to it. There was a girl about nineteen serving customers. Jaymie asked for Tami and was told she was out that moment but would be back soon. Jaymie decided to sit and wait.

She still had to process what the chief had told her. Jaymie should have asked the chief about Delores's natural family but she hadn't thought to, her mind full of other questions. It was a long time ago but there could still be an elderly mother out there, grieving for her kidnapped child, hoping for a reunion that was never going to happen. It hurt her heart to think about it.

Tami, dressed in white jeans and a pink blouse, which suited her pale coloring, came through the front door and saw Jaymie. "You made it!" she cried, slinging her purse over her shoulder.

"Of course. I never miss an appointment."

"You can have your break now," Tami said to the teenager, who smiled and nodded, then disappeared in back. "Did you like the chocolate cake?" she asked, turning to Jaymie.

"It was okay," Jaymie said, trying to find that fine line between honesty and cruelty. "To be frank, I'd prefer something a little . . . moister."

Tami nodded. "Yeah, I'm sorry. I think the batch of chocolate I was working with was too old." She ducked through the pass-through section of the counter and tossed her purse underneath. "People say it's okay to use no matter how old chocolate is, but I think it loses oil content. I'll make you another taster batch. I want you to be happy."

"I appreciate that," Jaymie said, relieved.

She didn't want to have to find a new baker for her wedding cake, but she also wanted her guests to enjoy it. "I stopped in to pick up the diary."

"Oh, right! I have it in back." Tami retreated. When she returned she handed over a small flowered book with a broken rusty lock.

As the baker grabbed a stack of flat bakery boxes and started constructing and stacking them on a shelf near the glass case, Jaymie opened the diary and glanced through. Much of it was blurry, the pale ink fuzzed as if it was being read through a steamy window. There were silly sayings, like *Kiss My Grits!* and *Where's the Beef?* and a whole page dedicated to Cyndi Lauper and "Girls Just Want to Have Fun." There were movie quotes like "Nobody puts baby in the corner." The passages that she could read, through the smudges, seemed to be the usual teen laments of boredom and boy problems. "What happened to it? It's all blurry and the pages are kind of warped."

"It got wet at some point, I guess. It was in a box that was in the basement. I doubt if it will help. I didn't write very much, sort of in fits and starts."

"I'm trying to get a feel for things," Jaymie admitted, closing the book and stuffing it in her purse. This was probably a forlorn hope, but Tami was the one who offered it. "Hey, I came across something interesting the other day. Among Delores's things was a photo from my sister's sixteenth birthday party and you were in it! I didn't know you were friends with Becca?"

A blank look on her face, Tami shrugged. "Isn't that funny? I don't remember that at *all*. Must've been a fluke."

Or maybe a birthday party was the kind of thing only the celebrant remembered, looking back, Jaymie thought. How many had she been to in childhood that she remembered, other than her own? As the baker continued building bakery boxes and stacking them neatly on the shelf, Jaymie leaned across the pass-through counter. "Tami, do you remember anything about that day, the day Delores disappeared?"

Tami paused and stared at her. "Good heavens, does anyone? I mean, it was a random day like any other, wasn't it?" She suddenly looked stricken, one hand over her heart. "I didn't mean . . . I mean, at the *time,* not knowing what happened, it seemed like a day like all the others."

"I get it," Jaymie replied, straightening. "But you'd be surprised. I'm piecing it together bit by bit. It has helped when I've been able to tell people things, like there was a football game after school that day, stuff like that. And others wrote diaries too, like Valetta. She was an *avid* diarist, recorded everything going on about herself, her brother, school . . . *every*thing. Right now I have a photographer from the school newspaper, the *Wolf Call,* sending me some photos from the football game."

Her face twisted in a puzzled look, Tami asked, "Why?"

Jaymie hesitated. She did not want to point a finger at Gus, especially not to his sister, who seemed to care for him a lot. "I'm just . . . like I said, getting a picture of the day. Who was there, who was playing . . . everything helps, right?"

"I don't think my diary will," Tami said. "In fact, you may as well leave it here," she said, holding out her hand. "It hasn't got anything in it, I can tell you that. I had a look already."

The instinct was to hand it back over, but . . . Jaymie held her purse close to her body. There might be some small detail that even Tami wouldn't have noticed, something about that day and Gus's movements. "I'll keep it, if that's okay." An older woman entered the bakery, the bells jingling over the door, and another followed. Jaymie waved and headed for the door, saying, "I'll leave you to it. Talk to you soon! Let me know when you have more cake for tasting."

Jaymie returned to her van and headed out of town. There were wedding details to take care of and she mustn't forget them in her determination to help solve the teen murders. There were several more things at the store that Heidi wanted to borrow to use for the wedding reception, which was going to take place on the lawn of the historic manor, with a rented marquee tent in case of inclement weather. She had found some vintage champagne glasses, a box of old wood frames, and assorted other items she had tagged for use. Storage space was tight at the store, so she'd use today to retrieve the stuff.

Jakob had told Jaymie the history of his and Gus's store. When they first got the idea for The Junk Stops Here, they ran it out of a storefront in Wolverhampton. But they outgrew that so fast that he and Gus rented an empty factory that had gone bankrupt during the recession. It was a huge empty space because the company had been forced to sell off all of the equipment to try to pay back their debts.

Though they had initially intended to

stock only reconstruction items like doors and doorknobs, windows, shutters, and vintage gingerbread from old houses torn down, as well as other vintage construction goods, they had swiftly realized that there was a lot of fast money in smaller items. They now sold everything from jewelry and china at the front in cases, to a vast array of furniture, books, clothes, luggage, as well as plumbing supplies, antique wrought-iron fencing . . . in short, anything and everything the lover of vintage and antiques could ever want. The stock changed every single day, as both men attended auctions and estate sales, as well as buying online.

Gus Majewski sat behind the glass counter at the front, hunched over and studying a business ledger with a worried frown. He wore smudged dollar store magnifying glasses that he threw down on the counter as she entered.

"Hey, Gus. How is everything?" She remembered what Jakob had said about Gus seeming on edge and examined him for signs of stress.

"Jaymie, how are you?" He came around the counter and gave her a big bear hug.

He certainly seemed fine today. "I'm good," she said with a gasp as he released her. He was very strong, and didn't always realize how tight his hugs were. "Is Jakob here?"

"No, he's picking some stuff up from an estate sale in Mount Clemens. Didn't he tell you?"

"Maybe he forgot."

"He'll be back in an hour or so, if you need him."

"No, it's okay. I'm here to pick up some stuff that we're using for the wedding. Did he tell you about it?"

"He sure did, and so did that bossy little wedding planner of yours. Come back and I'll help you load it into your van. You have someone to help on the other end?"

"Hopefully. If not, it'll ride around in my van until I do." She followed him back to a storage room, where there was a dolly cart loaded with stuff tagged "wedding" in Heidi's big looping handwriting.

He slipped the brake off the dolly cart. "Is this it?"

"I guess so." She followed him back through the cavernous warehouse. "Hey, I was just talking to your sister."

"Tami? Why?" he asked sharply, looking back over his shoulder.

Taken aback at his tone, she said, "Just . . . I had to pick something up. She . . . uh . . . she was giving me her diary from 1984. I'm trying to get a feel for that year at Wolver-hampton High; you know, because of Delores Paget and Rhonda."

"What does *she* know? She was hardly ever at school. She was in the same grade as me because she was left back. Did you know that? Spent all her time smoking with the stoners. She didn't even make it to the end of the school year."

Jaymie was silent; his criticism of his sister made her uncomfortable, but she was not going to go on the attack.

"Seriously! She's never been the brightest bulb in the package." He wheeled the dolly cart out the big double doors, open to the spring sunshine, and toward her vehicle.

Jaymie unlocked and opened the back doors of the van. Gus loaded the boxes containing stemware, vases and frames, a small mid-century modern side table, a pie-crust table and two bags of vintage crepe bells into the back of her van.

He dusted his hands and straightened from the task. "Tami's been a screwup her whole life."

"She's trying to help me out," Jaymie replied, feeling inclined to defend the woman.

He turned, his face twisted in an unhappy expression. "I wouldn't be so sure of that."

"What do you mean?"

"She's unhappy and confused. She always has been. I don't know what's wrong with her, but . . ." He shrugged. "Jaymie, if you want my advice, you'll drop all this investigation crap. He won't say it to your face, but Jakob doesn't like it."

Jaymie's heart thudded, but then she stiffened her spine and stared at him. Why was he trying to intimidate her to stop? "Gus, if Jakob had a problem with it he'd tell me. We're honest about things."

"I wouldn't bet on that. He doesn't want to piss you off." Looking broody, Gus jammed his hands in his pockets. "Look, if I tell you something, you have got to keep it a secret."

Jaymie was not about to promise anything, so she kept silent.

Maybe he took that for agreement, because he launched back into speech, staring down at a pothole in the parking lot pavement. "I saw Rhonda that day. She . . . uh . . . she told me she was going . . . going to pick Delores up at that farmhouse where she lived."

She watched him, her bull-crap meter was pinging loudly. "Why?"

"What?"

"*Why* was she picking Delores up?"

"I don't know. Why does anyone do anything? All I'm saying is, it was probably that whacko Clifford Paget who killed them both. But he's gone now, so . . . no one will ever know for sure."

Why was he lying? Didn't he realize that by saying he saw Rhonda he was making himself a suspect? Though in truth, she already suspected him. "How did she get hold of you?" she asked, thinking of what Sybil had said about Rhonda's phone calls. It's not like anyone had cell phones back then.

"She . . . called the school, I guess. I don't remember."

"Where did you two meet?"

"At school. In the parking lot."

"Why didn't you tell the police that at the time?"

"I don't know. I was scared, I guess."

"But no one knew she was dead at that point. They just thought she had taken off. *You* thought she left because she was pregnant." But the whole reason she wanted to see him that day was to tell him she *wasn't* pregnant. If they had actually met, wouldn't Rhonda have said that? Maybe there was more to this story. She opened her mouth to ask him more questions, but he waved

366

one hand and turned away. "Gus, can I ask —"

"No! Just drop it. Phone's ringing; gotta go." He slumped back into the store, shoving the empty dolly cart ahead of him.

She could go after him but he'd told his story now; he would no doubt stick to it. Jaymie got in the van and called Bernice. They were storing all the stuff in her garage until the wedding, so she may as well swing by there to drop it off. Bernie was home, so Jaymie headed there, mulling over Gus's foul mood, trying to decipher why he was so mad at his sister and trying to figure out why he was lying about seeing Rhonda. *If* he was lying about seeing Rhonda.

Maybe it was a lie, but not exactly a lie. Maybe he *did* meet up with her — not how and when he said, but somewhere else — killed her, and was now saying what he said to get it out there that when she left him, she was alive and well. It didn't make much sense, but trying to make sense of what people lied about was highly overrated. Sometimes people lied to get themselves out of one spot of trouble, not seeing traps they were walking right into, or how their lies were illogical or even couldn't be true. Some people lied reflexively, without even considering what they had already said. She hadn't noticed that about Gus in the past, but then, she didn't know him very well.

Her head was swimming with possibilities that she needed to sort out.

Bernie, in bare feet and exercise pants, came out to unlock the garage, and together they lugged the stuff into the rapidly filling space. Jaymie stared at the furniture and boxes and glanced over at Bernie. "You don't even have room in here for your car anymore. You're such a good sport about this," she said. "As if you don't have enough on your plate, with all of this wedding planning that Heidi is involving you in."

"Hey, it's fun! I was raised with brothers, and I didn't get to do a lot of girly stuff." She pushed the sleeves up on her long-sleeved baseball shirt, her dark skin a lovely contrast to the pale blue of the shirt. "Heidi has been good for me."

"You've been good for her, too," Jaymie said, reaching out and hugging her. She inhaled deeply her friend's scent, a lovely combination of soap and some product she used to keep her natural hair lustrous. It smelled deliciously of coconut and hibiscus. "You're like the sister she never had."

"*You're* the one who befriended her to get the whole town to accept her, and don't think she'll ever forget that."

Jaymie felt heat rush to her face as she released her friend from the hug. The May breeze cooled her skin. "Did Heidi say that? She wasn't supposed to figure that out."

"She's sharper than people think," Bernie said with a wide grin.

"You're right about that. She's a lot nicer than I ever expected, too." They closed the garage and Jaymie paced back to the van, slamming the back doors shut and locking it up. She turned back to Bernie. "You have to work tonight?"

Bernie nodded. "At least on the night shift I get to be more than the chief's chauffeur."

"He likes you, Bernie. I think he sees himself as your mentor."

"Yeah, well, I appreciate that, but he's not good at sharing his thought processes. Sometimes it's hard to figure out what's going on in that giant head."

"You'll have a new police chief soon enough, and then you'll have someone new to try to figure out."

"We all think it's going to be the assistant chief, Deborah Connolly. I'll be okay with that, she's cool." Bernie leaned back against Jaymie's van. "Has the chief been keeping you up to speed?"

"Kind of." Knowing it would go no further, she shared what the chief had told her about Clifford Paget. Bernie already knew most of the information anyway. "What's your take on that? The chief doesn't think he killed Delores, but it seems like the most likely solution." And maybe Rhonda, too, if what Gus had said was actually true; if so, that placed her at the farmhouse with Delores. "Clifford creeped my sister out. She thought he was a lech. And now we know he wasn't even related to Delores, and knew that the whole time. Maybe he was . . . I don't know, abusing her, and killed her to shut her up."

"Could be. But if he's willing to cop to helping kill his own mother, why wouldn't he admit to killing Delores?"

"And Rhonda."

"Right. Though we still don't know if she was killed by the same killer or if there were two murderers."

"True," Jaymie mused. "So you think I should trust the chief's feeling that Clifford isn't the killer?"

"I'd say that what seems like intuition is, in a highly trained and intelligent person, a lot more than just a gut instinct."

Jaymie nodded. "You know, I think you're right about that."

"I've learned at least as much from Chief Ledbetter as I have from all my textbooks."

"Though that won't stop you from hitting the textbooks," Jaymie said with a smile.

"You bet. Next stop, I make detective."

"You will, Bernie. We know you will. And when you do we will have one giant party." She gave her friend another hug. "I'd better get going. I promised to order the pamphlets from the printer for the Tea with the Queen event. I've pulled back this year on helping organize the whole thing with everything else I've got going on, but it's the least I can do."

Jaymie returned home and let Hoppy out, let Denver in, then set to work on organizing myriad details she had to take care of. First things first; she called in the order for the pamphlets, and sent over the graphic files via email. She then made a list of what *else* she had to do before the wedding. Now that the shower was over, the countdown to the day had truly begun.

The day dwindled. Should she call Jakob, see if he wanted her to come out and make dinner? Life was more complicated now than it used to be, but it was a *good* complicated, the kind of messy, busy, chaotic life she should hate, given her personality, but that she loved. Somehow, chaos was different when it was the busyness that came with love. She was secure in her trio of love: herself, Jakob and Jocie.

But the tangled mess of the murder investigation would not leave her alone. It was a hum of sad distraction in an otherwise happy time. She hauled out all the information she had and began to make notes. If she could construct a timeline of the day Rhonda and Delores disappeared and were murdered it might help pinpoint who could have done it. Maybe not why, or how, but who.

So . . .

Both girls were apparently at their schools in the morning. Both apparently left school at some point during the day. Rhonda was at her boarding school until lunch, Sybil helped her make phone calls on study break, and then she left. One brief call to Sybil set the time Rhonda left Chance Houghton, thirty miles from Wolverhampton, at about one thirty. So Rhonda took off, maybe to meet Gus at Wolverhampton High, maybe not. Jaymie was not sure when Delores left WH, nor where she went.

Hoppy started barking and almost immediately after there was a tapping at the back door. Jaymie jumped and looked up. Brock! Her heart thudding, she hurriedly covered up all the stuff she was looking through and crossed the room, unlocking the door. "Hey. Did Valetta tell you to come talk to me?"

He nodded. Brock was tall, with a full head of dark lank hair that looked greasy from some product he used. He was always neatly dressed, as befit a real estate salesman, but today, though he wore a sport coat and dress slacks, he looked rumpled and tired.

"Come on in," Jaymie said and let the door swing open. Hoppy darted out to the lawn. "Can I make you coffee?"

He nodded and slumped down in a chair at the table, passing one long-fingered hand over his face. She busied herself with making coffee and set a mug in front of him with the sugar bowl, milk pitcher and spoon close by. He ladled sugar into his cup and stirred.

"So you called the other day and wanted to talk to me but you never showed up. Why?"

He looked up with resentment etched in the deep lines on his face. "You *know* why."

"No, I honestly don't," she said, searching Brock's face for clues. He had bags under his eyes, which were bloodshot. Something was troubling him deeply.

"The moment you got off the phone with

me, you must have called your buddy the police chief," he said, his tone deeply resentful. "What did I ever do to you, Jaymie? Why don't you like me?"

Deciding to ignore the whining, Jaymie hit to the heart of his complaint. "If you had come in you would have discovered that the police chief actually called *me* wanting to come over, and I said sure. It was pure coincidence."

Brock snorted and glared down at his cup.

"I don't care if you believe me; it doesn't stop it from being true. Why did you call and want to come over? You said you had something to tell me."

He sighed and wiggled his shoulders. "Okay. All right." But still, he didn't say anything for a long time, gulping down his coffee and moodily glaring at the table.

She decided to wait it out. There was something on his mind, something important. She was curious as heck, but she wasn't going to badger him.

"It was all so long ago. I feel like I was someone else, you know? I can't get into my head, the mind of that teenage guy who was so hard up and miserable."

He was casting himself as a victim; this was not good. Jaymie was braced to hear anything and not react.

He was silent again for a while. "You know, I saw her that day."

"Delores. Yes, so you said."

"I wasn't exactly . . . truthful about what happened."

He lied; no surprise. But if he was about to tell Jaymie that he killed Delores, she was going to run out that back door and not stop.

"I took her for a ride."

Six words, so sinister. *I took her for a ride.* She could picture it, him taking her to a back road to neck, getting over-amorous, she begging him to stop . . . anxiety choked her. She wished he would just spit it out. But no, that picture in her mind was all wrong. She *knew* how Delores died, in her own kitchen with a cleaver in her head. So . . . he took her home and tried something, then . . . she shook her head and cleared her mind. She needed to *listen* instead of speculating. "Brock, why don't you tell me what happened?"

"I'm going to, from the beginning."

TWENTY-TWO

"I skipped school at lunch that day and hitched home," Brock said.

"Why?"

"I don't know. Bunch of guys were bugging me. Anyway, I was hanging around the Emporium when I saw Delores coming down the street toward the store. I talked to her. She was looking for a pay phone because she had to make a phone call. I think she was supposed to meet someone, but they weren't there."

"But you didn't ask her who she needed to call, or who she was meeting?"

"I don't think so. I don't remember."

"Okay." That was typical Brock, Jaymie thought; so self-involved he wouldn't even think to ask who she was calling.

"I told her she could use our phone at home for free instead of using a pay phone. Mom was at Mrs. Stubbs's. Val was at school."

He figured if he got her alone at his house he could make out with her. He didn't need to say it; the truth lingered in the air like a bad odor.

"So she came back home and used our phone." He wasn't looking up.

"How many calls? More than one? Did she actually talk to someone?"

"She got someone, yes. I heard her talking to someone. I *think* she made two calls, but I'm not sure."

"And?"

He shrugged. "She got off the phone and said she had to go home."

"Home? Why?"

"To meet someone, I guess."

"Hmm." She frowned and lifted the edge of one of the papers she had been reading. Did this revelation support Gus's assertion that Rhonda was going to the farmhouse to pick up Delores? "What did you say to her after that?"

"I asked how she was going to get there and she said she was hitching. So I offered her a ride."

"You drove her all the way out to the Paget house?"

He nodded.

"So you took her home. Was there anyone else there?"

He shrugged. "I don't know. I never got out of the car."

"Really? Why?"

He shrugged again and his cheeks turned red. "She told me to take off, to . . . to get lost."

She watched him for a minute. Jaymie slowly said, "There's more to it than that. What is it, Brock? I *know* there's more."

He hung his head and mumbled, "She told me I was a loser. A jerk. I had used her and then switched to Rhonda, she said, but Rhonda was too smart and too good for me. She let me have it, both barrels." He took in a deep breath and straightened, looking Jaymie directly in the eye for the first time. "And I *deserved* it. I was mad then, but looking back . . . if any guy ever uses Eva like that," he said about his daughter, ". . . just trying to cop a feel, I'll kill him. Having a daughter who's almost a teenager . . . it changes your perspective."

He seemed genuine, but most people try to show themselves as the good guy even after doing something despicable. "So you dropped her off and left?" she said, with heavy emphasis.

He nodded. "I peeled out of there so fast gravel flew."

"What time was that?"

378

He shrugged. "Maybe . . . two o'clock, two thirty? Not sure."

"And that was the last time you saw her?"

He nodded again.

"Where'd you go?" Would he lie, say he went home? He'd already lied to his sister and told her he went back to school. He likely didn't know how much Valetta had documented in her diary.

"Wolverhampton. I ended up in a filthy pool hall with some old dudes. They fed me a bottle of cheap wine. I got stinking drunk and threw up in the back alley."

"And then?"

He shrugged. "I slept it off on a bench in the back of the pool hall, sobered up and then drove home. I crawled into the house, sick as a dog."

"What time?"

He shrugged. "Hell if I know. Ten, maybe? Mom was already in bed. Val was mad. I was such a jerk; worried my mother to death." He took a heavy breath. "I'd love to say I straightened my life up and became a better son, but I didn't."

"And that was it?"

"That was it."

"So why didn't you tell the police you had given her a ride home when they asked if anyone knew anything?"

"I was scared. I'd been drinking the night before, and driving. And I didn't think it mattered. I wasn't lying, exactly; she *did* tell me once she was going to take off, just disappear. That's what I thought she was doing, arranging a ride to get out of town."

It made sense, but it had misled police for decades. "So, Brock . . . why did you lie to the chief now? You're not a kid anymore."

He shrugged. "It dredged it all back up and . . . I panicked. It doesn't exactly show me in a good light."

And that was Brock all over; he had never cared about his actual character, just how he appeared to others. But it seemed like he was having a crisis of conscience, so maybe there was hope for him yet. "You know what you have to do now, Brock. You *have* to tell the police the truth."

He swallowed. "Maybe you can tell Ledbetter for me. He'll believe *you.*"

"It's not my story, Brock." There was no way she was going to put herself on the line for him, especially since she wasn't positive she believed him.

After Brock left she doodled on a pad of paper. Some half-formed thoughts were bouncing around in her head. She did mindless chores: dishes, a load of laundry, some pre-cooking for the next meal she'd take out to Jakob's. She called him and they chatted, but Jocie had come home early from school. She wasn't feeling very well so he was going to tuck her in and have an early night himself.

"I miss you," he said. "I wish you were here."

"Me too," she confessed. She was tempted to tell him about her conversation with Gus but there was no point in upsetting him, not when he was worried about Jocie. "Call me later if she's feeling worse. And I'll call you in the morning to check in. I can come out and look after Jocie if she isn't well enough for school tomorrow."

"That's a relief; thanks, *liebchen.* Night."

She checked her email. The photographer had sent the photos. It was evident, and the photos confirmed, that Gus was there all afternoon as they practiced and then took to the field playing another local high school football team. It didn't seem possible that he was out at Delores's killing her and Rhonda and then taking Rhonda's body out to the island that evening to dispose of.

Despite multiple people lying about that day, it was most likely a case of that lowlife, Clifford Paget, killing two girls: Delores, who rejected his advances maybe — or who finally told him to lay off — and another,

Rhonda, who perhaps was collateral damage. Maybe Rhonda had arrived at the farmhouse to meet Delores and witnessed the murder.

Jaymie spread all the material out on the table and started going through it yet again. Maybe she had missed something. She looked at Valetta's diary entry about the day Rhonda and Delores died. Then she read Tami's diary. Thursday, November first, she simply wrote: *School all day, then caught Gus's football game. Went with him and some friends after to get a hamburger at Tovey's in Wolverhampton.*

Well, that was clear enough, and gave Gus an alibi for much later in the day. Except something was off about that. It was getting dark outside. She should be getting Denver to come in. Hoppy was outside again — he'd go in and out a million times a day, if she let him — and started barking. What now? Mr. Findley taking his evening walk? A cat other than Denver in their yard? A car going by?

She was about to go out to check when she saw a figure at the door. She ran to open it. "Tami! What a surprise!"

"Hey, Jaymie. Can I come in?" She was shivering. It was May, but evenings in Michigan were still coolish, and she was just wearing a hoodie over a T-shirt.

"Sure. Want a cup of tea?"

"I'd love one." Tami seemed nervous, but that was usual with her. As long as Jaymie had known her she was a nervous, pacing, agitated mess half the time.

Jaymie put her whistling teakettle on the burner, turned it on — the snap of the dial and poof of the flame so comforting, signaling tea would be ready soon — and sat back down.

Tami was staring at the papers laid out. "You're really into this, aren't you? Why don't you leave it up to the police to investigate? *They're* the professionals. It doesn't seem right that a citizen is getting so involved in police work."

Jaymie watched her fidget with her purse strap, her gloved hands twisting the strap over and over. She suddenly remembered what bothered her about the Thursday, November first, entry of Tami's in the diary. Tovey's in Wolverhampton had just celebrated their thirtieth anniversary in business in March. So unless there was a previous Tovey's Hamburger Joint, the entry was impossible. As was . . . gosh, she *knew* this. The movie *Dirty Dancing* didn't come out until 1987; it was one of Becca's favorites, and Jaymie had watched it many times with her sister, so it should not be mentioned in a diary from 1984.

The diary was a fake, an attempt to throw her off something. Tami must be covering up for Gus somehow, trying to alibi him for later that day, which indicated at the very least that she suspected him. "You and your brother were close when you were teenagers, right?" His stinging words about his sister came back to her. Gus had seemed intent on destroying Tami's credibility, looking back at her conversation earlier with him. What was he afraid she'd say? Did he not trust her to alibi him?

Tami nodded. "We were close. He's my little brother. I love him. I'd do anything for him."

Even lie, falsify a diary entry to alibi him that afternoon. Jaymie watched her gloved hands, twisting the purse strap. Twisting and twisting, hands in wool gloves too heavy for May. She swallowed hard. "You were angry that he wasted his chance to go to college. Why?"

"He could have *been* something. He could have . . . I don't know. Become a doctor, or a lawyer. Had a business. Instead he's running a junk store, stuck in the same stupid town his whole life."

"So you must have been upset when he

384

talked about dropping out of school and marrying Rhonda, when they thought she might be pregnant."

Tears welled in Tami's eyes and traced ribbons of pale skin through the makeup on her cheeks. "Scheming slut! Thought she was better than me. They *all* did, but she was the worst. And then she went to a *Christian* boarding school because her parents were missionaries! What a joke."

"You weren't in school that day, were you, Tami?" She held up the diary. "This is fake. You were home that day. Gus said you dropped out that year."

"I hated school. I never fit in."

Things were becoming clearer by the moment. Sometimes families pin all their hopes for the future on one member, the one who seems to stand out, the one with talent, or looks, or ambition. "No one fits in at high school," Jaymie said, gently. She slid her cell phone over and tapped the screen, hitting the icon for a handy app she often used when she was interviewing someone and wanted to remember their exact words.

"That's what everyone says, but every *single* kid I saw had friends, some place they fit, even the geeks like your friend Valetta. She had Dee and your sister. Not me. I didn't have *anyone.*"

"But someone invited you to Becca's birthday party."

She snorted. "Hah! That was a mistake. My mom worked at the grocery store, and your dad and mom shopped there. I guess they'd talk. Your father thought Becca and I were friends. He called our house and talked to my mom, telling her to bring me to the party. Mom *made* me go. No one wanted me there."

"I'm sorry," Jaymie said gently, her voice trembling ever so faintly. This was becoming troublesome; Tami's manner had gone from nervous to resentful, and the gloved hands were still twisting the purse strap. "So you were home that day, not at school."

Tami nodded.

"Did Rhonda call your place?"

Tami nodded again and stared off into space. "I knew you'd figure this all out," she said, her tone feathery and distracted. "As soon as we talked in the bakery I knew the diary was a mistake, but you wouldn't give it back." She shook her head. Her voice a whisper, she repeated, "You wouldn't give it back." She snatched it from the table and stuffed it in her purse. "I'll take it back now."

Jaymie swallowed. "Rhonda *did* call?"

"She wanted to know what time Gus

386

would be home. She'd completely forgotten he had a game that day. She said she had something important to discuss with him, but she wouldn't tell me what it was. I *knew* she was going to get him to run away with her." Tami frowned and looked across at Jaymie. She leaned forward, her eyebrows drawn down. "And then every *hope,* all his *plans,* would be washed down the drain. I was *furious.*"

Jaymie knew the truth from Sybil, that Rhonda was going to tell Gus she wasn't pregnant and that she thought they should cool it for a while. It would all have worked out if only Tami hadn't interfered. Rhonda had plans, ambitions. She also had no future past that afternoon, but she didn't know it.

Urgency coursed through Jaymie. This moment, at this exact time, Tami was ready to talk. Later, with a police warning and a lawyer, that might not necessarily be true. She had a feeling that didn't bode well for her, but she could take on Tami. She was strong and Tami was skinny as a rail. Consciously calming herself, slowing her breathing, Jaymie said, "So you told Rhonda . . . what?"

"I said that Gus was coming home early. If she wanted to see him, she should come to our house, not the school."

Jaymie swallowed, her suspicion confirmed. The murderer wasn't Gus at all. It was premeditated; Tami had planned to dispose of the woman she thought was carrying her brother's baby. This was even worse than she thought, not the impulse of the moment but a cold-blooded plan. "And then what?"

She shrugged, still twisting the purse strap, wearing her gloves so she wouldn't leave fingerprints in Jaymie's kitchen. Maybe this wasn't a good idea, leading her to confess. Jaymie should make an excuse to get out, but in the meantime she needed to keep Tami talking, make her calm, soothe her. She swallowed, hard, and was about to repeat her question, when Tami answered.

"So Rhonda came over, and I killed her."

Jaymie took in a swift breath; it was so harsh, so baldly put.

The confession seemed to act like a bomb, bursting the dam of reticence. In a rush, Tami leaned across the table and said, "I strangled her and she was dead and the phone was ringing. The *damn* phone, again! I answered and it was that little witch Delores, and she was asking was Gus home. I said no, of course not, and she said well, Rhonda was supposed to pick her up and then go see Gus before they took off, but things had gotten screwed up, and what should she do? Where should they meet?"

Delores had misunderstood; Rhonda must have said she was going to go see Gus and *then* pick up Delores, but the teen had gotten it backward. Jaymie's heart pounded and sweat started trickling down her back. In a movie it was never a good sign when the killer told you everything; they were venting, getting it all out to a person they knew wouldn't live to tell. After a lifetime of concealment there was a gush of words, a relief of sorts.

"I told her she had just missed Rhonda." Tami giggled and covered her mouth. "Oops, not funny, right?" But she giggled again, her eyes gleaming with manic humor. "But it *is* funny; just *missed* her! But, I said — and I thought quick about this, because I realized at that point that Delores knew too much already and could pin Rhonda down to our place — I said I knew where Rhonda was going to be. So I'd meet Delores at her house and take her to Rhonda. She wanted me to pick her up in Queensville at some guy's house but I only had Rhonda's Ford Falcon, and I didn't want to drive into town in that, so I said no, her house in the country."

Jaymie let out a long breath she hadn't

even known she was holding. *That* was how everything tied together.

"Stupid kid. She was rude. *So* rude! What a brat. I drove that freakin' Ford Falcon of Rhonda's, with her dead in the backseat covered in a blanket, and pulled right up to that dingy farmhouse." She stopped and looked at the stove, the burner aflame under the kettle, which was starting to simmer. "She lived like we did. Dirty, poor. Grubby. I should've felt sorry for her, I guess, but I didn't. It was her own fault, being rude to me like that. Disrespecting me. I walked right into that house, asked if anyone was home, and when I found out there wasn't anyone there but us I asked her for a drink of water. When she turned around, asking where Rhonda was as she did it, I picked up a cleaver off the counter and hit her *hard.* Shut her up for good."

Jaymie's head swam, and she felt nauseous. Now was the time to get out, out the back door and run. She got up casually as the kettle began to heat up. She crossed around back of Tami to the canister on the counter and got out the teabags, as if she was going to make a pot. "And then you put her in that trunk in the basement," Jaymie said.

"No way," Tami said, twisting and watching Jaymie. "I left her right there where she fell, with that cleaver still in her head."

Jaymie stopped, teabag in hand, and her breath caught; *that's* what Clifford had done, what he was feeling guilty about! He'd hidden the body, or started to. Maybe he came home and found Delores dead. Or maybe Jimbo and Olga did and thought Clifford had killed Delores. But whatever happened, they knew damn well they couldn't report Delores dead in their kitchen with their cleaver in her head, not with all they had done. So they hid her body in a trunk in their cellar and lied about it for decades. They must have been relieved as hell when Brock said Delores took off. All they had to do was go along with it, say yes, she'd talked about running off. The perfect cover. Hundreds, maybe thousands, of kids disappeared every year.

But when Jimbo died Clifford got scared and "disappeared" himself. Olga just kept on lying. "And so what about Rhonda?" Jaymie asked over her shoulder.

"Her?" Tami's chair creaked. "I took that car over to Heartbreak Island and drove it up to a place where I knew there was deep water, near the shipping channel. There's a spot we used to jump off for thrills, so I knew it was deep. There are cottages there now but it used to be a kind of park. You know, I'm a good driver. A *great* driver. Always have been. Used to have a boyfriend who did stupid stunts with his car, but I was even better at it than he was." She chuckled, seemingly becoming more relaxed as she talked. "Damned if I didn't almost kill myself that night! Put her in the front seat and gunned it, then jumped out. Almost took me with it. I could have died that night." She paused, then softly said, "But I didn't."

"And no one heard the noise and investigated?"

"I'm sure people heard. But there aren't that many people on the island that late in the year. *You* ought to know that."

Jaymie was startled by the implication; Tami apparently knew about the Leighton cottage on Heartbreak Island. But what she said was true. By November most of the island cottages were empty. Only a few, housing the island's permanent residents, were occupied.

Heart pounding, Jaymie glanced over at the back door, then at a rolling pin that was on the counter. Was her best plan to make a run for it, or hit Tami with the rolling pin? "You've done a good job of hiding it ever since."

"But I've *suffered*!" Tami cried, her words catching on a sob. She twisted in her seat, trying to look at Jaymie. She twisted the other way. "Every time I thought about Rhonda being pregnant, that I'd killed that poor little baby . . . I almost went crazy a time or two. Tried to kill myself once. Or twice. I've suffered enough, and all for nothing because she wasn't even pregnant. I'm *done.*" She was becoming agitated.

There was no more time to lose. Jaymie made a move to bolt for the door, but Tami seemed to anticipate it. She shrieked, "What are you doing, Jaymie? Don't get any —" The kettle started to scream as Tami, startled into action, jumped up and whirled, looping the purse strap around Jaymie's neck before she could bolt past her. It jerked Jaymie backward; she stumbled and the purse strap dug into her neck, choking her and making her cough. Hoppy, outside, began barking frantically and the phone started ringing, a din that was added to when Jaymie screamed as loud as she could while being choked as she clawed at the looped purse strap.

Tami was far stronger than Jaymie had expected. Too late she saw how she had underestimated Tami; how *everyone* had underestimated Tami.

They swayed and struggled. Jaymie, down on her knees, turned, reaching up and digging her fingernails into Tami's face as the woman tightened the leather purse strap around her victim's throat. Her breath cut off, stars began to dance in front of Jaymie and she felt herself sinking into unconsciousness, her flailing irresolute and frantic. That very moment she heard banging at the back door and Trip Findley, her back-lane neighbor, a dapper oldster with a cane, pelted into the house and began swinging his cane around so precipitously he knocked the kettle off the stove, sending boiling hot water streaming everywhere. Jaymie felt some splash on her, but more hit Tami, who shrieked in pain as Trip shouted expletives Jaymie never would have thought him capable of.

Finally Jaymie ducked out of the purse strap and was free.

It was a chilly evening, but Jaymie sat on an Adirondack chair in her backyard with a blanket wrapped around her. The police, summoned by multiple neighbors — including her next-door neighbor, Pam Driscoll, who ran the bed-and-breakfast for her friends — calling about a crime in progress, had an ambulance called for Tami, who had some pretty bad hot water scalds on her arms as well as bloody claw marks on her face from Jaymie. The paramedics had her bandaged and strapped to a gurney. They trundled her out the back door, through the summer porch, and down to the flagstone walk.

"Stop!" Tami screamed. "Jaymie, *Jaymie!* I'm s-sorry! Tell Gus I love him, and tell his little girl . . . my sweet niece . . ." She wailed and groaned, trying to sit up, struggling against the straps. "Tell my baby niece that her Auntie Tami loves her more than life. I didn't mean to do it. I didn't." She broke down weeping and the paramedic, at a sign from the police chief, wheeled her away carefully over the bumpy walkway.

Jaymie, after a brief check-over from the paramedics — she had a sore throat and some bruises, but she'd recover — had already told Chief Ledbetter everything that was recorded on her cell phone and he had confiscated it. Her voice was little more than a hoarse whisper. She wrote down her cell phone password for him and let him tag the phone as evidence. The roar of a motor echoed in the night and Jakob tore up the back lane in his pickup and skidded to a stop. He didn't even close the truck door in his haste. He squeezed past the paramedics and raced to Jaymie. He knelt by her and took her in his arms, pulling her gently close to his warmth.

"Jakob, who's with Jocie?" she whispered, her voice muffled by his plaid lumberman jacket.

Shakily, he laughed. "Stop worrying. Helmut is there. He came over for a coffee, so when I heard —"

"Who did you hear from?"

"Me," Valetta said out of the twilight dimness. She trotted up the walk to the couple. "Brock told me what he'd told you. I tried to call to talk it over but I didn't get an answer. Then I heard sirens and I *knew* something was up. So I called Jakob."

Shaking with a weird amalgam of relief, tears, laughter and love, Jaymie let herself be hugged and cosseted by her husband-to-be and maid of honor, all while Hoppy, finally released from the safe part of the house, jumped around them and barked and Denver huddled under Jaymie's chair and glared out at the cuckoo world of humans.

"Mr. Findley! Is he okay?" she finally asked her friends. She broke away and saw her neighbor talking to Chief Ledbetter, with Bernie Jenkins standing by as they took Trip's statement. She leaped up and hugged the slim elderly man, dressed in his best plaid pajamas. "You're my hero, Mr. Find-ley," she whispered. "Thank you."

"Something different about Hoppy's bark; that's how I knew something was wrong. I've got a dog. When they have that frantic tone, best to investigate. It's either a burglar or a skunk. I've chased away both from time to time."

Jaymie scooped up her little dog and held him close while he licked her face. "So I have Hoppy to thank, too," she whispered. "For that, I think he gets to be ring bearer." She looked over her shoulder toward Jakob. "Don't you think?"

"He sure does. Jocie is flower girl and Hoppy's the ring bearer; perfect."

TWENTY-THREE

A few days later Valetta, Dee, Johnny, Brock and Jaymie attended Rhonda's memorial service at Iona Welch's nursing home. There was a small activity room that was set aside that day for them, a cheerful sun-flooded space where crafts were done and teas were held, but today, a teenager who died decades ago was honored. Rhonda's frail mother wept through the whole thing, her pale, lined face twisted in grief. Petty sat beside her, holding her hand. Jaymie was touched when she saw that Delores Paget was being honored along with Rhonda Welch. She sobbed with grief herself, but also wept at the kindness that saw a forgotten teenager remembered.

Cyndi Lauper's "Time After Time" played, and then Petty took the podium and eulogized her beloved niece, Rhonda, remembering her as a witty, bright, lively girl with infinite capacity for love. She repeated what Jaymie had showed her in the journal, Rhonda's exhortation to herself to *Be kinder! Be smarter! Don't let my heart lead my head. Help and encourage others.* That, she said, was the kind of girl she was, showing the kind of woman she would have become.

She then introduced an older woman, with a deeply lined face and tightly curled gray hair, saying, "This is Marjorie Walker, who was Delores's mother."

"My baby would have been fifty years old soon," she said, then looked up from the podium. "My daughter's name was Cindy Lynn, and she was a *beautiful* baby, my very first, full of smiles and grace and funny spit bubbles. I was an overwhelmed young mom who trusted the wrong woman to care for her. I had her for just eight precious months, and when I look back I remember how tired I was, and how scared to be a mom, but also how much in love with my baby I was, how I *lived* for those smiles and spit bubbles and the very first laugh.

"And then she was *gone.* Just . . . gone. Like she was never there. I lived with all her little pink onesies and bibs and that empty cradle while the police did all they could, but still never found her. All those years — until a week ago — I have looked for my Cindy's face in every crowd. She was *never* forgotten." She paused and scanned the crowd. "I will always miss her. I wish someone could tell me what she was like."

Becca stood and approached her. "I can do that, ma'am," she said, touching the older woman's arm. Becca looked out to the crowd. "The Delores Paget I knew — Cindy Lynn Walker — had plans and dreams. She loved Tammy Wynette, blue jean jackets, the freedom of summer vacation, horses, and she *loved* life, even though it was hard for her. People at school saw that she was fierce, but sometimes she was *funny.* She was smart and the horses loved her. Horses are pretty good judges of character. She taught me how to ride and how to take care of the horses properly, how to brush them and talk to them. I will never forget the summer before she died, and how we spent almost every day riding horses, talking, and making plans for our futures." Becca paused and turned to the older woman, who stood by her side, tears sliding down her face. "I'll never forget her. All she wanted was to find her family."

Through tears, Jaymie proudly watched her sister. Becca was making sure *everyone* knew Delores just a little, and that her mother would know that she had one true friend, at least.

"She died looking for the truth about her life. I know that had she lived, she would have found you," Becca said to Marjorie Walker. "She was on her way to you, and somewhere, right now, I'm sure she's over-joyed to know that you never forgot her."

Delores's mother hugged Becca, thanked her, and then returned to her seat and her two other kids, two men who clutched her arms to them with sturdy love. Becca returned to her seat and Jaymie hugged her tightly. With prayers and music, the service was over. Two young women were lost no more, and those who loved them got the chance to mourn.

Tami Majewski was charged with one count of first-degree murder in the death of Rhonda and one count of second-degree murder in the death of Delores Paget, born Cindy Lynn Walker. Clifford Paget was charged with manslaughter in the death of his mother, so many years before, and with committing an indignity to a body for concealing Delores's body, which he had confessed to. He had been dragging her out of the kitchen, he said, when his father and stepmother returned. They assumed he had killed her and always believed that, no matter what he said. Shortly after his father died

Clifford decided to disappear, since his stepmother was making his life miserable by threatening to turn him in. He staged the drowning with the help of his friend. Henk Hofwegen was charged with misleading police officers and filing a false police report and pled guilty; his help in breaking the case would be taken into consideration.

On a slightly humorous note, Chief Ledbetter, one month away from retirement, told Jaymie what had been discovered among Tami's household garbage; there were five boxes of a well-known chocolate laxative, which she had used to flavor the chocolate cake she handed Jaymie at her wedding shower. The baker apparently thought it would give Jaymie so much discomfort she'd forget about investigating Rhonda and Delores's murders. As if *that* would ever happen, the chief said with a chuckle.

And so it was all over. And yet it would never be over in a sense, not for the families who had lost those two girls. Marjorie Walker had found a sister in grief, though, and she vowed to visit Iona Welch often.

TWENTY-FOUR

For Jaymie, May flew by with plans, work, fun with Jakob and Jocie, and the Tea with the Queen event, which went off smoothly, as usual. Jocie's oma made her a ruffled dress and parasol and she took part in the event as Princess Victoria, granddaughter of the queen, regally playing her part with both Mrs. Bellwood on the first day of the tea, and the new Queen Victoria, Imogene Frump, on the second day of the tea. She was so popular that many of the tea drinkers asked to have their photo taken with her and she was featured in the *Wolverhampton Weekly Howler*!

But finally, at long last, the big day arrived, the day that would unite Becca and Kevin, and Jaymie and Jakob, in wedded bliss. Despite fears of rain the day dawned brilliant, blue-domed and clear.

It was a Saturday in mid-June. The sun shone warmly, but without the heat that would come in full summer. The sky was still as blue as it had been at dawn, but a few puffy clouds now drifted lazily across it. Jaymie, in one of the bedrooms of the Queensville Historic Manor, eyed herself in a full-length mirror. She and Becca had been greeted early by a hairdresser, who came from Wolverhampton to their home and did their hair for the wedding. Becca's was a simple case of fluffing the curls, but Jaymie's long hair was now curled and dressed in a style with the long tail of the pony trimmed with flowers and draped over her shoulder. Her makeup was simple, not a whole lot more than she normally wore.

But the dress! The vintage dress was even more beautiful than it had been when she first tried it on. Heidi had it tailored to fit perfectly, and then had it trimmed by a professional with pearls that adorned the lace. Valetta, as her maid of honor, was Jaymie's dresser and was now done, but still fussed at a last tweak of her flower crown, which held a short lace veil that drifted over her shoulders.

Jaymie stared at herself in the mirror, unbelieving; she looked like someone out of a book of fairy tales, the long lace dress and laced bodice vintage and yet uniquely her. Becca entered the small room holding Jocie's hand. Jaymie turned. Both stared at her; tears gleamed in Becca's eyes behind her glasses. Her voice choked and thick, she said, "Oh, Jaymie, it's perfect! The dress is perfect."

Jocie was pure joy. She hopped on one foot, her pretty pink silk flower-girl dress billowing around her knees as Hoppy, with a dark pink bow around his neck, barked and jumped at her. The child then skipped across the space and hugged Jaymie as Hoppy still yapped, excited by all the commotion of the day.

Valetta, wearing her maid of honor attire, a rose wrap dress, gazed at the Leighton sisters, one to the other. "You both look so beautiful! I'm so happy for you both!"

"You two ready? Heidi's about to have a conniption fit, as my grandma would say," Bernie said, hustling in the door after Becca. "They're ready for you all!" She stopped, though, and smiled. "Wow. We all did it. You gals look so *beautiful*!" She eyed Becca's ivory Dupioni fitted silk suit. "This is *very* nice; more my style than a dress!"

"Thanks, Bernie, but I don't think I can see anything right now, much less myself, with how Jaymie looks. My little sister!" She swiped at a tear that welled from her eyes and dripped down, leaving a makeup-less rivulet.

"Becca, no tears!" Dee, who hustled into the room, said. "Your makeup will be smudged!" She got out a compact and patted at her friend's face. She was dressed in pale blue, as Becca's matron of honor.

"Nothing can happen until I've had a moment with my two girls," Jaymie's dad, Alan, said, following Dee into the room.

Valetta took Jocie's hand and led her out the door, beckoning Hoppy, who, for once, obeyed. "We'll wait for you downstairs in the entry with Heidi," she said. Dee smiled and followed their friend out, taking Jocie's other hand.

Becca hustled to her younger sister and hugged her carefully. "You look so beautiful," she whispered, touching the silken curl that lay over her shoulder. She turned to her father. "Daddy, we've already done this before a time or two. I'm going to leave you with Jaymie."

"Hold it! You're not getting away without at least one word, sweetie." He hugged his oldest daughter and kissed her cheek. "This is the last time I walk you down the aisle, I *know* it. Kevin is a keeper."

"I know he is." Becca turned and said, "Take your time, Jaymie. Don't let *anyone* hurry you. This is your day. Jakob will wait." She retreated to the hall and clattered down the stairs.

Her dad, looking dapper in a beautiful charcoal gray suit with a pink carnation as a boutonniere, held her at arms' length. "My beautiful baby girl," he said.

Jaymie was nervous, but calm; nervous for the day, and calm about the ever-after part. Every moment of the last year had brought her to this, the gift of a relationship and love she knew would stand the test of time. She had something to say to her father, though, and this was the moment. "Dad, in the last couple of months I've gotten a good look at how hard it was for you and mom when I was born." Reading Valetta's diaries and talking to Becca about that time had been illuminating.

"Honey, I —"

"No, I know," she said, patting his hand where it clutched her arm and gazing steadily into his blue eyes. "I know you wouldn't undo any of it. I want to say thank you. You've always been there for me, and you raised Becca to be such a good sister, and . . . and Mom . . . I love her *so* much. We may not understand each other some-times, but I love her. I want to make sure I tell her that more often." Her voice choked and she cleared her throat. "And thank you for bringing Grandma Leighton into our home when I was a baby. I think it gave Becca her teenage freedom back, and it gave Mom time to . . . to recover. I know how hard it was for her, having me."

Joy Leighton had done her very best to be a good mother to Jaymie despite having some problems after giving birth. People didn't understand postpartum depression then as much as they now did. She had recently confessed to her younger daughter how much shame she felt over her depression and sense of failure, and they had made peace.

"Jaymie, I know you and Joy haven't always had the best mother-daughter relationship," her dad said gently. "But there was never *ever* a time when she didn't love you, when she wasn't grateful you were born. I *never* want you to mistake that."

"I know that now."

They spent some more private moments together, and then he led her down the stairs to join Becca, Dee, Valetta, and the two "groomsmen," Kevin's sister Georgina and Jakob's brother Helmut. Jocie was acting as flower girl for both couples and Hoppy, with two tiny velvet pouches tied to his collar, was the rings bearer.

Denver got to stay home in peace and be the grouch.

Heidi, her eyes gleaming with happiness, hugged both brides and consulted her clipboard, a happy Miss Bossy as she whispered orders to everyone, arranging them to suit her. They had decided the weather was too chancy, so they'd hold the ceremony inside, in the large parlors of the Queensville Historic Manor, with the sliding doors opened between the two large rooms and rented chairs placed so there was an aisle for the brides to walk. The brides and their attendants gathered in the large open hall, and the music started.

The sisters had decided to have their father walk them down the aisle separately, so Heidi sent Dee and Kevin's sister, Georgina, dressed in coordinating blue and peach skirt suits, down the aisle together. Then Becca, on their father's arm, headed to her groom, Kevin, to the tune of Elton John's "Your Song." Both brides had decided that since it was a nontraditional wedding, they'd walk toward their grooms to nontraditional wedding songs that suited their tastes and personalities. It was all being filmed at Jaymie's insistence because her one regret was that she would miss some of her sister's ceremony — the walk down the aisle, at least — while she waited for her own to begin.

Heidi dashed into the parlor and beckoned Jaymie's father with a hissed *"Come back!"* reminding him to come back for his second daughter. Alan Leighton returned, to a ripple of laughter from the crowd; Jaymie couldn't see him as he trotted back up the aisle, but she *could* hear the chuckles and thought he was probably mugging for the crowd.

Heidi then dashed back to the entrance and sent Valetta and Helmut down the aisle together, very slowly, to the strains of Jaymie's choice of wedding song, Christina Perry's "A Thousand Years." Alan joined Jaymie, slightly out of breath, gazed at her, misty-eyed, and kissed her cheek. "You're so beautiful," he whispered.

"You two, *now*!" Heidi whispered, her face glowing with joy. "Good luck, Jaymsie!"

As Jaymie's head swam she took a deep breath, remembering Becca's advice to be mindful, and started. This was her one and only wedding day. She made sure to look to the left and to the right as they slowly walked. There was Chief Ledbetter, now retired, and a stout smiling woman with him who must be his wife. There was Nan Goodenough with her husband, newspaper

410

owner Joe Goodenough. There were Mrs. Bellwood and Imogene Frump, Bill Waterman, Cynthia Turbridge and Jewel Dandridge, who sat on either side of Petty Welch. Joel Lockland grinned, his fond gaze swiftly drifting to Heidi at the back of the room with her clipboard. The Klausners, Brock Nibley with his two kids, Trip Findley and many, many others were in the audience.

Then there were their families, Jakob's large and loving clan, and her own smaller group, including her beloved Grandma Leighton, who sat with her old friend Mrs. Stubbs, both in wheelchairs. And Jaymie's mother. She paused and caught her mother's eye; the slim, eager, tiny and perfectly dressed woman blew her a kiss, tears making mascara trails in her makeup.

Then Jaymie looked ahead and all she saw was Jakob, handsome in a dark suit and rose-colored silk tie. He looked . . . *miserable*! Her heart constricted, but as she walked toward him, her view changed. He wasn't miserable at all; his face was twisted because he was trying not to cry, she knew it because she knew *him*. He stood with his little girl, hand on her shoulder. So Jaymie smiled, and in that moment she felt the thread of their connection tug. He smiled too, as tears coursed down his cheeks and started down hers. She wasn't normally a crier but there was nothing ordinary about this day.

Her father kissed her cheek and handed her to her groom, and they all faced the officiant, the kindly pastor from the local Methodist church, who Jaymie well knew from past Sunday-school attendance and numerous town events. Becca and Kevin were wed, in the first of the two ceremonies. They then stood to one side and witnessed the second part.

The next minutes were a happy blur until they came to their vows.

"Jakob, one night I stumbled into your cabin, scared and alone," she said. "I think I knew, in that moment, that I wanted to come back, that I'd seek the comfort of your arms again. I do that now and forever, and I know I'll never be alone again." Jakob smiled, teary-eyed. She looked down at Jocie. "Jocie, you are the daughter of my heart. I . . ." She swallowed hard. "I want to thank your mama in heaven for bringing you into the world. And I hope she knows now that she can trust me with you, now and forever."

The pastor prompted Jakob. In an oddly choked voice, he said, "Jaymie, the night you came to my cabin I feel like fate had her hand in it. She brought me a woman I adored right away, a woman who looked on my daughter with so much love, and who has a heart so big . . . I'm grateful and forever thankful. I love you, now and forever."

Jaymie and Jakob were pronounced husband and wife, and with Jocie were pronounced family; the two kissed, a lingering kiss interrupted only by Jocie, bouncing impatiently by their side. As cameras flashed, she and Jakob kissed Jocie's cheeks, too, while Hoppy yapped impatiently.

Both couples returned down the aisle to applause and cheering, but Jakob pulled her aside and they hid behind a curtain in the front hall. "I love you so much, Mrs. Jaymie Leighton Müller."

"And I love you, *forever.*"

Pictures were taken in various locations; with the two couples alone, with family members, including one tiny bouncy child and one tiny bouncy three-legged pooch. On the porch, in the meadow, by a rustic fence. It took a while. Wedding guests drank cocktails served by Bernice at a vintage bar and ate appetizers prepared and served by a three-woman catering company from a town nearby. The sun descended toward the horizon, the angle of sunlight giving everything a golden glow.

The big back lawn of the historic home had been transformed, with a large white marquee tent, a wooden dance floor and tables adorned with white damask tablecloths and centerpieces of aqua-tinged Mason jars holding pretty bouquets of late spring blooms. Dinner was a relatively simple meal served buffet-style. Picnic foods were featured: potato and pasta salads provided by local friends, cold meats, salads, fried chicken. But there were plenty of hot entrees too: meat loaf, mac and cheese, and more. The caterers provided roasted chicken and prime rib, as well as homey desserts like peach cobbler and an abundance of fruit pies. Toasts were made, jokes were told, speeches were listened to and bouquets were tossed . . . all the usual wedding ingredients were there times two.

Finally it was wedding cake time. They weren't the ones Jaymie and Becca had planned for or expected, but as the Wolverhampton bakery's professional cake baker, Tami Majewski, was now in jail awaiting trial, they had brought in outside help. A baker who was on maternity leave came forward, drew up pictures, and baked two lovely cakes, one chocolate and one buttercream vanilla. They were perfectly lovely and delicious.

No one mentioned Tami, but she was not forgotten. Gus, accompanied by his wife and toddler, attended the wedding of his best friend and business partner. But he was somber throughout and slipped away early. Jaymie had hoped to talk to him, to see how he was doing in all the tumult, but she knew that Jakob was helping him through it.

Gus had confided in his friend and partner that he hadn't known what Tami did all those years ago. But he acknowledged that when he finally figured it out, upset and confused about what to do, he did try to muddle the investigation. It was a rash act he regretted, but as angry as he was with her, his sister had always been dear to him. Though horrified at the lives she took, he was doing his best to help Tami now.

Jaymie and Jakob, Becca and Kevin, approached their cakes. Bernie and Heidi had done a wonderful job of refurbishing Delores Paget's old dressing table, giving it a shabby chic patina and adorning it with swoops of rose and aqua tulle and big silk cabbage roses. They cut their cakes to cheers from the audience, and then started cutting pieces for guests, Kevin and Jakob commandeered to hand out the cake.

Once they were done, Becca returned to their guests but Jaymie lingered at the dressing table. "It's so beautiful," Jaymie said, touching the surface on which their cakes rested. "I wonder if I can find a home for it after this." She didn't want Delores's dressing table to go to some stranger.

Valetta materialized beside her. "If you don't mind . . ." She hesitated.

"Go on?"

"My niece is into the shabby chic stuff. Could I buy it for her? I'll look after it, I promise."

Jaymie nodded, feeling the tears well in her eyes and not trusting her voice. She was so happy but her heart hurt, remembering Delores and Rhonda, denied the fullness of adult life, on this day.

"Take it for Eva; our gift," Jakob said as he returned to his wife's side and squeezed her close to him. "Another young girl should have better memories with it and give it the home it needs."

Jaymie buried her face in his chest. Jakob understood her feeling about vintage pieces; he felt the way she did, that some things deserved to be treated well after a life of neglect.

Twilight had deepened into a rich indigo and the sky was scattered with stars. As the evening began to wind down, Jaymie went looking for Heidi. Her friend had gone above and beyond what was expected, and Jaymie wanted her to know how much she appreciated it. Where the heck was she? Joel was getting drunk with a couple of Jakob's brothers and couldn't give her a coherent answer, so she hoisted her skirts and went looking. She found her friend sitting alone on the front steps of the house. That was extremely unlike her.

"Hey, girlfriend, what are you doing out here sitting alone?" Jaymie plopped down on the step next to her and put her arm around Heidi's shoulders. The moon was rising, casting a pale white glow over the forest opposite the house.

"Just a quiet moment," she said.

That was even *more* unusual. "Is everything okay?"

Heidi turned her face to Jaymie and smiled, but it was tremulous. "I'm fine. A little tired."

"Honey, after the Herculean effort you put into my and Becca's wedding you deserve a week in the Bahamas."

"Joel can't get away right now."

"You could go alone."

She shook her head. "Maybe in a few months."

"Heidi, are you sure everything is okay? You seem —"

"Jaymie, *there* you are!" A strident voice that Jaymie knew too well cut through the still air. "I've been looking for you for a half hour." It was Becca, stalking around the corner to the front of the house. "We need you! Mom and Dad are heading back to Canada with Grandma Leighton and they want to say goodbye." Becca and Kevin were staying in Queensville and looking after the house and the animals while Jaymie and Jakob had their honeymoon. Alan and Joy Leighton were taking his mother back to London, where they'd stay in Becca's house for a month, while both couples had their honeymoons.

"I'll be there in a minute," Jaymie said. "Heidi and I are just —"

"No, *now*!" Becca insisted.

"You can't keep your grandma waiting," Heidi said, pushing Jaymie. "I'll come with you."

And so the wedding came to an end, with a bustle of people heading off to various places, kisses, hugs, well-wishes and teary smiles. Jocie, exhausted as she was, was desperately trying to stay awake for every single minute, though her cousins had long ago fallen asleep in the back of their parents'

SUV. Jaymie had a quiet moment with her new daughter and assured her that once Jaymie and Jakob were back, they would all have a wonderful family week at the cottage on Heartbreak Island.

Finally Jakob's mother and father, with whom Jocie was staying for a week, claimed they were oh, *so* tired and must go home to bed. Jocie reluctantly agreed and they headed off for the Müllers' farmhouse, where Jocie's kitten, Little Bit, awaited them. The little girl twisted in her seat and waved to Jaymie and Jakob as they drove away, the moonlight glinting in the car windows. Becca and Kevin left soon after to return to the Queensville house to feed Denver and get some well-deserved rest on their wedding night. They'd leave for their fortnight in England when Jaymie and Jakob got back.

As the crew Heidi had hired to clean up after the wedding were toting away rented chairs and china and taking down the giant marquee by the light of portable floods, there were a few chairs left, sitting out under the stars in the dew-dampened lawn where croquet and badminton would be played all summer. Jakob held Jaymie close in a teak double Adirondack glider chair, with a sleepy Hoppy curled up on her lap, supported by his strong hands. That was the benefit of marrying a big guy, Jaymie thought, leaning her beribboned and bedecked head on his shoulder; he could cuddle Jocie, Jaymie, and her little dog, too.

She had cake smeared on her dress. And wine. And maybe even some gravy. She smiled. The lovely dress had served its purpose well. Jaymie looked around the circle. Heidi was sitting alone and so was Joel, and both looked kind of miserable. Trouble in paradise? Jaymie wondered. She watched through half-closed eyes. She'd have to explore the problem between them when she got back from her honeymoon.

Valetta and Dee were chatting quietly about some village tangle, as Dee's husband, Johnny, helped the crew.

"Jaymie, Mrs. Klausner has a problem with one of her grandkids who has been working part-time in the store," Valetta said. She looked tired, her eyes behind the glasses rimmed in dark smudges.

"Who, Gracey?"

"No, one of the others. I tried to help, but I think I made things worse. She asked me to ask you if you could come and see her once you're back from your honeymoon."

Jakob chuckled, a sound deep in his chest that rumbled through her at the same time.

"That's my Jaymie; problem solver to the world."

She picked up and kissed his broad hand as Hoppy grumbled in his sleep. "I will. Remind me, though. This is going to be a busy summer."

"Why do you think you're so good at the problem solving and mystery figuring out?" Dee asked, yawning. "I have my own theory, but I'd be interested in your take on it. It's your life, after all."

Jaymie thought it over, gazing up at the stars that blanketed the dark night sky. A nighthawk circled above them, screeching. "I guess . . . these things gnaw away in my brain until I have to start asking questions. Asking questions — and really listening to the answers and putting them together with what other people have told me — is the best way to figure things out. If I hadn't kept hold of Tami's fake diary, read it, and realized there were things wrong with it, I never would have figured out she killed poor Rhonda and Delores."

"*And* there was that little matter of her coming to your back door and trying to kill you," Valetta said.

"Yes, there was that."

Jaymie felt Jakob's hold on her tighten, enough that Hoppy whimpered in his sleep;

in that moment she knew that when something like that happened it would always upset him, but he would never try to stop her from doing what she needed to do. He was *so* the right husband for her.

Husband! She was *married*! Despite her curiosity about Dee's comment that she had her own theory about why Jaymie was good at solving puzzles, she was too tired to pursue it. She stirred. "It's time to go home," she murmured. It was her wedding night. In the modern era, maybe that didn't hold the same weight and meaning that it once did, but she didn't want to miss it. She got up, took Hoppy out of Jakob's arms, where he had crept to snuggle, and said, "I think it's time for this honeymooning couple to go to their cabin in the country." They would be leaving in the morning for the camping trip, but were spending their first night as a married couple at home, in the cabin.

A long round of hugs, kisses and well-wishes followed, while Hoppy ran off, did his business, and returned. Jaymie, still in her wedding dress, then had to hike up her skirts and go on poop patrol, while everyone watched and laughed hysterically, the result of exhaustion and wine. She discarded the baggie of poo in the appropriate container with much catcalling from her friends and laughter about doggie bags.

And *finally,* they headed home, happy silence in the pickup truck cab, her in her stained wedding dress and he jacketless in his suit pants and white shirt, undone at the neck. She glanced over. She found him impossibly handsome and loved everything about his face, including his slight beard. She reached over and caressed his cheek as he kissed her palm. He was her Jakob, and she loved him.

The cabin was a warm island of comfort and solitude. As they turned all the lights off, locked up and carried Hoppy upstairs with them, arms around each other's waists, she knew that ahead lie her biggest adventures yet. And as her stained wedding dress pooled on the floor beside the four-poster rustic log bed in the big master suite of the log cabin, the gown swiftly claimed by Hoppy as his bed for the night, she gave herself over to complete joy, down to the bedrock of her soul.

FROM JAYMIE'S
VINTAGE KITCHEN

Salmon Loaf with Mushroom Cream Sauce
by Jaymie Leighton

Sometimes when you try to cook from an old recipe there are techniques or ingredients that mystify you. Sometimes, though, the puzzle is something else entirely. In the case of this Salmon Loaf from my grandmother's cookbook, it was the handwriting that was hard to decipher. She must have been in a hurry, because her normally elegant script is a scrawled mess. I can relate; occasionally in the kitchen I'm in a slapdash hurry too!

Salmon Loaf is one of those ubiquitous recipes from the Depression era, when high-quality protein was too expensive for many households. As surprising as it seems today, canned salmon was considered a cheap alternative to beef. I think its popularity was due to the fact that the tins stored well. The taste for salmon loaf lasted well into the fifties. On Pinterest I saw a 1950s ad for a popular brand of canned soup that included a recipe for Salmon Loaf; it encouraged the home cook to heat up a can of mushroom soup as a sauce, but I guarantee you my Mushroom Cream Sauce is a thousand times better and almost as easy!

I have considerably altered Grandma Leighton's recipe and added the delicious mushroom sauce. I think it takes what could have been a mundane recipe over the top!

Baked Salmon Loaf
Serves: 4 generously

Ingredients:
Note: the original recipe called for a one-pound can of salmon, but I don't think they make that size anymore. So I improvised! Also, while I used the less-expensive pink salmon, to keep it budget-friendly, I think it would be delicious with good red salmon!

1 14.75-ounce can of salmon and 1
   6-ounce can, skin and bones removed
   and flaked
2 eggs, lightly beaten
1/2 cup milk
1/2 cup breadcrumbs (I used seasoned, and

it turned out just fine!)
1 tbsp lemon juice
1 tsp Old Bay seasoning (optional; use 1/2
 tsp salt if omitting)
Freshly ground pepper, about half a
 teaspoon
1 tbsp melted butter
1 tbsp finely minced fresh dill

Preheat oven to 350 degrees. Butter an 8 1/2 by 4 1/2 by 2 1/2 loaf pan. Combine ingredients in order given and pack firmly into the pan (mine was nonstick, but I buttered it anyway!). Bake for 40 minutes; remove from oven, and let stand for 5 to 10 minutes before trying to slice! I turned it out onto a plate for slicing, and it worked beautifully.

Mushroom Cream Sauce

Ingredients:
3 tbsp butter
1 cup sliced button mushrooms
1 tbsp all-purpose flour
Freshly ground sea salt and pepper
1 cup milk
1/2 cup heavy cream

In a medium saucepan melt the butter and sauté the mushrooms until soft. Add flour and freshly ground sea salt and pepper, whisk together, then let combine for a couple of minutes over low heat. Add the milk and heavy cream, whisk and let simmer, thickening. Pour over slices of salmon loaf and enjoy!

ABOUT THE AUTHOR

Victoria Hamilton is the pseudonym of nationally bestselling romance author Donna Lea Simpson.

She now happily writes about vintage kitchen collecting, muffin baking, and dead bodies in the Vintage Kitchen Mysteries and Merry Muffin Mystery series. Besides writing about murder and mayhem, and blogging at Killer Characters, Victoria collects vintage kitchen wares and old cookbooks, as well as teapots and teacups.

Visit Victoria at: http://www.victoriahamilton mysteries.

The employees of Thorndike Press hope you have enjoyed this Large Print book. All our Thorndike, Wheeler, and Kennebec Large Print titles are designed for easy reading, and all our books are made to last. Other Thorndike Press Large Print books are available at your library, through selected bookstores, or directly from us.

For information about titles, please call:
    (800) 223-1244

or visit our website at:
    gale.com/thorndike

To share your comments, please write:
    Publisher
    Thorndike Press
    10 Water St., Suite 310
    Waterville, ME 04901

П/19

DATE DUE

DEC 3 0 2019	
JAN 2 3 2020	
FEB 0 4 2020	
AUG 1 2 2022	
Barrett How	
4-3-24	
7-23-21	
	PRINTED IN U.S.A.